POPULAR PUBLICATIONS · FACSIMILE EDITIONS

# Famous Fantastic Mysteries #1 (September–October 1939)

Initially published by The Frank A. Munsey Company, *Famous Fantastic Mysteries* was dedicated to reprinting the rare science fiction and fantasy stories from the early years of *Argosy*, *The All-Story*, and *The Cavalier*. *Famous Fantastic Mysteries* is one of the most important science fiction pulps. The first issue contains classic stories by A. Merritt, Manly Wade Wellman, Tod Robbins, Ray Cummings, and Donald Wandrei, among others.

Authors:

*A. Merritt, Manly Wade Wellman, Tod Robbins, Robert Neal Leath, Ray Cummings, Donald Wandrei, J.U. Giesy*

Illustrators:

*Samuel Cahan, Joseph A. Farren*

NOTE: We have attempted to restore the original page scans in this facsimile in order to provide an enjoyable reading experience. However, in some cases there can be text loss due to damage to the original pulp, tight bindings, or other reasons.

# Famous FANTASTIC Mysteries

**Vol. 1**  **SEPTEMBER-OCTOBER, 1939**  **No. 1**

THIS magazine is the answer to thousands of requests that we have received over a period of years, demanding a second look at famous fantasies which, since their original publication, have become accepted classics. Our choice has been dictated by *your* requests and our firm belief that these are the aces of imaginative fiction.

—*The Editors.*

THE FRANK A. MUNSEY COMPANY, Publisher, 280 Broadway, New York, N. Y.
WILLIAM T. DEWART, *President*

THE CONTINENTAL PUBLISHERS & DISTRIBUTORS, LTD.
3 La Belle Sauvage, Ludgate Hill, London, E.C., 4
Paris: HACHETTE & CIE, 111 Rue Reaumur

# The Moon Pool

## By A. MERRITT

**Three times the Moon Door had swung closed on the prey of the Moon Dweller.
Could science save the fourth victim of that ancient curse?**

### CHAPTER I

#### THE THROCKMARTIN MYSTERY

I AM breaking a long silence to clear
the name of Dr. David Throckmartin
and to lift the shadow of scandal
from that of his wife and of Dr. Charles
Stanton, his assistant. That I have not
found the courage to do so before, all
men who are jealous of their scientific
reputations will understand when they have
read the facts entrusted to me alone.

I shall first recapitulate what has
actually been known of the Throckmartin
expedition to the island of Ponape in the
Carolines—the Throckmartin Mystery, as
it is called.

Dr. Throckmartin set forth, you will
recall, to make some observations of
Nan-Matal, that extraordinary group of
island ruins, remains of a high and pre-

historic civilization, that are clustered along the east shore of Ponape. With him went his wife to whom he had been wedded less than half a year. The daughter of Professor Frazier-Smith, she was as deeply interested and almost as well informed as he, upon these relics of a vanished race that titanically strew certain islands of the Pacific and form the basis for the theory of a submerged Pacific continent.

Mrs. Throckmartin, it will be recalled, was much younger, fifteen years at least, than her husband. Dr. Charles Stanton, who accompanied them as Dr. Throckmartin's assistant, was about her age. These three and a Swedish woman, Thora Helversen, who had been Edith Throckmartin's nurse in babyhood and who was entirely devoted to her, made up the expedition.

Dr. Throckmartin planned to spend a year among the ruins, not only of Ponape, but of Lele—the twin centers of that colossal riddle of humanity whose answer has its roots in immeasurable antiquity; a weird flower of man-made civilization that blossomed ages before the seeds of Egypt were sown; of whose arts we know little and of whose science and secret knowledge of nature nothing.

He carried with him complete equipment for his work and gathered at Ponape a dozen or so natives for laborers. They went straight to Metalanim harbor and set up their camp on the island called Uschen-Tau in the group known as the Nan-Matal. You will remember that these islands are entirely uninhabited and are shunned by the people on the main island.

Three months later Dr. Throckmartin appeared at Port Mooresby, Papua. He came on a schooner manned by Solomon Islanders and commanded by a Chinese half-breed captain. He reported that he was on his way to Melbourne for additional scientific equipment and whites to help him in his excavations, saying that the superstition of the natives made their aid negligible. He went immediately on board the steamer Southern Queen which was sailing that same morning. Three nights later he disappeared from the Southern Queen and it was officially reported that he had met death either by being swept overboard or by casting himself into the sea.

A relief-boat sent with the news to Ponape found the Throckmartin camp on the island Uschen-Tau and a smaller camp on the island called Nan-Tanach. All the equipment, clothing, supplies were intact. But of Mrs. Throckmartin, of Dr. Stanton, or of Thora Helversen they could find not a single trace!

The natives who had been employed by the archeologist were questioned. They said that the ruins were the abode of great spirits—*ani*—who were particularly powerful when the moon was at the full. On these nights all the islanders were doubly careful to give the ruins wide berth. Upon being employed, they had demanded leave from the day before full moon until it was on the wane and this had been granted them by Dr. Throckmartin. Thrice they had left the expedition alone on these nights. On their third return they had found the four white people gone and they "knew that the *ani* had eaten them." They were afraid and had fled.

That was all.

The Chinese half caste was found and reluctantly testified at last that he had picked Dr. Throckmartin up from a small boat about fifty miles off Ponape. The scientist had seemed half mad, but he had given the seaman a large sum of money to bring him to Port Moresby and to say, if questioned, that he had boarded the boat at Ponape harbor.

That is all that has been known to anyone of the fate of the Throckmartin expedition.

Why, you will ask, do I break silence now; and how came I in possession of the facts I am about to set forth?

To the first I answer: I was at the Geographical Club recently and I overheard two members talking. They mentioned the name of Throckmartin and I became an eavesdropper. One said:

"Of course what probably happened was that Throckmartin killed them all. It's a dangerous thing for a man to marry a woman so much younger than himself and then throw her into the necessarily close company of exploration with a man as young and as agreeable as Stanton was. The inevitable happened, no doubt. Throckmartin discovered; avenged himself. Then followed remorse and suicide."

"Throckmartin didn't seem to be that kind," said the other thoughtfully.

"No, he didn't," agreed the first.

"Isn't there another story?" went on the second speaker. "Something about Mrs. Throckmartin running away with Stanton and taking the woman, Thora, with her? Somebody told me they had been recognized in Singapore recently."

"You can take your pick of the two stories," replied the other man. "It's one or the other I suppose."

It was neither one nor the other of them. I know—and I will answer now the second question—because I was with Throckmartin when he—vanished. I know what he told me and I know what my own eyes saw. Incredible, abnormal, against all the known facts of our science as it was, I testify to it. And it is my intention, after this is published, to sail to Ponape, to go to the Nan-Matal and to the islet beneath whose frowning walls dwells the mystery that Throckmartin sought and found—and that at the last sought and found Throckmartin!

I will leave behind me a copy of the map of the islands that he gave me. Also his sketch of the great courtyard of Nan-Tanach, the location of the moon door, his indication of the probable location of the moon pool and the passage to it and his approximation of the position of the shining globes. If I do not return and there are any with enough belief, scientific curiosity and courage to follow, these will furnish a plain trail.

I will now proceed straightforwardly with my narrative.

For six months I had been on the d'Entrecasteaux Islands gathering data for the concluding chapters of my book upon "Flora of the Volcanic Islands of the South Pacific." The day before, I had reached Port Moresby and had seen my specimens safely stored on board the Southern Queen. As I sat on the upper deck that morning I thought, with homesick mind, of the long leagues between me and Melbourne and the longer ones between Melbourne and New York.

It was one of Papua's yellow mornings, when she shows herself in her most somber, most baleful mood. The sky was a smoldering ocher. Over the island brooded a spirit sullen, implacable and alien; filled with the threat of latent, malefic forces waiting to be unleashed. It seemed an emanation from the untamed, sinister heart of Papua herself—sinister even when she smiles. And now and then, on the wind, came a breath from unexplored jungles, filled with unfamiliar odors, mysterious, and menacing.

It is on such mornings that Papua speaks to you of her immemorial ancientness and of her power. I am not unduly imaginative but it is a mood that makes me shrink—I mention it because it bears directly upon Dr. Throckmartin's fate. Nor is the mood Papua's alone. I have felt it in New Guinea, in Austraila, in the Solomons and in the Carolines. But it is in Papua that it seems most articulate. It is as though she said: "I am the ancient of days; I have seen the earth in the throes of its shaping; I am the primeval; I have seen races born and die and, lo, in my breast are secrets that would blast you by the telling, you pale babes of a puling age. You and I ought not be in the same world; yet I am and I shall be! Never will you fathom me and you I hate though I tolerate! I tolerate—but how long?"

And then I seem to see a giant paw that reaches from Papua toward the outer world, stretching and sheathing monstrous claws.

All feel this mood of hers. Her own people have it woven in them, part of their web and woof; flashing into light unexpectedly like a soul from another universe; masking itself as swiftly.

I fought against Papua as every white man must on one of her yellow mornings.

And as I fought I saw a tall figure come striding down the pier. Behind him came a Kapa-Kapa boy swinging a new valise. There was something familiar about the tall man. As he reached the gangplank he looked up straight into my eyes, stared at me for a moment and waved his hand. It was Dr. Throckmartin!

Coincident with my recognition of him there came a shock of surprise that was definitely—unpleasant. It was Throckmartin—but there was something disturbingly different about him and the man I had known so well and had bidden farewell less than a year before. He was then, as you know, just turned forty, lithe, erect, muscular; the face of a student and of a seeker. His controlling expression was one of enthusiasm, of intellectual keenness, of —what shall I say—expectant search. His ever eagerly questioning brain had stamped itself upon his face.

I sought in my mind for an explanation of that which I had felt on the flash of his greeting. Hurrying down to the lower deck I found him with the purser. As I spoke he turned and held out to me an eager hand—and then I saw what the change was that had come over him!

He knew, of course, by my face the uncontrollable shock that my closer look had given me. His eyes filled and he turned briskly to the purser; then hurried off to his stateroom, leaving me standing, half dazed.

At the stair he half turned.

"Oh, Goodwin," he said. "I'd like to see you later. Just now—there's something I must write before we start—"

He went up swiftly.

" 'E looks rather queer—eh?" said the purser. "Know 'im well, sir? Seems to 'ave given you quite a start, sir."

I made some reply and went slowly to my chair. I tried to analyze what it was that had disturbed me so; what profound change in Throckmartin that had so shaken me. Now it came to me. It was as though the man had suffered some terrific soul searing shock of rapture and horror combined; some soul cataclysm that

in its climax had remolded his face deep from within, setting on it the seal of wedded joy and fear. As though indeed ecstasy supernal and terror infernal had once come to him hand in hand, taken possession of him, looked out of his eyes and, departing, left behind upon him ineradicably their shadow.

Alternately I looked out over the port and paced about the deck, striving to read the riddle; to banish it from my mind. And all the time still over Papua brooded its baleful spirit of ancient evil, unfathomable, not to be understood; nor had it lifted when the Southern Queen lifted anchor and steamed out into the gulf.

## CHAPTER II

### DOWN THE MOON PATH

I WATCHED with relief the shores sink down behind us; welcomed the touch of the free sea wind. We seemed to be drawing away from something malefic; something that lurked within the island spell I have described, and the thought crept into my mind, spoke—whispered rather—from Throckmartin's face.

I had hoped—and within the hope was an inexplicable shrinking, an unexpressed dread—that I would meet Throckmartin at lunch. He did not come down and I was sensible of a distinct relief within my disappointment. All that afternoon I lounged about uneasily but still he kept to his cabin. Nor did he appear at dinner.

Dusk and night fell swiftly. I was warm and went back to my deck-chair. The Southern Queen was rolling to a disquieting swell and I had the place to myself.

Over the heavens was a canopy of cloud, glowing faintly and testifying to the moon riding behind it. There was much phosphorescence. Now and then, before the ship and at the sides, arose those strange little swirls of mist that steam up from the Southern Ocean like the breath of sea monsters, whirl for a moment and disappear. I lighted a cigarette and tried once more to banish Throckmartin's face from my mind.

Suddenly the deck door opened and through it came Throckmartin himself. He paused uncertainly, looked up at the sky with a curiously eager, intent gaze, hesitated, then closed the door behind him.

"Throckmartin," I called. "Come sit with me. It's Goodwin."

Immediately he made his way to me, sitting beside me with a gasp of relief that I noted curiously. His hand touched mine and gripped it with a tenseness that hurt. His hand was icelike. I puffed up my cigarette and by its glow scanned him closely. He was watching a large swirl of the mist that was passing before the ship. The phosphorescence beneath it illumined it with a fitful opalescence. I saw fear in his eyes. The swirl passed; he sighed; his grip relaxed and he sank back.

"Throckmartin," I said, wasting no time in preliminaries. "What's wrong? Can I help you?"

He was silent.

"Is your wife all right and what are you doing here when I heard you had gone to the Carolines for a year?" I went on.

I felt his body grow tense again. He did not speak for a moment and then:

"I'm going to Melbourne, Goodwin," he said. "I need a few things—need them urgently. And more men—white men."

His voice was low; preoccupied. It was as though the brain that dictated the words did so perfunctorily, half impatiently; aloof, watching, strained to catch the first hint of approach of something dreaded.

"You are making progress then?" I asked. It was a banal question, put forth in a blind effort to claim his attention.

"Progress?" he repeated. "Progress— "

He stopped abruptly; rose from his chair, gazed intently toward the north. I followed his gaze. Far, far away the moon had broken through the clouds. Almost on the horizon, you could see the faint luminescence of it upon the quiet sea. The distant patch of light quivered and shook. The clouds thickened again and it was gone. The ship raced southward, swiftly.

Throckmartin dropped into his chair. He lighted a cigarette with a hand that trembled. The flash of the match fell on his face and I noted with a queer thrill of apprehension that its unfamiliar expression had deepened; become curiously intensified as though a faint acid had passed over it, etching its lines faintly deeper.

"It's the full moon tonight, isn't it?" he asked, palpably with studied inconsequence.

"The first night of full moon," I answered. He was silent again. I sat silent too, waiting for him to make up his mind to speak. He turned to me as though he had made a sudden resolution.

"Goodwin," he said. "I do need help. If ever man needed it, I do. Goodwin—can you imagine yourself in another world, alien, unfamiliar, a world of terror, whose unknown joy is its greatest terror of all; you all alone there; a stranger! As such a man would need help, so I need—"

He paused abruptly and arose to his feet stiffly; the cigarette dropped from his fingers. I saw that the moon had again broken through the clouds, and this time much nearer. Not a mile away was the patch of light that it threw upon the waves. Back of it, to the rim of the sea was a lane of moonlight; it was a gleaming gigantic serpent racing over the rim of the world straight and surely toward the ship.

Throckmartin gazed at it as though turned to stone. He stiffened to it as a pointer does to a hidden covey. To me from him pulsed a thrill of terror—·but terror tinged with an unfamiliar, an infernal joy. It came to me and passed away—leaving me trembling with its shock of bitter sweet.

He bent forward, all his soul in his eyes. The moon path swept closer, closer still. It was now less than half a mile away. From it the ship fled; almost it came to me, as though pursued. Down upon it, swift and straight, a radiant torrent cleaving the waves, raced the moon stream. And then—

"Good God!" breathed Throckmartin, and if ever the words were a prayer and an invocation they were.

And then, for the first time—I saw—*it!*

The moon path, as I have said, stretched

to the horizon and was bordered by darkness. It was as though the clouds above had been parted to form a lane—drawn aside like curtains or as the waters of the Red Sea were held back to let the hosts of Israel through. On each side of the stream was the black shadow cast by the folds of the high canopies. And straight as a road between the opaque walls gleamed, shimmered and danced the shining, racing, rapids of moonlight.

Far, it seemed immeasurably far, along this stream of silver fire I sensed, rather than saw, something coming. It drew into sight as a deeper glow within the light. On and on it sped toward us—an opalescent mistiness that swept on with the suggestion of some winged creature in darting flight. Dimly there crept into my mind memory of the Dyak legend of the winged messenger of Buddha—the Akla bird whose feathers are woven of the moon rays, whose heart is a living opal, whose wings in flight echo the crystal clear music of the white stars—but whose beak is of frozen flame and shreds the souls of unbelievers. Still it sped on, and now there came to me sweet, insistent tinklings—like a pizzicati on violins of glass, crystalline, as purest, clearest glass transformed to sound. And again the myth of the Akla bird came to me.

But now it was close to the end of the white path; close up to the barrier of darkness still between the ship and the sparkling head of the moon stream. And now it beat up against that barrier as a bird against the bars of its cage. And I knew that this was no mist born of sea and air. It whirled with shimmering plumes, with swirls of lacy light, with spirals of living vapor. It held within it odd, unfamiliar gleams as of shifting mother-of-pearl. Coruscations and glittering atoms drifted through it as though it drew them from the rays that bathed it.

Nearer and nearer it came, borne on the sparkling waves, and less and less grew the protecting wall of shadow between it and us. The crystalline sounds were louder —rhythmic as music from another planet.

Now I saw that within the mistiness was a core, a nucleus of intenser light—veined, opaline, effulgent, intensely alive. And above it, tangled in the plumes and spirals that throbbed and whirled were seven glowing lights.

Through all the incessant but strangely ordered movement of the—*thing*—these lights held firm and steady. They were seven—like seven little moons. One was of a pearly pink, one of delicate nacreous blue, one of lambent saffron, one of the emerald you see in the shallow waters of tropic isles; a deathly white; a ghostly amethyst; and one of the silver that is seen only when the flying fish leap beneath the moon. There they shone—these seven little varicolored orbs within the opaline mistiness of whatever it was that, poised and expectant, waited to be drawn to us on the light filled waves.

The tinkling music was louder still. It pierced the ears with a shower of tiny lances; it made the heart beat jubilantly— and checked it dolorously. It closed your throat with a throb of rapture and gripped it tight like the hand of infinite sorrow!

Came to me now a murmuring cry, stilling the crystal clear notes, it was articulate —but as though from something utterly foreign to this world. The ear took the cry and translated with conscious labor into the sounds of earth. And even as it compassed, the brain shrank from it irresistibly and simultaneously it seemed, reached toward it with irresistible eagerness.

"Av-o-lo-ha! Av-o-lo-ha!" So the cry seemed to throb.

The grip of Throckmartin's hand relaxed. He walked stiffly toward the front of the deck, straight toward the vision, now but a few yards away from the bow. I ran toward him and gripped him—and fell back. For now his face had lost all human semblance. Utter agony and utter ecstasy— there they were side by side, not resisting each other; unholy inhuman companions blending into a look that none of God's creatures should wear—and deep, deep as his soul! A devil and a god dwelling harmoniously side by side! So must Satan, newly fallen, still divine, seeing heaven and contemplating hell, have looked.

And then—swiftly the moon path faded! The clouds swept over the sky as though a hand had drawn them together. Up from the south came a roaring squall. As the moon vanished what I had seen vanished with it—blotted out as an image on a magic lantern; the tinkling ceased abruptly—leaving a silence like that which follows an abrupt and stupendous thunder clap. There was nothing about us but silence and blackness!

Through me there passed a great trembling as one who had stood on the very verge of the gulf wherein the men of the Louisades say lurks the fisher of the souls of men, and has been plucked back by sheerest chance.

Throckmartin passed an arm around me.

"It is as I thought," he said. In his voice was a new note; of the calm certainty that has swept aside a waiting terror of the unknown. "Now I know! Come with me to my cabin, old friend. For now that you too have seen I can tell you"—he hesitated—"what it was you saw," he ended.

As we passed through the door we came face to face with the ship's first officer. Throckmartin turned quickly, but not soon enough for the mate not to see and stare with amazement. His eyes turned questioningly to me.

With a strong effort of will Throckmartin composed his face into at least a semblance of normality.

"Are we going to have much of a storm?" he asked.

"Yes," said the mate. Then the seaman, getting the better of his curiosity, added, profanely: "We'll probably have it all the way to Melbourne."

Throckmartin straightened as though with a new thought. He gripped the officer's sleeve eagerly.

"You mean at least cloudy weather—for"—he hesitated—"for the next three nights, say?"

"And for three more," replied the mate.

"Thank God!" cried Throckmartin, and

I think I never heard such relief and hope as was in his voice.

The sailor stood amazed. "Thank God?" he repeated. "Thank—what d'ye mean?"

But Throckmartin was moving onward to his cabin. I started to follow. The first officer stopped me.

"Your friend," he said, "is he ill?"

"The sea!" I answered hurriedly. "He's not used to it. I am going to look after him."

I saw doubt and disbelief in the seaman's eyes but I hurried on. For I knew now that Throckmartin was ill indeed—but that it was a sickness neither the ship's doctor nor any other could heal.

## CHAPTER III

### "DEAD! ALL DEAD!"

THROCKMARTIN was sitting on the side of his berth as I entered. He had taken off his coat. He was leaning over, face in hands.

"Lock the door," he said quietly, not raising his head. "Close the port-holes and draw the curtains—and—have you an electric flash in your pocket—a good, strong one?"

He glanced at the small pocket flash I handed him and clicked it on. "Not big enough I'm afraid," he said. "And after all"—he hesitated—"it's only a theory."

"What's only a theory?" I asked in astonishment.

"Thinking of it as a weapon against—what you saw," he said, with a wry smile.

"Throckmartin," I cried. "What was it? Did I really see—that thing—there in the moon path? Did I really hear—"

"This for instance," he interrupted.

Softly he whispered: "Av-o-lo-ha!" With the murmur I seemed to hear again the crystalline unearthly music; an echo of it, faint, sinister, mocking, jubilant.

"Throckmartin," I said. "What was it? What are you flying from, man? Where is your wife—and Stanton?"

"Dead!" he said monotonously. "Dead! All dead!" Then as I recoiled in horror—

"All dead. Edith, Stanton, Thora—dead—or worse. And Edith in the moon pool—with them—drawn by what you saw on the moon path—and that wants me—and that has put its brand upon me—and pursues me."

With a vicious movement he ripped open his shirt.

"Look at this," he said. I gazed. Around his chest, an inch above his heart, the skin was white as pearl. The whiteness was sharply defined against the healthy tint of the body. He turned and I saw it ran around his back. It circled him. The band made a perfect cincture about two inches wide.

"Burn it!" he said, and offered me his cigarette. I drew back. He gestured—peremptorily. I pressed the glowing end of the cigarette into the ribbon of white flesh. He did not flinch nor was there odor of burning nor, as I drew the little cylinder away, any mark upon the whiteness.

"Feel it!" he commanded again. I placed my fingers upon the band. It was cold—like frozen marble.

He handed me a small penknife.

"Cut!" he ordered. This time, my scientific interest fully aroused, I did so without reluctance. The blade cut into flesh. I waited for the blood to come. None appeared. I drew out the knife and thrust it in again, fully a quarter of an inch deep. I might have been cutting paper so far as any evidence followed that what I was piercing was human skin and muscle.

Another thought came to me and I drew back, revolted.

"Throckmartin," I whispered. "Not leprosy!"

"Nothing so easy," he said. "Look again and find the places you cut.

I looked, as he bade me, and in the white ring there was not a single mark. Where I had pressed the blade there was no trace. It was as though the skin had parted to make way for the blade and closed.

Throckmartin arose and drew his shirt about him.

"Two things you have seen," he said. "It—and its mark—the seal it placed on me that gives it, I think, the power to follow me. Seeing, you must believe my story. Goodwin, I tell you again that my wife is dead—or worse—I do not know; the prey of—what you saw; so, too, is Stanton; so Thora. How—" He stopped for a moment. Then continued:

"And I am going to Melbourne for the things to empty its den and its shrine; for dynamite to destroy it and its lair—if anything made on earth will destroy it; and for white men with courage to use them. Perhaps—perhaps after you have heard, you will be one of these men?" He looked at me a bit wistfully. "And now—do not interrupt me, I beg of you, till I am through—for"—he smiled wanly—"the mate may be wrong. And if he is"—he arose and paced twice about the room—"if he is I may not have time to tell you."

"Throckmartin," I answered, "I have no closed mind. Tell me—and if I can I will help."

He took my hand and pressed it.

"Goodwin," he began, "if I have seemed to take the death of my wife lightly—or rather"—his face contorted—"or rather—if I have seemed to pass it by as something not of first importance to me—believe me it is not so. If the rope is long enough—if what the mate says is so—if there is cloudy weather until the moon begins to wane—I can conquer—that I know. But if it does not—if the dweller in the moon pool gets me—then must you or some one avenge my wife—and me—and Stanton. Yet I cannot believe that God would let a thing like that conquer! But why did He then let it take my Edith? And why does He allow it to exist? Are there things stronger than God, do you think, Goodwin?"

He turned to me feverishly. I hesitated.

"I do not know just how you define God," I said. "If you mean the will to know, working through science—"

He waved me aside impatiently.

"Science," he said. "What is our science against—that? Or against the science of whatever cursed, vanished race that made it—or made the way for it to enter this world of ours?"

With an effort he regained control of himself.

"Goodwin," he said, "do you know at all of the ruins on the Carolines; the cyclopean, megolithic cities and harbors of Ponape and Lele, of Kusaie, of Ruk and Hogolu, and a score of other islets there? Particularly, do you know of the Nan-Matal and Metalanim?"

"Of the Metalanim I have heard and seen photographs," I said. "They call it, don't they, the Lost Venice of the Pacific?"

"Look at this map," said Throckmartin. He handed me the map. "That," he went on, "is Christian's map of Metalanim harbor and the Nan-Matal. Do you see the rectangles marked Nan-Tanach?"

"Yes," I said.

"There," he said, "under those walls is the moon pool and the seven gleaming lights that raise the dweller in the pool and the altar and shrine of the dweller. And there in the moon pool with it lie Edith and Stanton and Thora."

"The dweller in the moon pool?" I repeated half-incredulously.

"The thing you saw," said Throckmartin solemnly.

A solid sheet of rain swept the ports, and the Southern Queen began to roll on the rising swells. Throckmartin drew another deep breath of relief, and drawing aside a curtain peered out into the night. Its blackness seemed to reassure him. At any rate, when he sat again he was calm.

"There are no more wonderful ruins in the world than those of the island Venice of Metalanim on the east shore of Ponape," he said almost casually. "They take in some fifty islets and cover with their intersecting canals and lagoons about twelve square miles. Who built them? None knows! When were they built? Ages before the memory of present man, that is sure. Ten thousand, twenty thousand, a hundred thousand years ago—the last more likely.

"All these islets, Goodwin, are squared, and their shores are frowning sea-walls of gigantic basalt blocks hewn and put in place by the hands of ancient man. Each inner water-front is faced with a terrace of those basalt blocks which stand out six feet above the shallow canals that meander between them. On the islets behind these walls are cyclopean and time-shattered fortresses, palaces, terraces, pyramids; immense courtyards, strewn with ruins—and all so old that they seem to wither the eyes of those who look on them.

"There has been a great subsidence. You can stand out of Metalanim harbor for three miles and look down upon the tops of similar monolithic structures and walls twenty feet below you in the water.

"And all about, strung on their canals, are the bulwarked islets with their enigmatic giant walls peering through the dense growths of mangroves—dead, deserted for incalculable ages; shunned by those who live near.

"You as a botanist are familiar with the evidence that a vast shadowy continent existed in the Pacific—a continent that was not rent asunder by volcanic forces as was that legendary one of Atlantis in the Eastern Ocean. My work in Java, in Papua, and in the Ladrones had set my mind upon this Pacific lost land. Just as the Azores are believed to be the last high peaks of Atlantis, so evidence came to me steadily that Ponape and Lele and their basalt bulwarked islets were the last points of the slowly sunken western land clinging still to the sunlight, and had been the last refuge and sacred places of the rulers of that race which had lost their immemorial home under the rising waters of the Pacific.

"I believed that under these ruins I might find the evidence of what I sought. Time and again I had encountered legends of subterranean networks beneath the Nan-Matal, of passages running back into the main island itself; basalt corridors that followed the lines of the shallow canals and ran under them to islet after islet, linking them in mysterious chains.

"My—my wife and I had talked before we were married of making this our great work. After the honeymoon we prepared for the expedition. It was to be my monument. Stanton was as enthusiastic as ourselves. We sailed, as you know, last May in fulfilment of our dreams.

"At Ponape we selected, not without difficulty, workmen to help us—diggers I had to make extraordinary inducements before I could get together my force. Their beliefs are gloomy, these Ponapeans. They people their swamps, their forests, their mountains and shores with malignant spirits—*ani* they call them. And they are afraid—bitterly afraid of the isles of ruins and what they think the ruins hide. I do not wonder—now! For their fear has come down to them, through the ages, from the people 'before their fathers,' as they call them, who, they say, made these mighty spirits their slaves and messengers.

"When they were told where they were to go, and how long we expected to stay, they murmured. Those who, at last, were tempted made what I thought then merely a superstitious proviso that they were to be allowed to go away on the three nights of the full moon. If only I had heeded them and gone, too!"

He stopped and again over his face the lines etched deep.

"We passed," he went on, "into Metalanim harbor. Off to our left—a mile away arose a massive quadrangle. Its walls were all of forty feet high and hundreds of feet on each side. As we passed it our natives grew very silent; watched it furtively, fearfully. I knew it for the ruins that are called Nan-Tanach, the 'place of frowning walls.' And at the silence of my men I recalled what Christian had written of this place; of how he had come upon its 'ancient platforms and tetragonal enclosures of stonework; its wonder of tortuous alleyways and labyrinth of shallow canals; grim masses of stonework peering out from behind verdant screens; cyclopean barricades. And now, when we had turned into its ghostly shadows, straightway the merriment of our guides was hushed and conversation died down to whispers. For we were close to Nan-Tanach—the place of lofty walls, the most remarkable of all the Metalanim ruins." He arose and stood over me.

"Nan-Tanach, Goodwin," he said solemnly—"a place where merriment is hushed indeed and words are stifled; Nan-Tanach—where the moon pool lies hidden —lies hidden behind the moon rock, but sends its diabolic soul out—even through the prisoning stone." He raised clenched hands. "Oh, Heaven," he breathed, "grant me that I may blast it from earth!"

He was silent for a little time.

"Of course I wanted to pitch our camp there," he began again quietly, "but I soon gave up that idea. The natives were panic-stricken—threatened to turn back. 'No,' they said, 'too great *ani* there. We go to any other place—but not there.' Although, even then, I felt that the secret of the place was in Nan-Tanach, I found it necessary to give in. The laborers were essential to the success of the expedition, and I told myself that after a little time had passed and I had persuaded them that there was nothing anywhere that could molest them, we would move our tents to it. We finally picked for our base the islet called Uschen-Tau—you see it here—" He pointed to the map. "It was close to the isle of desire, but far enough away from it to satisfy our men. There was an excellent camping-place there and a spring of fresh water. It offered, besides, an excellent field for preliminary work before attacking the larger ruins. We pitched our tents, and in a couple of days the work was in full swing."

## CHAPTER IV

### THE MOON ROCK

"I DO not intend to tell you now," Throckmartin continued, "the results of the next two weeks, Goodwin, nor of what we found. Later—if I am allowed I will lay all that before you. It is sufficient to say that at the end of those two weeks I had found confirmation of many of my theories, and we were well under way to solve a mystery of humanity's youth— so we thought. But enough. I must hurry on to the first stirrings of the inexplicable thing that was in store for us.

"The place, for all its decay and desolation, had not infected us with any touch of morbidity—that is not Edith, Stanton or myself. My wife was happy—never had she been happier. Stanton and she, while engrossed in the work as much as I, were of the same age, and they frankly enjoyed the companionship that only youth can give youth. I was glad—never jealous.

"But Thora was very unhappy. She was a Swede, as you know, and in her blood ran the beliefs and superstitions of the Northland—some of them so strangely akin to those of this far southern land; beliefs of spirits of mountain and forest and water— werewolves and beings malign. From the first she showed a curious sensitivity to what, I suppose, may be called the 'influences' of the place. She said it 'smelled' of ghosts and warlocks.

"I laughed at her then—but now I believe that this sensitivity of what we call primitive people is perhaps only a clearer perception of the unknown which we, who deny the unknown, have lost.

"A prey to these fears, Thora always followed my wife about like a shadow; carried with her always a little sharp hand-ax, and although we twitted her about the futility of chopping fantoms with such a weapon she would not relinquish it.

"Two weeks slipped by, and at their end the spokesman for our natives came to us. The next night was the full of the moon, he said. He reminded me of my promise. They would go back to their village next morning; they would return after the third night, as at that time the power of the *ani* would begin to wane with the moon. They left us sundry charms for our 'protection,' and solemnly cautioned us to keep as far away as possible from Nan-Tanach during their absence—although their leader politely informed me that, no doubt, we were stronger than the spirits. Half-exasperated, half-amused I watched them go.

"No work could be done without them, of course, so we decided to spend the days of their absence junketing about the southern islets of the group. Under the moon the ruins were inexpressibly weird and beautiful. We marked down several spots

for subsequent exploration, and on the morning of the third day set forth along the east face of the breakwater for our camp on Uschen-Tau, planning to have everything in readiness for the return of our men the next day.

"We landed just before dusk, tired and ready for our cots. It was only a little after ten o'clock when Edith awakened me.

"'Listen!' she said. 'Lean over with your ear close to the ground!' I did so, and seemed to hear, far, far below, as though coming up from great distances, a faint chanting. It gathered strength, died down, ended; began, gathered volume, faded away into silence.

"'It's the waves rolling on rocks somewhere,' I said. 'We're probably over some ledge of rock that carries the sound.'

"'It's the first time I've heard it,' replied my wife doubtfully. We listened again. Then through the dim rhythms, deep beneath us, another sound came. It drifted across the lagoon that lay between us and Nan-Tanach in little tinkling waves. It was music—of a sort; I won't describe the strange effect it had upon me. You've felt it—"

"You mean on the deck?" I asked. Throckmartin nodded.

"I went to the flap of the tent," he continued, "and peered out. As I did so Stanton lifted his flap and walked out into the moonlight, looking over to the other islet and listening. I called to him.

"'That's the queerest sound!' he said. He listened again. 'Crystalline! Like little notes of translucent glass. Like the bells of crystal on the sistrums of Isis at Dendarah Temple,' he added half-dreamily. We gazed intently at the island. Suddenly, on the gigantic sea-wall, moving slowly, rhythmically, we saw a little group of lights. Stanton laughed.

"'The beggars!' he exclaimed. 'That's why they wanted to get away, is it? Don't you see, Dave, it's some sort of a festival— rites of some kind that they hold during the full moon! That's why they were so eager to have us *keep* away, too.'

"I felt a curious sense of relief, although

I had not been sensible of any oppression. The explanation seemed good. It explained the tinkling music and also the chanting—worshipers, no doubt, in the ruins—their voices carried along passages I now knew honeycombed the whole Nan-Matal.

" 'Let's slip over,' suggested Stanton—but I would not.

" 'They're a difficult lot as it is,' I said. 'If we break into one of their religious ceremonies they'll probably never forgive us. Let's keep out of any family party where we haven't been invited.'

" 'That's so,' agreed Stanton.

"The strange tinkling music, if music it can be called, rose and fell, rose and fell—now laden with sorrow, now filled with joy.

" 'There's something—something very unsettling about it,' said Edith at last soberly. 'I wonder what they make those sounds with. They frighten me half to death, and, at the same time, they make me feel as though some enormous rapture was just around the corner.'

"I had noted this effect, too, although I had said nothing of it. And at the same time there came to me a clear perception that the chanting which had preceded it had seemed to come from a vast multitude—thousands more than the place we were contemplating could possibly have held. Of course, I thought, this might be due to some acoustic property of the basalt; an amplification of sound by some gigantic sounding-board of rock; still—

" 'It's devilish uncanny!' broke in Stanton, answering my thought.

"And as he spoke the flap of Thora's tent was raised and out into the moonlight strode the old Swede. She was the great Norse type—tall, deep-breasted, molded on the old Viking lines. Her sixty years had slipped from her. She looked like some ancient priestess of Odin." He hesitated. "She knew," he said slowly, "something more far-seeing than my science had given her sight. She warned me—she warned me! Fools and mad that we are to pass such things by without heed!" He brushed a hand over his eyes.

"She stood there," he went on. "Her eyes were wide, brilliant, staring. She thrust her head forward toward Nan-Tanach, regarding the moving lights; she listened. Suddenly she raised her arms and made a curious gesture to the moon. It was—an archaic—movement; she seemed to drag it from remote antiquity—yet in it was a strange suggestion of power. Twice she repeated this gesture and—the tinkling died away! She turned to us.

" 'Go!' she said, and her voice seemed to come from far distances. 'Go from here—and quickly! Go while you may. They have called—' She pointed to the islet. 'They know you are here. They wait.' Her eyes widened further. 'It is there,' she wailed. 'It beckons—the—the—'

"She fell at Edith's feet, and as she fell over the lagoon came again the tinklings, now with a quicker note of jubilance—almost of triumph.

"We ran to Thora, Stanton and I, and picked her up. Her head rolled and her face, eyes closed, turned as though drawn full into the moonlight. I felt in my heart a throb of unfamiliar fear—for her face had changed again. Stamped upon it was a look of mingled transport and horror—alien, terrifying, strangely revolting. It was"—he thrust his face close to my eyes—"what you see in mine!"

For a dozen heart-beats I stared at him, fascinated; then he sank back again into the half-shadow of the berth.

"I managed to hide her face from Edith," he went on. "I thought she had suffered some sort of a nervous seizure. We carried her into her tent. Once within the unholy mask dropped from her, and she was again only the kindly, rugged old woman. I watched her throughout the night. The sounds from Nan-Tanach continued until about an hour before moon-set. In the morning Thora awoke, none the worse, apparently. She had had bad dreams, she said. She could not remember what they were—except that they had warned her of danger. She was oddly sullen, and I noted that throughout the morning her gaze returned again half-fascinatedly, half-wonderingly to the neighboring isles.

"That afternoon the natives returned. They were so exuberant in their apparent relief to find us well and intact that Stanton's suspicions of them were confirmed. He slyly told their leader that 'from the noise they had made on Nan-Tanach the night before they must have thoroughly enjoyed themselves.'

"I think I never saw such stark terror as the Ponapean manifested at the remark! Stanton himself was so plainly startled that he tried to pass it over as a jest. He met poor success! The men seemed panic-stricken, and for a time I thought they were about to abandon us—but they did not. They pitched their camp at the western side of the island—out of sight of Nan-Tanach. I noticed that they built large fires, and whenever I awoke that night I heard their voices in slow, minor chant—one of their song 'charms,' I thought drowsily, against evil *ani*. I heard nothing else; the place of frowning walls was wrapped in silence—no lights showed. The next morning the men were quiet, a little depressed, but as the hours wore on they regained their spirits, and soon life at the camp was going on just as it had before.

"You will understand, Goodwin, how the occurrences I have related would excite the scientific curiosity. We rejected immediately, of course, any explanation admitting the supernatural. Why not? Except the curiously disquieting effects of the tinkling music and Thora's behavior there was nothing to warrant any such fantastic theories—even if our minds had been the kind to harbor them.

"We came to the conclusion that there must be a passageway between Ponape and Nan-Tanach, known to the natives—and used by them during their rites. Ceremonies were probably held in great vaults or caverns beneath the ruins.

"We decided at last that on the next departure of our laborers we would set forth immediately to Nan-Tanach. We would investigate during the day, and at evening my wife and Thora would go back to camp, leaving Stanton and me to spend the night on the island, observing from some safe hiding-place what might occur.

"The moon waned; appeared crescent in the west; waxed slowly toward the full. Before the men left us they literally prayed us to accompany them. Their importunities only made us more eager to see what it was that, we were now convinced, they wanted to conceal from us. At least that was true of Stanton and myself. It was not true of Edith. She was thoughtful, abstracted—reluctant. Thora, on the other hand, showed an unusual restlessness, almost an eagerness to go. Goodwin"—he paused—"Goodwin, I know now that the poison was working in Thora—and that women have perceptions that we men lack—forebodings, sensings. I wish to Heaven I had known it then—Edith!" he cried suddenly. "Edith—come back to me! Forgive me!"

I stretched the decanter out to him. He drank deeply. Soon he had regained control of himself.

"When the men were out of sight around the turn of the harbor," he went on, "we took our boat and made straight for Nan-Tanach. Soon its mighty sea-wall towered above us. We passed through the water-gate with its gigantic hewn prisms of basalt and landed beside a half-submerged pier. In front of us stretched a series of giant steps leading into a vast court strewn with fragments of fallen pillars. In the center of the court, beyond the shattered pillars, rose another terrace of basalt blocks, concealing, I knew, still another enclosure.

"And now, Goodwin, for the better understanding of what follows and to guide you, should I—not be able—to accompany you when you go there, listen carefully to my description of this place: Nan-Tanach is literally three rectangles. The first rectangle is the sea-wall, built up of monoliths. Gigantic steps lead up from the landing of the sea-gate through the entrance to the courtyard.

"This courtyard is surrounded by another, inner basalt wall.

"Within the courtyard is the second enclosure. Its terrace, of the same basalt as the outer walls, is about twenty feet high.

Entrance is gained to it by many breaches which time has made in its stonework. This is the inner court, the heart of Nan-Tanach! There lies the great central vault with which is associated the one name of living being that has come to us out of the mists of the past. The natives say it was the treasure-house of Chau-te-leur, a mighty king who reigned long 'before their fathers.' As Chau is the ancient Ponapean word both for sun and king, the name means 'place of the sun king.'

"And opposite this place of the sun king is the moon rock that hides the moon pool.

"It was Stanton who first found what I call the moon rock. We had been inspecting the inner courtyard; Edith and Thora were getting together our lunch. I forgot to say that we had previously gone all over the islet and had found not a trace of living thing. I came out of the vault of Chau-te-leur to find Stanton before a part of the terrace studying it wonderingly.

"What do you make of this?" he asked me as I came up. He pointed to the wall. I followed his finger and saw a slab of stone about fifteen feet high and ten wide. At first all I noticed was the exquisite nicety with which its edges joined the blocks about it. Then I realized that its color was subtly different—tinged with gray and of a smooth, peculiar—deadness.

"'Looks more like calcite than basalt,' I said. I touched it and withdrew my hand quickly, for at the contact every nerve in my arm tingled as though a shock of frozen electricity had passed through it. It was not cold as we know cold that I felt. It was a chill force—the phrase I have used—frozen electricity—describes it better than anything else. Stanton looked at me oddly.

"'So you felt it, too,' he said. 'I was wondering whether I was developing hallucinations like Thora. Notice, by the way, that the blocks beside it are quite warm beneath the sun.'

"I felt them and touched the grayish stone again. The same faint shock ran through my hand—a tingling chill that had in it a suggestion of substance, of force.

We examined the slab more closely. Its edges were cut as though by an engraver of jewels. They fitted against the neighboring blocks in almost a hair-line. Its base, we saw, was slightly curved, and fitted as closely as top and sides upon the huge stones on which it rested. And then we noted that these stones had been hollowed to follow the line of the gray stone's foot. There was a semicircular depression running from one side of the slab to the other. It was as though the gray rock stood in the center of a shallow cup—revealing half, covering half. Something about this hollow attracted me. I reached down and felt it. Goodwin, although the balance of the stones that formed it, like all the stones of the courtyard, were rough and age-worn—this was as smooth, as even surfaced as though it had just left the hands of the polisher.

"'It's a door!' exclaimed Stanton. 'It swings around in that little cup. That's what makes the hollow so smooth.'

"'Maybe you're right,' I replied. 'But how the devil can we open it?'

"We went over the slab again—pressing upon its edges, thrusting against its sides. During one of those efforts I happened to look up—and cried out. For a foot above and on each side of the corner of the gray rock's lintel I had seen a slight convexity, visible only from the angle at which my gaze struck it. These bosses on the basalt were circular, eighteen inches in diameter, as we learned later, and at the center extended two inches only beyond the face of the terrace. Unless one looked directly up at them while leaning against the moon rock—for this slab, Goodwin, is the moon rock—they were invisible. And none would dare stand there!

"We carried with us a small scaling-ladder, and up this I went. The bosses were apparently nothing more than chiseled curvatures in the stone. I laid my hand on the one I was examining, and drew it back so sharply I almost threw myself from the ladder. In my palm, at the base of my thumb, I had felt the same shock that I had in touching the slab below. I put my hand back. The impression came from a spot not more than an inch wide. I went carefully over the entire convexity, and six times more the chill ran through my arm. There were, Goodwin, seven circles an inch wide in the curved place, each of which communicated the precise sensation I have described. The convexity on the opposite side of the slab gave precisely the same results. But no amount of touching or of pressing these spots singly or in any combination gave the slightest promise of motion to the slab itself.

" 'And yet—they're what open it,' said Stanton positively.

" 'Why do you say that?' I asked.

" 'I—don't know,' he answered hesitatingly. 'But something tells me so. Throck,' he went on half earnestly, half laughingly, 'the purely scientific part of me is fighting the purely human part of me. The scientific part is urging me to find some way to get that slab either down or open. The human part is just as strongly urging me to do nothing of the sort and get away while I can!'

"He laughed again—shamefacedly.

" 'Which will it be?' he asked—and I thought that in his tone the human side of him was ascendant.

" 'It will probably stay as it is—unless we blow it to bits,' I said.

" 'I thought of that,' he answered, 'and—I wouldn't dare,' he added soberly enough. And even as I had spoken there came to me the same feeling that he had expressed. It was as though something passed out of the gray rock that struck my heart as a hand strikes an impious lip. We turned away—uneasily, and faced Thora coming through a breach in the terrace.

" 'Miss Edith wants you quick,' she began—and stopped. I saw her eyes go past me and widen. She was looking at the gray rock. Her body grew suddenly rigid; she took a few stiff steps forward and then ran straight to it. We saw her cast herself upon its breast, hands and face pressed against it; heard her scream as though her very soul were being drawn from her—and watched her fall at its foot. As we picked her up I saw steal from her face the look I had observed when first we heard the crystal music of Nan-Tanach—that unhuman mingling of opposites!"

## CHAPTER V

### AV-O-LO-HA

"WE CARRIED Thora back, down to where Edith was waiting. We told her what had happened and what we had found. She listened gravely, and as we finished Thora sighed and opened her eyes.

" 'I would like to see the stone,' she said. 'Charles, you stay here with Thora.' We passed through the outer court silently—and stood before the rock. She touched it, drew back her hand as I had; thrust it forward again resolutely and held it there. She seemed to be listening. Then she turned to me.

" 'David,' said my wife, and the wistfulness in her voice hurt me—'David, would you be very, very disappointed if we went from here—without trying to find out any more about it—would you?'

"Goodwin, I never wanted anything so much in my life as I wanted to learn what that rock concealed. You will understand—the cumulative curiosity that all the happenings had caused; the certainty that before me was an entrance to a place that, while known to the natives—for I still clung to that theory—was utterly unknown to any man of my race; that within, ready for my finding, was the answer to the stupendous riddle of these islands and a lost chapter of the history of humanity. There before me—and was I asked to turn away, leaving it unread!

"Nevertheless, I tried to master my desire, and I answered—'Edith, not a bit if you want us to do it.'

"She read my struggle in my eyes. She looked at me searchingly for a moment and then turned back toward the gray rock. I saw a shiver pass through her. I felt a tinge of remorse and pity!

" 'Edith,' I exclaimed, 'we'll go!'

"She looked at me hard. 'Science is a jealous mistress,' she quoted. 'No, after all it may be just fancy. At any rate, you can't run away. No! But, Dave, I'm going to stay too!'

" 'You are not!' I exclaimed. 'You're going back to the camp with Thora. Stanton and I will be all right.'

" 'I'm going to stay,' she repeated. And there was no changing her decision. As we neared the others she laid a hand on my arm.

" 'Dave,' she said, 'if there should be something — well — inexplicable tonight— something that seems—too dangerous—will you promise to go back to our own islet tomorrow, or, while we can, and wait until the natives return?'

"I promised eagerly—for the desire to stay and see what came with the night was like a fire within me.

"And would to Heaven I had not waited another moment, Goodwin; would to Heaven I had gathered them all together then and sailed back on the instant through the mangroves to Uschen-Tau!

"We found Thora on her feet again and singularly composed. She claimed to have no more recollection of what had happened after she had spoken to Stanton and to me in front of the gray rock than she had after the seizure on Uschen-Tau. She grew sullen under our questioning, precisely as she had before. But to my astonishment, when she heard of our arrangements for the night, she betrayed a febrile excitement that had in it something of exultance.

"We had picked a place about five hundred feet away from the steps leading into the outer court.

"We settled down just before dusk to wait for whatever might come. I was nearest the giant steps; next me Edith; then Thora, and last Stanton. Each of us had with us automatic pistols, and all, except Thora, had rifles.

"Night fell. After a time the eastern sky began to lighten, and we knew that the moon was rising; grew lighter still, and the orb peeped over the sea; swam suddenly into full sight. Edith gripped my hand, for, as though the full emergence into the heavens had been a signal, we heard begin

beneath us the deep chanting. It came from illimitable depths.

"The moon poured her rays down upon us, and I saw Stanton start. On the instant I caught the sound that had roused him. It came from the inner enclosure. It was like a long, soft sighing. It was not human; seemed in some way—mechanical. I glanced at Edith and then at Thora. My wife was intently listening. Thora sat, as she had since we had placed ourselves, elbows on knees, her hands covering her face.

"And then suddenly from the moonlight flooding us there came to me a great drowsiness. Sleep seemed to drip from the rays and fall upon my eyes, closing them—closing them inexorably. I felt Edith's hand relax in mine, and under my own heavy lids saw her nodding. I saw Stanton's head fall upon his breast and his body sway drunkenly. I tried to rise—to fight against the profound desire for slumber that pressed in on me.

"And as I fought I saw Thora raise her head as though listening; saw her rise and turn her face toward the gateway. For a moment she gazed, and my drugged eyes seemed to perceive within it a deeper, stronger radiance. Thora looked at us. There was infinite despair in her face—and expectancy. I tried again to rise—and a surge of sleep rushed over me. Dimly, as I sank within it, I heard a crystalline chiming; raised my lids once more with a supreme effort, saw Thora, bathed in light, standing at the top of the stairs, and then —sleep took me for its very own—swept me into the very heart of oblivion!

"Dawn was breaking when I wakened. Recollection rushed back on me and I thrust a panic-stricken hand out toward Edith; touched her and felt my heart give a great leap of thankfulness. She stirred, sat up, rubbing dazed eyes. I glanced toward Stanton. He lay on his side, back toward us, head in arms.

"Edith looked at me laughingly. 'Heavens! What sleep!' she said. Memory came to her. Her face paled. 'What happened?' she whispered. 'What made us sleep like that?' She looked over to

Stanton, sprang to her feet, ran to him, shook him. He turned over with a mighty yawn, and I saw relief lighten her face as it had lightened my heart.

"Stanton raised himself stiffly. He looked at us. 'What's the matter?' he exclaimed. 'You look as though you've seen ghosts!'

"Edith caught my hands. 'Where's Thora?' she cried. Before I could answer she ran out into the open calling: 'Thora! Thora!'

"Stanton stared at me. 'Taken!' was all I could say. Together we went to my wife, now standing beside the great stone steps, looking up fearfully at the gateway into the terraces. There I told them what I had seen before sleep had drowned me. And together then we ran up the stairs, through the court and up to the gray rock.

"The gray rock was closed as it had been the day before, nor was there trace of its having opened. No trace! Even as I thought this Edith dropped to her knees before it and reached toward something lying at its foot. It was a little piece of gray silk. I knew it for part of the kerchief Thora wore about her hair. Edith took the fragment; hesitated. I saw then that it had been *cut* from the kerchief as though by a razor-edge; I saw, too, that a few threads ran from it—down toward the base of the slab; ran to the base of the gray rock and—under it! The gray rock was a door! And it had opened and Thora had passed through it!

"I think, Goodwin, that for the next few minutes we all were a little insane. We beat upon that diabolic entrance with our hands, with stones and clubs. At last reason came back to us. Stanton set forth for the camp to bring back blasting powder and tools. While he was gone Edith and I searched the whole islet for any other clue. We found not a trace of Thora nor any indication of any living being save ourselves. We went back to the gateway to find Stanton returned.

"Goodwin, during the next two hours we tried every way in our power to force entrance through the slab. The rock within

effective blasting radius of the cursed door resisted our drills. We tried explosions at the base of the slab with charges covered by rock. They made not the slightest impression on the surface beneath, expending their force, of course, upon the slighter resistance of their coverings.

"Afternoon found us hopeless, so far as breaking through the rock was concerned. Night was coming on and before it came we would have to decide our course of action. I wanted to go to Ponape for help. But Edith objected that this would take hours and after we had reached there it would be impossible to persuade our men to return with us that night, if at all. What then was left? Clearly only one of two choices: to go back to our camp and wait for our men to return and on their return try to persuade them to go with us to Nan-Tanach. But this would mean the abandonment of Thora for at least two days. We could not do it; it would have been too cowardly.

"The other choice was to wait where we were for night to come; to wait for the rock to open as it had the night before, and to make a sortie through it for Thora before it could close again. With the sun had come confidence; at least a shattering of the mephitic mists of superstition with which the strangeness of the things that had befallen us had clouded for a time our minds. In that brilliant light there seemed no place for fantoms.

"The evidence that the slab had opened was unmistakable, but might not Thora simply have *found* it open through some mechanism, still working after ages, and dependent for its action upon laws of physics unknown to us upon the full light of the moon? The assertion of the natives that the *ani* had greatest power at this time might be a far-flung reflection of knowledge which had found ways to use forces contained in moonlight, as we have found ways to utilize the forces in the sun's rays. If so, Thora was probably behind the slab, sending out prayers to us for help.

"But how explain the sleep that had descended upon us? Might it not have been some emanation from plants or gaseous emanations from the island itself? Such things were far from uncommon, we agreed. In some way, the period of their greatest activity might coincide with the period of the moon, but if this were so why had not Thora also slept?

"As dusk fell we looked over our weapons. Edith was an excellent shot with both rifle and pistol. With the idea that the impulse toward sleep was the result either of emanations such as I have described or man made, we constructed rough-and-ready but effective neutralizers, which we placed over our mouths and nostrils. We had decided that my wife was to remain in the hollow spot. Stanton would take up a station on the far side of the stairway and I would place myself opposite him on the side near Edith. The place I picked out was less than five hundred feet from her, and I could reassure myself now as to her safety, as I looked down upon the hollow wherein she crouched. As the phenomena had previously synchronized with the rising of the moon, we had no reason to think they would occur any earlier this night.

"A faint glow in the sky heralded the moon. I kissed Edith, and Stanton and I took our places. The moon dawn increased rapidly; the disk swam up, and in a moment it seemed was shining in full radiance upon ruins and sea.

"As it rose there came as on the night before the curious little sighing sound from the inner terrace. I saw Stanton straighten up and stare intently through the gateway, rifle ready. Even at the distance he was from me, I discerned amazement in his eyes. The moonlight within the gateway thickened, grew stronger. I watched his amazement grow into sheer wonder.

"I arose.

"'Stanton, what do you see?' I called cautiously. He waved a silencing hand. I turned my head to look at Edith. A shock ran through me. She lay upon her side. Her face was turned full toward the moon. She was in deepest sleep!

"As I turned again to call to Stanton, my eyes swept the head of the steps and stopped, fascinated. For the moonlight had thickened more. It seemed to be—curdled—there; and through it ran little gleams and veins of shimmering white fire. A languor passed through me. It was not the ineffable drowsiness of the preceding night. It was a sapping of all will to move. I tore my eyes away and forced them upon Stanton. I tried to call out to him. I had not the will to make my lips move! I had struggled against this paralysis and as I did so I felt through me a sharp shock. It was like a blow. And with it came utter inability to make a single motion. Goodwin, I could not even move my eyes!

"I saw Stanton leap upon the steps and move toward the gateway. As he did so the light in the courtyard grew dazzlingly brilliant. Through it rained tiny tinklings that set the heart to racing with pure joy and stilled it with terror.

"And now for the first time I heard that cry '*Av-o-lo-ha! Av-o-lo-ha!*' the cry you heard on deck. It murmured with the strange effect of a sound only partly in our own space—as though it were part of a fuller phrase passing through from another dimension and losing much as it came; infinitely caressing, infinitely cruel!

"On Stanton's face I saw come the look I dreaded—and yet knew would appear; that mingled expression of delight and fear. The two lay side by side as they had on Thora, but were intensified. He walked on up the stairs; disappeared beyond the range of my fixed gaze. Again I heard the murmur—'*Av-o-lo-ha!*' There was triumph in it now and triumph in the storm of tinklings that swept over it.

"For another heart-beat there was silence. Then a louder burst of sound and ringing through it Stanton's voice from the courtyard—a great cry—a scream—filled with ecstasy insupportable and horror unimaginable! And again there was silence. I strove to burst the invisible bonds that held me. I could not. Even my eyelids were fixed. Within them my eyes, dry and aching, burned.

"Then Goodwin—I first saw the inexplicable! The crystalline music swelled. Where I sat I could take in the gateway and its basalt portals, rough and broken, rising to the top of the wall forty feet above, shattered, ruined portals—unclimbable. From this gateway an intenser light began to flow. It grew, it gushed, and into it, into my sight, walked Stanton.

"Stanton! But—Goodwin! What a vision!" He ceased. I waited—waited.

## CHAPTER VI

### INTO THE MOON POOL

"GOODWIN," Throckmartin said at last, "I can describe him only as a thing of living light. He radiated light; was filled with light; overflowed with it. Around him was a shining cloud that whirled through and around him in radiant swirls, shimmering tentacles, luminescent, coruscating spirals.

"I saw his face. It shone with a rapture too great to be borne by living men, and was shadowed with insuperable misery. It was as though his face had been remolded by the hand of God and the hand of Satan, working together and in harmony. You have seen it on my face. But you have never seen it in the degree than Stanton bore it. The eyes were wide open and fixed, as though upon some inward vision of hell and heaven! He walked like the corpse of a man damned who carried within him an angel of light.

"The music swelled again. I heard again the murmuring—'Av-o-lo-ha!' Stanton turned, facing the ragged side of the portal. And then I saw that the light that filled and surrounded him had a nucleus, a core—something shiftingly human shaped —that dissolved and changed, gathered itself, whirled through and beyond him and back again. And as this shining nucleus passed through him Stanton's whole body pulsed with light. As the luminescence moved, there moved with it, still and serene always, seven tiny globes of light like seven little moons.

"So much I saw and then swiftly Stanton seemed to be lifted—levitated—up the unscalable wall and to its top. The glow faded from the moonlight, the tingling music grew fainter. I tried again to move. The spell still held me fast. The tears were running down now from my rigid lids and brought relief to my tortured eyes.

"I have said my gaze was fixed. It was. But from the side, peripherally, it took in a part of the far wall of the outer enclosure. Ages seemed to pass and I saw a radiance stealing along it. Soon there came into sight the figure that was Stanton. Far away he was—on the gigantic wall. But still I could see the shining spirals whirling jubilantly around and through him; felt rather than saw his tranced face beneath the seven lights. A swirl of crystal notes, and he had passed. And all the time, as though from some opened well of light, the courtyard gleamed and sent out silver fires that dimmed the moon-rays, yet seemed strangely to be a part of them.

"Ten times he passed before me so. The luminescence came with the music; swam for a while along the man-made cliff of basalt and passed away. Between times eternities rolled and still I crouched there, a helpless thing of stone with eyes that would not close!

"At last the moon neared the horizon. There came a louder burst of sound; the second, and last, cry of Stanton, like an echo of the first! Again the soft sigh from the inner terrace. Then—utter silence. The light faded; the moon was setting and with a rush life and power to move returned to me, I made a leap for the steps, rushed up them, through the gateway and straight to the gray rock. It was closed— as I knew it would be. But did I dream it or did I hear, echoing through it as though from vast distances a triumphant shouting—'Av-o-lo-ha! Av-o-lo-ha!'?

"I remembered Edith. I ran back to her. At my touch she wakened; looked at me wonderingly; raised herself on a hand.

"'Dave!' she said, 'I slept—after all.' She saw the despair on my face and leaped to her feet. 'Dave!' she cried. 'What is it? Where's Charles?'

"I lighted a fire before I spoke. Then I told her. And for the balance of that night we sat before the flames, arms around each other—like two frightened children."

Suddenly Throckmartin held his hands out to me appealingly.

"Goodwin, old friend!" he cried. "Don't look at me as though I were mad. It's truth, absolute truth. Wait—" I comforted him as well as I could. After a little time he took up his story.

"Never," he said, "did man welcome the sun as we did that morning. As soon as it was light we went back to the courtyard. The basalt walls whereon I had seen Stanton were black and silent. The terraces were as they had been. The gray slab was in its place. In the shallow hollow at its base was—nothing. Nothing—nothing was there anywhere on the islet of Stanton—not a trace, not a sign on Nan-Tanach to show that he had ever lived.

"What were we to do? Precisely the same arguments that had kept us there the night before held good now—and doubly good. We could not abandon these two; could not go as long as there was the faintest hope of finding them—and yet for love of each other how could we remain? I loved my wife, Goodwin—how much I never knew until that day; and she loved me as deeply.

"'It takes only one each night,' she said. 'Beloved, let it take me.'

"I wept, Goodwin. We both wept.

"'We will meet it together,' she said. And it was thus at last that we arranged it."

"That took great courage indeed, Throckmartin," I interrupted. He looked at me eagerly.

"You do believe then?" he exclaimed.

"I believe," I said. He pressed my hand with a grip that nearly crushed it.

"Now," he told me, "I do not fear. If I—fail, you will prepare and carry on the work."

I promised. And—Heaven forgive me—that was three years ago.

"It did take courage," he went on, again quietly. "More than courage. For we knew it was renunciation. Each of us in our hearts felt that one of us would not be there to see the sun rise. And each of us prayed that the death, if death it was, would not come first to the other.

"We talked it all over carefully, bringing to bear all our power of analysis and habit of calm, scientific thought. We considered minutely the time element in the phenomena. Although the deep chanting began at the very moment of moonrise, fully five minutes had passed between its full lifting and the strange sighing sound from the inner terrace. I went back in memory over the happenings of the night before. At least fifteen minutes had intervened between the first heralding sigh and the intensification of the moonlight in the courtyard. And this glow grew for at least ten minutes more before the first burst of the crystal notes.

"The sighing sound—of what had it reminded me? Of course—of a door revolving and swishing softly along its base.

"'Edith!' I cried. 'I think I have it! The gray rock opens five minutes after upon the moonrise. But whoever or whatever it is that comes through it must wait until the moon has risen higher, or else it must come from a distance. The thing to do is not to wait for it, but to surprise it before it passes out the door. We will go into the inner court early. You will take your rifle and pistol and hide yourself where you can command the opening—if the slab does open. The instant it moves I will enter. It's our best chance, Edith. I think it's our only one.'

"My wife demurred strongly. She wanted to go with me. But I convinced her that it was better for her to stand guard without, prepared to help me if I were forced from what lay behind the rock again into the open.

"The day passed too swiftly. In the face of what we feared our love seemed stronger than ever. Was it the flare of the spark before extinguishment? I wondered. We prepared and ate a good dinner. We tried to keep our minds from anything but the scientific aspect of the phenomena.

We agreed that whatever it was its cause must be human, and that we must keep that fact in mind every second. But what kind of men could create such prodigies? We thrilled at the thought of finding perhaps the remnants of a vanished race, living perhaps in cities over whose rocky skies the Pacific rolled; exercising there the lost wisdom of the half-gods of earth's youth.

"At the half-hour before moonrise we two went into the inner courtyard. I took my place at the side of the gray rock. Edith crouched behind a broken pillar twenty feet away, slipped her rifle-barrel over it so that it would cover the opening.

"The minutes crept by. The courtyard was very quiet. The darkness lessened and through the breaches of the terrace I watched the far sky softly lighten. With the first pale flush the stillness became intensified. It deepened—became unbearably- expectant. The moon rose, showed the quarter, the half, then swam up into full sight like a great bubble.

"Its rays fell upon the wall before me and suddenly upon the convexities I have described seven little circles of light sprang out. They gleamed, glimmered, grew brighter—shone. The gigantic slab before me turned as though on a pivot, sighing softly as it moved.

"For a moment I gasped in amazement. It was like a conjurer's trick. And the moving slab I noticed was also glowing, becoming opalescent like the little shining circles above.

"Only for a second I gazed and then with a word to Edith flung myself through the opening which the slab had uncovered. Before me was a platform and from the platform steps led downward into a smooth corridor. This passage was not dark; it glowed with the same faint silvery radiance as the door. Down it I raced. As I ran, plainer than ever before, I heard the chanting. The passage turned abruptly, passed parallel to the walls of the outer courtyard and then once more led abruptly downward. Still I ran, and as I ran I looked at the watch on my wrist. Less than three minutes had elapsed.

"The passage ended. Before me was a high vaulted arch. For a moment I paused. It seemed to open into space; a space filled with lambent, coruscating, many-colored mist whose brightness grew even as I watched. I passed through the arch and stopped in sheer awe!

"In front of me was a pool. It was circular, perhaps twenty feet wide. Around it ran a low, softly curved lip of glimmering silvery stone. Its water was palest blue. The pool with its silvery rim was like a great blue eye staring upward.

"Upon it streamed seven shafts of radiance. They poured down upon the blue eye like cylindrical torrents; they were like shining pillars of light rising from a sapphire floor.

"One was the tender pink of the pearl; one of the aurora's green; a third a deathly white; the fourth the blue in mother-of-pearl; a shimmering column of pale amber; a beam of amethyst; a shaft of molten silver. Such are the colors of the seven lights that stream upon the moon pool. I drew closer, awestricken. The shafts did not illumine the depths. They played upon the surface and seemed there to diffuse, to melt into it. The pool drank them!

"Through the water tiny gleams of phosphorescence began to dart, sparkles and coruscations of pale incandescence. And far, far below I sensed a movement, a shifting glow as of something slowly rising.

"I looked upward, following the radiant pillars to their source. Far above were seven shining globes, and it was from these that the rays poured. Even as I watched their brightness grew. They were like seven moons set high in some caverned heaven. Slowly their splendor increased, and with it the splendor of the seven beams streaming from them. It came to me that they were crystals of some unknown kind set in the roof of the moon pool's vault and that their light was drawn from the moon shining high above them. They were wonderful, those lights—and what must have been the knowledge of those who set them there!

"Brighter and brighter they grew as the

moon climbed higher, sending its full radiance down through them. I tore my gaze away and stared at the pool. It had grown milky, opalescent. The rays gushing into it seemed to be filling it; it was alive with sparklings, scintillations, glimmerings. And the luminescence I had seen rising from its depths was larger, nearer!

"A swirl of mist floated up from its surface. It drifted within the embrace of the rosy beam and hung there for a moment. The beam seemed to embrace it, sending through it little shining corpuscles, tiny rosy spiralings. The mist absorbed the rays, was strengthened by it, gained substance. Another swirl sprang into the amber shaft, clung and fed there, moved swiftly toward the first and mingled with it. And now other swirls arose, here and there, too fast to be counted, hung poised in the embrace of the light streams; flashed and pulsed into each other.

"Thicker and thicker still they arose until the surface of the pool was a pulsating pillar of opalescent mist; steadily growing stronger; drawing within it life from the seven beams falling upon it; drawing to it from below the darting, red atoms of the pool. Into its center was passing the luminescence I had sensed rising from the far depths. And the center glowed, throbbed—began to send out questing swirls and tendrils.

"There forming before me was *that* which had walked with Stanton, which had taken Thora—the thing I had come to find!

"With the shock or realization my brain sprang into action. My hand fell to my pistol and I fired shot after shot into its radiance. The place rang with the explosions and there came to me a sense of unforgivable profanation. Devilish as I knew it to be, that chamber of the moon pool seemed also—in some way—holy. As though a god and a demon dwelt there, inextricably commingled.

"As I shot the pillar wavered; the water grew more disturbed. The mist swayed and shook; gathered itself again. I slipped a second clip into the automatic and, another idea coming to me, took careful aim at one of the globes in the roof. From thence I knew came the force that shaped the dweller in the pool. From the pouring rays came its strength. If I could destroy them I could check its forming. I fired again and again. If I hit the globes I did no damage. The little motes in their beams danced with the motes in the mist, troubled. That was all.

"Up from the pool like little bells, like bubbles of crystal notes rose the tinklings. Their notes were higher, had lost their sweetness, were angry, as it were, with themselves.

"And then out from the Inexplicable, hovering over the pool, swept a shining swirl. It caught me above the heart; wrapped itself around me. I felt an icy coldness and then there rushed over me a mingled ecstasy and horror. Every atom of me quivered with delight and at the same time shrank with despair. There was nothing loathsome in it. But it was as though the icy soul of evil and the fiery soul of good had stepped together within me. The pistol dropped from my hand.

"So I stood while the pool gleamed and sparkled; the streams of light grew more intense and the mist glowed and strengthened. I saw that its shining core had shape—but a shape that my eyes and brain could not define. It was as though a being of another sphere should assume what it might of human semblance, but was not able to conceal that what human eyes saw was but a part of it. It was neither man nor woman; it was unearthly and androgynous. Even as I found its human semblance it changed. And still the mingled rapture and terror held me. Only in a little corner of my brain dwelt something untouched; something that held itself apart and watched. Was it the soul? I have never believed—and yet—

"Over the head of the misty body there sprang suddenly out seven little lights. Each was the color of the beam beneath which it rested. I knew now that the dweller was—complete!

"And then—behind me I heard a scream.

It was Edith's voice. It came to me that she had heard the shots and followed me. I felt every faculty concentrate into a mighty effort. I wrenched myself free from the gripping tentacle and it swept back. I turned to catch Edith, and as I did so slipped—fell. As I dropped I saw the radiant shape above the pool leap swiftly for me!

"There was the rush past me and as the dweller paused, straight into it raced Edith, arms outstretched to shield me from it!"

He trembled.

"She threw herself squarely within its diabolic splendor," he whispered. "She stopped and reeled as though she had encountered solidity. And as she faltered it wrapped its shining self around her. The crystal tinklings burst forth jubilantly. The light filled her, ran through and around her as it had with Stanton, and I saw drop upon her face—the look. From the pillar came the murmur—'Av-o-lo-ha!' The vault echoed it.

"'Edith!' I cried. 'Edith!' I was in agony. She must have heard me, even through the—thing. I saw her try to free herself. Her rush had taken her to the very verge of the moon pool. She tottered; and in an instant—she fell—with the radiance still holding her, still swirling and winding around and through her—into the moon pool! She sank, Goodwin, and with her went—the dweller!

"I dragged myself to the brink. Far down I saw a shining, many-colored nebulous cloud descending; caught a glimpse of Edith's face, disappearing; her eyes stared up to me filled with supernal ecstasy and horror. And—vanished!

"I looked about me stupidly. The seven globes still poured their radiance upon the pool. It was pale-blue again. Its sparklings and coruscations were gone. From far below there came a muffled outburst of triumphant chanting!

"'Edith!' I cried again. 'Edith, come back to me!' And then a darkness fell upon me. I remember running back through the shimmering corridors and out into the courtyard. Reason had left me. When it

returned I was far out at sea in our boat wholly estranged from civilization. A day later I was picked up by the schooner in which I came to Port Moresby.

"I have formed a plan; you must hear it, Goodwin—" He fell upon his berth. I bent over him. Exhaustion and the relief of telling his story had been too much for him. He slept like the dead.

## CHAPTER VII

### THE DWELLER COMES

ALL that night I watched over him. When dawn broke I went to my room to get a little sleep myself. But my slumber was haunted.

The next day the storm was unabated. Throckmartin came to me at lunch. He looked better. His strange expression had waned. He had regained much of his old alertness.

"Come to my cabin," he said. There, he stripped his shirt from him. "Something is happening," he said. "The mark is smaller." It was as he said.

"I'm escaping," he whispered jubilantly. "Just let me get to Melbourne safely, and then we'll see who'll win! For, Goodwin, I'm not at all sure that Edith is dead—as we know death—nor that the others are. There was something outside experience there—some great mystery."

And all that day he talked to me of his plans.

"There's a natural explanation, of course," he said. "My theory is that the moon rock is of some composition sensitive to the action of moon rays; somewhat as the metal selenium is to sun rays. There is a powerful quality in moonlight, as both science and legends can attest. We know of its effect upon the mentality, the nervous system, even upon certain diseases.

"The moon slab is of some material that reacts to moonlight. The circles over the top are, without doubt, its operating agency. When the light strikes them they release the mechanism that opens the slab, just as you can open doors with sunlight by an ingenious arrangement of selenium-cells. Apparently it takes the strength of the full moon to do this. We will first try a concentration of the rays of the *nearly* full moon upon these circles to see whether that will open the rock. If it does we will be able to investigate the pool without interruption from—from—what emanates.

"Look, here on the chart are their locations. I have made this in duplicate for you in the event of something happening to me."

He worked upon the chart a little more.

"Here," he said, "is where I believe the seven great globes to be. They are probably hidden somewhere in the ruins of the islet called Tau, where they can catch the first moon rays. I have calculated that when I entered I went so far this way— here is the turn; so far this way, took this other turn and ran down this long, curving corridor to the hall of the moon pool. That ought to make lights, at least approximately, here." He pointed.

"They are certainly cleverly concealed, but they must be open to the air to get the light. They should not be too hard to find. They must be found." He hesitated again. "I suppose it would be safer to destroy them, for it is clearly through them that the phenomena of the pool is manifested; and yet, to destroy so wonderful a thing! Perhaps the better way would be to have some men up by them, and if it were necessary, to protect those below, to destroy them on signal. Or they might simply be covered. That would neutralize them. To destroy them—" He hesitated again. "No, the phenomena is too important to be destroyed without fullest investigation." His face clouded again. "But it is *not* human; it can't be," he muttered. He turned to me and laughed. "The old conflict between science and too frail human credulity!" he said.

Again—"We need half a dozen diving-suits. The pool must be entered and searched to its depths. That will indeed take courage, yet in the time of the new moon it should be safe, or perhaps better after the dweller is destroyed or made safe."

We went over plans, accepted them, rejected them, and still the storm raged— and all that day and all that night.

I hurry to the end. That afternoon there came a steady lightening of the clouds which Throckmartin watched with deep uneasiness. Toward dusk they broke away suddenly and soon the sky was clear. The stars came twinkling out.

"It will be tonight," Throckmartin said to me. "Goodwin, friend, stand by me. To-night it will come, and I must fight."

I could say nothing. About an hour before moonrise we went to his cabin. We fastened the port-holes tightly and turned on the lights. Throckmartin had some queer theory that the electric rays would be a bar to his pursuer. I don't know why. A little later he complained of increasing sleepiness.

"But it's just weariness," he said. "Not at all like that other drowsiness. It's an hour till moonrise still," he yawned at last. "Wake me up a good fifteen minutes before."

He lay upon the berth. I sat thinking. I came to myself with a start. What time was it? I looked at my watch and jumped to the port-hole. It was full moonlight; the orb had been up for fully half an hour. I strode over to Throckmartin and shook him by the shoulder.

"Up, quick, man!" I cried. He rose sleepily. His shirt fell open at the neck and I looked, in amazement, at the white band around his chest. Even under the electric light it shone softly, as though little flecks of light were in it.

Throckmartin seemed only half-awake. He looked down at his breast, saw the glowing cincture, and smiled.

"Oh, yes," he said drowsily, "it's coming—to take me back to Edith! Well, I'm glad."

"Throckmartin!" I cried. "Wake up! Fight."

"Fight!" he said. "No use; keep the maps; come after us."

He went to the port and drowsily drew aside the curtain. The moon traced a broad path of light straight to the ship. Under its rays the band around his chest gleamed brighter and brighter; shot forth little rays; seemed to move.

He peered out intently and, suddenly, before I could stop him, threw open the port. I saw a glimmering presence moving swiftly along the moon path toward us, skimming over the waters.

And with it raced little crystal tinklings and far off I heard a long-drawn murmuring cry.

On the instant the lights went out in the cabin, evidently throughout the ship, for I heard shoutings above. I sprang back into a corner and crouched there. At the porthole was a radiance; swirls and spirals of living white cold fire. It poured into the cabin and it was filled with dancing motes of light, and over the radiant core of it shone seven little lights like tiny moons. It gathered Throckmartin to it. Light pulsed through and from him. I saw his skin turn to a translucent, shimmering whiteness like illumined porcelain. His face became unrecognizable, inhuman with the monstrous twin expressions. So he stood for a moment. The pillar of light seemed to hesitate and the seven lights to contemplate me. I shrank further down into the corner. I saw Throckmartin drawn to the port. The room filled with murmuring. I fainted.

When I awakened the lights were burning again.

But of Throckmartin there was no trace!

There are some things that we are bound to regret all our lives. I suppose I was unbalanced by what I had seen. I could not think clearly. But there came to me the sheer impossibility of telling the ship's officers what I had seen; what Throckmartin had told me. They would accuse me, I felt, of his murder. At neither appearance of the phenomena had any save our two selves witnessed it. I was certain of this because they would surely have discussed it. Why none had seen it I do not know.

The next morning when Throckmartin's absence was noted, I merely said that I had left him early in the evening. It occurred to no one to doubt me, or to question me further. His strangeness had caused much comment; all had thought him half-mad. And so it was officially reported that he had fallen or jumped from the ship during the failure of the lights, the cause of which was another mystery of that night.

Afterward, the same inhibition held me back from making his and my story known to my fellow scientists.

But this inhibition is suddenly dead, and I am not sure that its death is not a summons from Throckmartin.

And now I am going to Nan-Tanach to make amends for my cowardice by seeking out the dweller. So sure am I that all I have written here is absolutely true.

---

They wrestled
wildly in space

*A Vivid*
*Tale of*
*Martian Conquest*
By
MANLY WADE WELLMAN

# Space Station No. 1

IN ITS time Space Station No. 1 was
unique in the solar system and probably the universe, for, of all the worlds
that swung around the sun, it alone was a
creation of mortal engineers and me-
chanics, built of materials artificially prepared, shaped and joined, for civilized purposes and profit.

Without it the Martio-Terrestrial

League's Jovian colonies might well have
failed at the start. Jupiter's moons abound-
ed in valuable minerals, offered broad lands
for development and settlement by emi-
grants, but they were almost too far away.
Only once in two years were Mars and
Jupiter in conjunction, close enough for
liners and freighters to ply between. A
few days thus, then the planets drifted

27

apart on their orbits, the gap widening to an impossible distance for two years more.

Wherefore the League's experts planned and built Space Station No. 1, to circle the sun along Mars' orbit, but on the far side of the sun from Mars. Old Sol's gravity carried the synthetic planetoid in approximate position, as the current of a whirlpool carries a chip of wood in an endless circle. Occasional rocket blasts kept the station exactly where it should be. Thus, when the planet was in opposition and at its farthest from Jupiter, the station was at its closest, a half-way house for the refueling of Jupiter-bound ships from Earth and Mars. Supplies and other relief could reach the colonists once each year instead of once each two years.

Viewed from afar against the star-dusted black of space, the station looked like an exaggerated mimicry of ringed Saturn. The spherical center was an outmoded and awkward space-hulk two hundred meters in diameter. Construction ships had towed it into position, then clamped great girders all around its equator to extend like spokes from a hub. These in turn were braced with smaller crosswise girders and cables and the whole decked over with metal plates to make a circular plane a mile across, extending collar-like from and around the ball-shaped center. This deck was the landing port. The hulk in the middle did duty as administration building, storehouse, and living quarters.

For men lived there. And though the League and the colonies found Space Station No. 1 practical and valuable, its attendants found it all but unendurable.

There were two of them, standing just now on the outer rim of the deck, clad in space-overalls of insulated fabric, magnetized boots that held them to the almost gravityless plating, and bell-like glass helmets, slightly clouded against the sun's unimpeded glare. The taller was Lane Everitt, a tough-bodied young Terrestrial, who was glaring as fiercely as the sun itself. He had had enough of Space Station No. 1, this cramped corner where he must live in dingy cabins, corridors and holds, and swaddle himself in glass and fabric whenever he ventured out for exercise.

A full year of this prison-like boredom, and why? Because he, a simple navigator of Spaceways, Inc., had loved and been loved by Fortuna Sidney, daughter of the corporation's director-general. Now he was out here, doomed to the most deadly routine job in the universe, while she was shut up in the strictest schools with instructions to forget him.

"Rats!" he growled aloud, and his own voice, echoing inside the helmet, startled him. He must stop mumbling to himself—yes, and lying awake, and cheating at solitaire—or he'd go crazy, like that chap Ropakihn he had relieved out here. And if he went crazy, he, too, would be clapped in an asylum. No job, no freedom. No Fortuna. He gazed down from the deck's verge into the endlessness of space, found no comfort there, then turned his head inside the transparent helmet to glance back along the level expanse of deck. He felt like a very small fly on the rim of a very big tray, with the hulk for an apple in its center. And Earth and the solar system valued him at less than a fly.

"Did you mention rats, Ev? You require rodents for some purpose?"

IT WAS the mechanically expressionless voice of Zeoui, his Martian associate, who stood beside him. Zeoui's chrysanthemum-like face—if face it really was—tilted toward him questioningly.

Zeoui was one of those Martians destined from birth and before to live and work with Terrestrials. Eugenic breeding and medical alteration had brought his shape to approximate that of an Earth man. His soft, bladder-like body had been elongated, stiffened with artificial spine, and raised erect upon two slender limbs. Its upper corners were even shaped into shoulders, and bore in lieu of arms two tentacles with sensitive tips, just now concealed in his space-mittens. At the top, under the helmet, was his large and fragile braincase, shaggy all over with the petal-like fronds and tags of tissue housing his Martian awareness of conditions that approximated the five Terrestrial senses. Thus developed and equipped, Zeoui could walk and work with Earth's mankind, could talk—he favored ultra-pedantic and exact poly-syllables—by stirring air through an arti-ficial larynx. He was more at home among Terrestrials than among the jelly-like bodies and feeler-appendages of his fellow-Martians.

He spoke again: "A rocket vessel, swift and small, approaches."

"Coming here? Already?" Everitt glanced up. "They aren't due, not for hours yet."

The thought of ships depressed him. For five days they would be passing him, heading for Jupiter, and in a few weeks the craft from the colonies would be stop-ping off on the inner trail—worse than no company at all. He and Zeoui would mix liquid oxygen and other ingredients into fuel and operate the pumps, but there would be no chatting or fraternizing. Skip-pers might transmit formal orders, receive reports, no more. No word from home or friends, no mail. . . .

"Observe. It is approaching rapidly." Zeoui pointed a tentacle. In the blackness far above circled a tiny gray dart of a space-craft, cutting speed, and preparing to land. Everitt scowled in perplexity, lift-ing a hand to his helmet as if to rumple his bright hair inside.

"That's not a Spaceways job," he said in mystified tones. "It looks like a war craft. What—"

The lead-colored cigar burst into a dazzling flare at the nose, and the gush of the forward rockets braked it sharply. As the two watchers stood at gaze, it fell to a swaying crawl directly overhead. Then it curved in, around, and down to the deck not a hundred yards away.

Almost before its rocket blasts had sub-sided a panel sprang open in its side and a helmeted head popped out.

"Someone disembarks," commented Zeoui's maddeningly dry voice. "Yes, and makes significant motions of the hand."

The first figure to reach the deck was small and slight, even in space-overall.

"Ev!" came a soft, trembling cry to Everitt's earphones, and his heart stirred. He had never expected to hear that voice again.

"Ev, dear!" The little figure was run-ning toward him, and he found his own voice.

"Fortuna!" he cried back, and sped to meet her. A moment later he had clutched the newcomer in his arms, was pressing her close to him and gazing at a dear white face through two thicknesses of clouded glass. Her big, storm-dark eyes swam with tears of mingled joy and concern, her full lips trembled.

Then more motion from the direction of the ship caught Everitt's eye. A towering form in full space-armor stepped into view. Then another, then four more in a group. They bore arms in their hands or belts— the big leader an electro-automatic rifle, his stunted neighbor a lantern-like rust-ray, the other pistols. Everitt stiffened in startled wonder.

"It's all right, they're my men," came Fortuna's voice to his ears. "Let's go some-where and talk, Ev. It's important."

"Right, Fortuna," he agreed, making his voice steady. To Zeoui he spoke crisply. "Stay on deck, will you? I'm tak-ing her inside."

Zeoui's face-petals stirred and curled against his helmet-glass, as if in worried fidgets. "These individuals," he ventured. "Is it to be understood that—"

"Steady, old man," cautioned Everitt quickly. "You aren't supposed to speak to visitors."

"The same restriction applies to your-self," reminded Zeoui.

"But I must speak," Everitt said flatly. "I'll handle this situation alone, though. No need for you to be involved."

IT WAS half a warning, half a snub, and Zeoui fell silent. Taking Fortuna's arm, Everitt led her toward the hulk. Their eyes were ever upon each other, and their emotion was too deep for smiles. Behind them came the armed half dozen companions of the girl.

The lock-panel in the hulk slid back at Everitt's touch and first he and Fortuna, then the others, stepped into the little air-lock chamber. A moment later they had passed the inner panel. Inside the old control room that, stripped of instruments and fitted with a desk, chairs and cabinets, served as an office, they felt the comforting pull of the artificial gravity that the outer deck lacked.

All began to unship their helmets. Everitt and Fortuna freed their faces first and at once kissed with hungry violence. Everitt thought that the biggest of Fortuna's companions chuckled derisively under his half-doffed headpiece, but was too happy to resent it.

"And now," Fortuna murmured, freeing her lips, "I'll tell you how we are working your escape."

"Escape?" repeated Everitt sharply. "You don't mean—"

"I tried to get you relieved," the girl said, with a serious wag of her dark, curly head, "but daddy turned obdurate. Said he'd keep you here until you rotted. And so, in desperation, I went at it another way." Half turning in Everitt's embrace, she nodded to the big man. "Tell him, Ropakihn."

"Ropakihn?" said Everitt. "Are you—?" He paused.

The giant's head was out of the helmet now. It showed huge, heavy-jowled, with bright, piggy eyes, a mighty blade of a nose and a crimson complexion. The coarse, well-combed thatch of hair was a good six feet six above the office floor, and the armored body was heavy, even for that height. A loose smile crossed the big, red countenance as a raspy voice answered Everitt's half-voiced question.

"Yes, I'm Ropakihn, the man who played—well, eccentric—to get away from here." The lips grew looser, writhing a bit. "They shut me up in a comfortable but boresome asylum, until Miss Fortuna here came to visit me. She arranged for a leave of absence for me and these other inmates. You see," and his rasp grew smug, "I knew about the new type of war-craft and their MS-ray. Knew it from a retired officer— also eccentric enough to be shut up. He babbled out the location of a hangar where an ultra-fast experimental ship was kept."

Everitt puzzled over this information. "MS-ray—metal-solvent? I heard it was being developed, an advance on the rust-ray principle."

"Since you were exiled it became a reality," Ropakihn informed him. "There's one on that super-speed ship out there— the one we took a few nights ago from its hangar."

He paused, grinning in a self-congratulatory manner, while Fortuna took up the tale. "I guessed," she said, "that Ropakihn wasn't as afflicted as they thought. I also guessed that he would be miffed enough at the people who had exiled and imprisoned him to be an ally. He was good enough to listen and to pick these other friends."

For the first time Everitt looked at Ropakihn's five companions, also helmet-less by now. And he was genuinely shocked.

Not one of them was normal. The man with the rust-ray was a hunched and twisted dwarf with the face of a cunning weasel. Two of the others were well set up, but they wore expressions of brutal stupidity. The remaining two were patently imbecilic, fidgety and grimacing. No wonder both Fortuna and Ropakihn had avoided saying "crazy"—had employed such words as "eccentric" and "afflicted." The other expression would have been too pointed to use in this company.

Ropakihn continued, amusedly:

"In any case, Everitt, Miss Fortuna got us out. Now she wants us to try to get you out."

"Exactly," added Fortuna in happy triumph. "What with our extra speed, we have a start of hours on the rest of the ships. Have you any baggage? We'll head back to Earth at once."

"I can't go," said Everitt.

THERE was silence for a moment, and they all looked at him—Fortuna uncomprehending, Ropakihn somewhat scornful, the others foolishly querulous. Then Fortuna began to argue.

"You don't understand, darling. It isn't as though they were out patrolling the space-lanes for you. Why, they won't even know you've deserted until we're safely landed and lost, in Africa or Brazil or—"

"I can't go," said Everitt again.

Ropakihn chuckled, as he had when Fortuna and Everitt had kissed each other.

"Do I read you rightly?" he inquired with the hint of a sneer. "Do you feel that your duty lies here?"

"Duty!" snapped Fortuna heatedly. "This routine job? Why, Ev, darling, a child could do it, mixing fuel and filling tanks."

"Without me the Jovian route will be broken in two," he reminded her. "Zeoui couldn't handle things alone."

Fortuna clenched her little fists in despair. "Don't you want me? Don't I love you, and didn't Spaceways do you a shabby trick? Your every instinct—"

"There are many instincts," he interrupted gently. "One is for love, and heaven knows that it's strong in me. But another's for honor and loyalty. That keeps me at my post."

Another silence, with all eyes on Everitt. Finally Fortuna shrugged, though not in complete resignation.

"Maybe you're right," she said slowly.

"I know I am," Everitt rejoined. "You can go home, dear, and wait for the thing to work out properly."

"That," growled Ropakihn in a new, grim voice, "is where you are wrong."

HE TOOK a step forward. The five grouped behind him suddenly brought their weapons to the ready. Ropakihn himself shifted his right hand to the trigger-switch of his rifle.

"Corby," he said crisply to the twisted man with the rust-ray, "go out on deck and bring that Martian in here."

"Yop." The man called Corby made a sloppy gesture of salute and turned to enter the air-lock, putting on his helmet as he did so.

Everitt tightened his muscles as if to spring, but Ropakihn lifted his weapon warningly. "Steady," said the giant. "You're my prisoners."

"Ropakihn!" called Fortuna. "I'm giving orders here."

"Not now." The heavy, red face crinkled in a broader grin. "You think I'll go back to that asylum? Think again, lady. We're going to go to Jupiter instead."

Everitt had not shrunk back from the menace of the guns. "You're outlaws, then?" he demanded accusingly. "You mean to defy Earth and Mars together?"

"Outlaws—for today," agreed Ropakihn in high good humor. "But in a few weeks we'll be conquerors. That MS-ray will blow the defenses loose from the whole Jovian colonial setup. They'll have to surrender to us. Instead of outlaws—rulers!" He grew exultant. "And Earth and Mars will have to treat with us."

Then he grew blustery. "Get ready to mix us some fuel, Everitt. Enough for the jump to Jupiter."

Everitt shook his head. "I serve no ship without a voucher from the Interplanetary Commerce Commission," he said flatly.

"Here's my voucher," and Ropakihn twiddled his rifle. "It's electric powered, but bored for lead-and-powder cartridges —fifty— just like the guns of the ancients. A novelty piece." His grin grew cruel. "No merciful death by shock, Everitt. How would you like me to start shooting your toes off, one at a time?"

Everitt was disdainfully silent.

"Or Miss Fortuna's toes, perhaps? Does that intrigue you?"

Everitt felt a chill creep along his spine. Fortuna tortured! . . .

"There's no fuel mixed as yet," he announced. "We didn't expect a ship so soon."

"No? Then we'll start the machinery going. And when we've fueled ourselves, we'll try out our MS-ray—wash this station clear out of the universe."

One or two of Ropakihn's followers giggled inanely at the thought, and Fortuna shivered. The sense of her danger and his own helplessness infuriated Everitt. "You'll destroy the station!" he cried.

"Of course," Ropakihn's face turned harsh. "It doesn't fill me with affectionate memories. And with it gone, police craft can't refuel and follow."

"Next year Mars will be in the halfway station spot," Everitt reminded him. "There'll be plenty of trouble flying out to Jupiter after you."

"When we're holding all the colonies as hostage?" laughed Ropakihn. "Don't be absurd. They'll be glad to meet whatever terms we make. Freedom, money, recognition as governors even."

Everitt said nothing. The scheme was as practicable as it was daring. Such a weapon as the MS-ray, unknown as yet on the Jovian moons, would spell victory for this handful of insane adventurers. What fantastic rulers for the unlucky settlers!

The air-lock opened and two figures entered—Zeoui and Corby, taking off their helmets. The Martian's chrysanthemum face turned toward Ropakihn.

"Your lieutenant has been explaining to me your stratagem for the invasion and conquest of Jupiter's satellites," he volunteered in his precise manner. "Have you accommodations in your ship for a recruit?"

Everitt gasped. Was Zeoui, the pedant, inflamed by dreams of piracy? Ropakihn grinned welcome.

"Certainly we have room, for several recruits. But how about the fuel? You, Martian—what's your name?"

"Zeoui," was the reply. "You want fuel? Expediently? Give me two men to help."

Ropakihn waved forward the two brutal-faced outlaws. Zeoui led them through the inner door of the office and down the passage toward the fuel-mixing chamber. Everitt watched with rage-darkened face, much to Ropakihn's amusement.

"Your partner seems to be reasonable," he commented. "How about you two?"

Everitt shook his head. "You want somebody normal to leaven your crazy crew." He exulted at the flinch that the word "crazy" wrung from his captors, and went on. "Nothing doing, Ropakihn. If you're destroying the space station, destroy me with it. You won't have long to enjoy the sensation."

Ropakihn turned toward Fortuna, but she shook her head. "It's unnecessary to ask me," she said.

The big man chuckled, his gaze feasting on her trim lines which the collapsed space-overall could not disguise. "I'm not asking," he replied. "You're coming along—to help shorten the journey . . ." His greedy eyes never left her. "You'll be queen of my new Jovian empire. . . ."

EVERITT could stand no more. He made a lunge at his towering foe. But the magnetism in his shoes, augmented by the floor's artificial gravity, slowed his charge for a second. In that second Ropakihn was on guard, fending him off with the rifle barrel across his chest, while Corby and the two others had fallen upon him.

For full half a minute Everitt battled, his angry strength almost a match for his three assailants, but then they forced him down and began to bind his limbs with a belt from his own overall. Fortuna, seeing his defeat, made a dash as if to help him. Ropakihn, laughing, clutched at her, and she swerved away, then ran for the door that led to the hulk's interior.

A form popped into view on the threshold, barring her retreat. It was Zeoui. A quick clutch with a tentacle-tip, and he had her by the wrist. "Was she endeavoring to depart?" he enunciated dryly.

"She tried to fight," growled Ropakihn. "I'll take the fight out of her before we've been aboard a quarter of an hour. How's the fuel job?"

"Going expeditiously," retorted the Martian. "The assistants you placed at my disposal are supervising the mixing-pumps. May I be assigned others to aid in extending the feed conduits to your vessel?"

"Right." Ropakihn turned his eyes to his three remaining henchmen. "Corby, stay here to keep an eye on Everitt. You others, on with your helmets and go with Zeoui."

Zeoui still held Fortuna, who had quieted, but still glared angrily. "It would be well," he suggested, "to confine this person likewise."

He himself assisted in tying her arms and ankles. Then he bustled about, helping his two new companions to put on their helmets. Finally he led them out upon the deck.

TIME passed. Everitt and Fortuna, helpless in their bonds, lay propped against a bulkhead under Corby's guard. Ropakihn, lolling on the desk, talked. He throve on his own boasting, telling enthusiastically of his enterprise in planning the theft of the speed-craft with its new ray equipment, his courage and resource in executing that theft, of his daring in conceiving the idea of conquering Jupiter's moons.

Half an hour was gone before he wearied at the sound of his voice. Breaking his stream of self-praise then he moved to a port and looked out.

"Where's Zeoui?" he demanded, half aloud. "I don't see him or the others. They must be in the cruiser itself."

Again he studied the deck outside. "They've got the pipe drawn out to the ship," he continued after a moment, "but it's limp—there can't be a very big stream of fuel. Probably none at all."

Swinging around, he glared at the prisoners and at Corby. "Say," he blustered at the universe in general, "are those lazy limpets soldiering on their mixing jobs? I'll show them how!" He started to tramp across the floor, but the loud clang of his magnetized boots halted him. Lifting one foot, then the other, he pulled the metal footgear away. "No need for them to know I'm coming," he commented. "Corby, you're in charge until I get back."

He was gone into the inner passage. Corby, his slow mind groping after the reason for his chief's ire, took a step as if to follow, then stared stupidly in Ropakihn's wake. For the moment he was not watching Everitt or Fortuna.

Everitt felt a tug at his bonds. A hand was freeing him—Fortuna's hand. She had won loose! He wasted no time in pondering now, but as his own arms felt the strap draw away, sprang to his feet.

Corby heard the motion and turned, but before he lifted his ray-tube Everitt's hard fist connected with the loose-hung jaw. The hunchback went hurtling backward, his skull ringing on the floor before his weapon fell with a shattering sound. He lay still.

Everitt caught up the ray-tube, saw that it was jammed, and dropped it with an exclamation of impatience. From the desk he seized his helmet.

"What are you going to do?" he asked Fortuna breathlessly, sitting up to untie her ankles.

"Stay where you are," he cautioned her hastily. "Leave your feet tied and your hands behind you. Then Ropakihn and his men will think you're still helpless, and leave you alone for a minute." He poised the helmet above his head. "I'm making a dash for the ship outside. Zeoui and his playmates may not recognize me at once. If I get in among them and smash them, I'll have the MS-ray. Give me a moment to learn how to work it, and it'll be our saving."

Clamping his helmet in place, he stepped to the inner lock-panel. Behind him rose the panicky roar of Ropakihn, hurrying back from his inspection. The bellowed words penetrated even the helmet-glass.

"Corby!" the giant was shouting. "Look alive! The fuel-mixer went wrong somehow —liquid oxygen escaped, and both the boys are frozen stiff as boards!"

He came into view, and saw Everitt.

"You loose?" he bawled, but his erstwhile captive was into the air-lock, then through it and upon the deck.

No motion, no life met Everitt's eyes outside. The outlaw ship was where it had been, half the radius of the deck away, and to it extended the jointed metal pipe that carried fuel.

Ropakihn was right, no liquid was coursing through that flaccid conduit. Everitt started at a half-run for the cruiser.

But a savage voice rang in his earphones: "Stand still, or I'll plug you!"

Everitt whirled around. Ropakihn had come out, helmet hastily donned and rifle poised. His huge body almost fell at the outer threshold of the lock, and only a clutch at a port-rim saved it.

The outlaw, in his haste to pursue, had left off his magnetic boots. Outside the hulk he had only the tiny gravity-pull of the deck to govern him, and his huge body weighed but a few ounces. An unconsidered touch of toe-pressure was enough to unbalance him, even hurl him clear of the deck.

"Take off your shoes and throw them to me!" he yelled at Everitt.

The smaller man stood still, making no motion to obey.

Ropakihn's beaked face darkened with rage. "Off with them, or—"

Steadying himself with his left hand on the port-rim, Ropakihn pointed his rifle with the other. Everitt ducked out of the line of fire, himself slipping to one knee. At once Ropakihn floundered forward and upon him, clutching one foot and fairly ripping the shoe from it. "I'll do the walking, you do the stumbling," he taunted.

Everitt lay still beneath the outlaw, but not in submission. He was analyzing the situation—so logical, though he had never thought of it before. Inside the hulk you had weight and never stopped to realize that out here you needed magnets to hold you down lest—

Ropakihn had tucked his rifle under an elbow and was pulling off the other shoe. That vast mass of flesh, sprawling upon Everitt, was no heavier than a silk handkerchief. Even as the second shoe fell to the deck, Everitt summoned his strength and surged upward, thrusting his enemy along and traveling with him. Next instant they floundered in emptiness, the deck dropping from beneath them as if snatched by the hand of a prank-playing Titan.

THEY wrestled wildly in space, weightless as swimmers and clumsy as dreamers. It was like a dream at that, a horrible nightmare in which one strikes or grapples but encounters no resistance. Arms around Ropakihn's body, Everitt stared over the crag of the giant's shoulder at Space Station No. 1—dwindling, falling down and away, shrinking to a lump-centered shield on a starry curtain of black. The very heave of Everitt's body had been enough to send them both flying like stones from a sling, unfettered by gravity, unimpeded by air, hundreds of yards, a mile.

They wrenched and tore at each other's throats for a time, baffled by the folds of fabric. Then Ropakihn, letting go, struck Everitt clumsily on the breast-bone. The buffet dashed them violently apart.

Everitt saw the jetty sky and its stars whirl, saw the disk that was the station whip from underfoot to overhead, then back out of sight to appear underfoot again. He was somersaulting in space. Ropakihn, too, was flying backward, head over heels over head, shrinking to the apparent size of a squirming doll.

Everitt gave vent to a hysterical laugh over their ridiculous plight. Strong as lions but light as feathers they were losing themselves in nothingness by their own undirectible exertions. Even now they had no power to come together or to return to the deck after they had left. He had a mental picture of himself falling to an orbit, circling the man-made planetoid like a satellite. Ropakihn, caught in another orbit, might make the same circuit at a slower or faster pace. Drawing into conjunction, perhaps they would be close enough to resume hostilities.

Everitt laughed again more wildly.

A shout assailed his earphones. Ropakihn, far away, was doing something with the rifle. Yes, firing it, not at Everitt, but into space behind himself. Flash after flash of detonation and Ropakihn seemed to grow in size.

Oh, that was it. The weapon carried explosive charges and its recoil, though barely enough to stir a proper weight, could propel the few ounces that its operator scaled just now. The rocket was definitely approaching. He grew bigger, bigger, like a rubber figure swelling with gas.

Now he was aiming the gun at Everitt, firing once. The bullet missed, and the recoil slowed Ropakihn. Again they collided and grappled.

The smaller, more agile Everitt managed to seize and clamp his enemy's massive rifle arm. Ropakihn tried to shove him loose, but Everitt wrung the wrist he held with desperate vigor. He heard the giant's involuntary grunt of pain, saw the huge, mittened hand sag open. The weapon swam slowly out of it.

Darting out his own hand, Everitt clutched the receding barrel. He had no time to find trigger or grip, but struck as with a club.

The shock of the blow, falling on Ropakihn's shoulder, almost drove them apart again, but they clung somehow as the giant tried to snatch back his rifle. Everitt threw his legs up and forward, clamping them around his foe's great waist as around a wild horse. He took a rib-buckling punch over the heart, but next moment had struck once more with the rifle-butt, this time full on the front of Ropakihn's helmet.

The clouded glass splintered, and suddenly the outlaw's red visage showed plain and monstrous in the unfiltered sunlight. A breath's space, then the red turned blue, the great mouth gaped after the fleeting air. Bulging eyes fixed Everitt with dire hate and abruptly fell blank and dull as pebbles. The blueness deserted the face in turn, and went tallow-pale. The heaving cask-like body between Everitt's clamping knees gave a final convulsive shudder and relaxed.

Everitt had won.

H E DID not feel elated, only weary. Kicking loose from the senseless, dying Ropakihn, he stared frantically around to locate the station. It was behind his shoulder. Pointing the rifle into space before him, he fired it again and again. The recoil made itself felt. Again and again he fired.

A full minute elapsed before he approached the deck of the little island in space. His sense of direction changed—the station was no longer before or behind, but beneath. He glanced upward once. Afar he saw the silhouette of Ropakihn, quite motionless and limp in the sky. Then he drifted down like a leaf from a tree. An overalled figure dashed across the deckplates to meet him.

"An outstanding exhibition of valor and physical prowess, Ev!"

No mistaking that affected voice. It was the traitor Zeoui. Did he think to mock and sneer? Everitt clutched his rifle to fire. But the Martian stood still beneath him, holding up something. A weapon? Everitt's magnetic shoes!

Zeoui was trying to help him then! Puzzled, unable to comprehend the Martian's sudden change of front, still Everitt held his fire as he floated slowly down.

A moment later the Terrestrial had landed, and Zeoui was steadying him with a careful tentacle.

"Once more assume your metal footgear," came the dry accents of advice. "As I have already observed, it was a splendid and satisfactory encounter, not lacking in scientific interest. I dared hope that, when I left Miss Fortuna's encircling cords somewhat loose, she would find opportunity to set you at liberty."

Everitt was beginning to realize. "The other outlaws—" he began.

"They have been dealt with decisively," Zeoui reassured him. "I profited by the patent stupidity of the first contingent in the mixing-shop. Catching them off guard, I released upon them a flood of liquid oxygen. The sudden drop in temperature accomplished their demise.

"The others, who accompanied me out here, suffocated for want of air. I, affecting to assist them in donning their helmets, fastened only half the clamps. The air gradually but completely departed."

"And Corby?" asked Everitt. "The man I knocked out?"

"The charming and capable young object of your admiration, Miss Fortuna Sidney, has locked him up."

ONCE more in the office together, Zeoui, Everitt and Fortuna seated themselves around the desk. From the ventilator of the locker-closet where the madman Corby was imprisoned came the occasional grumpy pleas for freedom.

"And in that manner," the Martian finished his story, "I found it extremely simple. So simple, in truth, that Ropakihn, who considered himself the only astute person in the situation, was disposed to trust me. My pretense at helping to capture Miss Fortuna clinched it. Thereafter he thought nothing of counter-treachery on my part, but allowed me to conduct his unfortunate lunatic associates to their destruction."

Everitt made a rueful grimace. "You had me fooled, too," he confessed humbly.

Again Corby pleaded from his prison: "Who shut me up here? What happened?"

"He seems dazed by Ev's blow," explained Fortuna. "Claims not to remember coming here, or anything about Ropakihn's attempt."

Zeoui nodded sagely. "Such mental derangements frequently follow head injuries," he said weightily. "Perhaps he is only feigning amnesia, to obtain mercy. In that case, however, he would not dare amend my report to the police ship."

"Police ship?" gasped Everitt. "Is one coming?"

"I took opportunity to broadcast an emergency message with the radio in the war-craft. Immediately thereafter I was in receipt of a reply from a patrol ship. At the request of Director-General Sidney himself—he was aboard—I told the story."

"He must have been furious at me," cried Fortuna.

"Let me amend my statement," went on Zeoui. "I told only a portion of the story. I led them to believe that the theft and flight were Ropakihn's idea exclusively, and that the outlaws kidnaped Miss Fortuna from her school on Earth. The director-general expressed great satisfaction in your activities, Ev, and intimated that he would release you from exile. He will also cease his objections to your marriage—"

"Zeoui, you flower-faced sap!" exploded Everitt. "You've given me all the credit."

Again Zeoui nodded gravely.

"But what about you?" Fortuna demanded.

"Yes, you're screwier than Ropakihn's whole mob put together," Everitt chimed in. "If you take no credit, they'll keep you on duty here."

The Martian nodded.

"That is eminently correct." Both Everitt and Fortuna could have sworn that the petals of Zeoui's weird visage were wreathed into something like a grin of satisfaction. "To be sure I shall remain on duty here. I enjoy it."

# The Whimpus

## BY TOD ROBBINS

**If you are a militant materialist, with no belief in anything but that which you see with your eyes or touch with your own hands, this story is not for you. But, "There are more strange things hidden away in the sea than ever man heard tell of."**

## CHAPTER I

### THE BOX ON THE BEACH

"THERE'S things out there, Miss Bessie, that you never heard tell of. I know you're school-learned and all, but the old sea's got more secrets hid away than there are shells on this beach."

Elizabeth Wilkinson smiled down on the garrulous old fisherman, who sat cross-legged on the sand patiently mending the broken strands of a net. He had been in her father's employ since she could first remember and had always had that quality, so endearing to the very young, of being able to lie prodigiously and convincingly. Even now she enjoyed his wild tales. The savor of the sea was in them. While listening to them, she felt very childlike and very frightened. It was just as though she were swept off her feet and carried away in a heavy surf.

"Now, own up, Captain Ben," she said, attempting to make his watery blue eyes drop before her steady brown ones, "you just thought of that on the spur of the moment. There never was such a creature as a whimpus."

The old man's under-lip shot out as it always did when his word was doubted. He assumed a grieved and disgusted expression. His thick, blunt fingers once more busied themselves with their task.

"What's the use of tellin' you anythin', Miss Bessie?" he mumbled. "You're gettin' to be just like your pop, with no belief in nothin' but what you sees with your own eyes. If all folks was like you there wouldn't be no religion, even. It ain't what we see what makes life interestin', it's what's just around the corner. There's things happenin' right now that ain't never been writ up in books, and there's creatures crawlin' about what would make Ringling Brothers' head animal-trainer take to his heels if he ever suddenly happened to catch sight of 'em."

"But a whimpus, Captain Ben! You say it has a tail and fins like a fish?"

"It has so, Miss Bessie; and big blue eyes, most like a gal's. Leastwise, so Dick Jamieson told me—him who was wrecked in the China Sea. And Dick was a truthful man when not in liquor."

"How long are they, Captain Ben?"

"About the length of my arm, missy, with pointed teeth which can give a man a cruel bite if they catched him in the calf of the leg."

"And hair, Captain Ben? I believe you said they had long, curly hair?"

"So Dick told me, missy. With a flash to it like gold in the sunlight. He leaned down and put his hand on one of 'em, thinkin' he had found a treasure or somethin'. It was nothin' more or less than a whimpus sleepin', her hair slung over her like

37

a net; and she wakes up, fightin'-mad, and bites a piece off his little finger for his boldness. Then she gives a flip to her tail and away she sails as saucy as you please —leavin' Dick on the bank, jumpin' with pain."

For a long moment there was silence. The girl had half turned away from the old fisherman and was looking out to sea. It was a day in late August. Above the gray tumbling waste of waters, a pale opalescent curtain of fog was slowly descending. The Adventurer—Mr. Wilkinson's yacht—rode at anchor barely two hundred yards from shore. Already she was swathed in drifting tides of vapor. Like a fantom ship, she appeared and disappeared. At one moment she seemed to be scarcely a stone's throw from the beach; at the next, a mile or so offshore. It had been blowing hard on the preceding night. The waves were like an army coming home with victory on their shields. They thundered out their deep-throated war song on the beach. Far out in the impenetrable mist, like a voice from another world, the melancholy call of a seagull rose for a moment above the tumult of tumbling waters.

"No, Miss Bessie," Captain Ben continued with a shake of his head, "there's more things hid away in the sea than ever man heard tell of. But the fog's gettin' precious thick. I think you'd best be off to the house or you'll get wet to the skin."

But Elizabeth had caught sight of something in the surf which held her undivided attention. It was a large box which, at that moment, was riding the snowy crest of a wave. On it came smoothly, like a miniature ship, sinking at last into a milky chasm as the billow tripped on the beach with its treasure and fell sprawling. For an instant the box was left high and dry.

Moved by a sudden impulse which she was soon to regret, Elizabeth ran forward across the wet, quivering sand and bent over the box.

"Come back, missy!" Captain Ben called in a shrill, quavering voice. "What ever are ye thinkin' of? Come back this instant afore one of them big waves catches yer!"

Elizabeth raised the box. Holding it tight to her breast, she hurried back just as another huge wave charged down on her with a threatening roar. Lowering her prize to the sand beyond the reach of its many long arms, she surveyed Captain Ben triumphantly.

"This belongs to me now, doesn't it?" she asked, indicating the box with a slender, moist finger.

"Aye, aye, missy," Captain Ben said solemnly. "What a man fishes out of the sea belongs to him, no matter who it belonged to afore. The King of England's crown jewels might be in this here box and they wouldn't be no more his now than Mike Rafferty's pig." He paused and scratched his grizzled chin. "But I guess these ain't crown jewels," he added rather sorrowfully. "They're more like to be lemons."

"Why lemons?"

"'Cause a tramp steamer run aground in the fog last night off Wishbone Point. They had to lighten her cargo afore they got her off; and they do say she was loaded down with crates of lemons. Some of the boys in the village was fishin' for 'em all mornin'."

"I don't believe it is a crate of lemons," Elizabeth said with a shake of her head. Once more she bent down and turned the box over on its side. At the next moment, with a stifled cry, she stepped back so hurriedly that she nearly tripped over the old man's outstretched legs.

"Why, what's the matter, missy?" Captain Ben asked, looking up from the net in surprise. "You looks as if somethin' had bit yer!"

"There's something alive in that box," she said in a rather unsteady voice. "I heard it move. Do you suppose it could be a baby, Captain Ben?"

The old fisherman's mouth extended from ear to ear. A glimpse of his gums could be seen, with here and there a single discolored tooth rising from them like so many weatherbeaten tombstones. He was laughing silently.

"Don't laugh at me!" Elizabeth cried

angrily. "I tell you there *is* something
alive in that box! I heard it rattling about
when I moved it!"

Captain Ben rose stiffly to his feet and
bent over the box. "I misdoubt it's a baby,
Miss Bessie," he mumbled. "A baby
wouldn't have much chance of weatherin'
through such a sea in this old craft. Mebbe
the lemons ain't packed very tight. Let's
see."

He put one of his gnarled hands on the
box and turned it over. On the instant a
strange flapping sound could be heard issu-
ing from the interior, followed almost immediately by a loud scratching as though
long, sharp nails were at work.

Captain Ben uttered an ejaculation of
amazement. "That's mighty strange!" he
muttered. "There must be fish and crabs
in this box. But who ever heard tell of—"
He paused and scratched the top of his
weatherbeaten hat. "Shall I open it?"

" No," Elizabeth murmured. "I don't
want to see what's in it. There's something
horrible, I know. I wish I hadn't taken
that box out of the water."

"Why, what's the matter, missy? You
look all upset. It's only fish and crabs
thrown in higgledy-piggledy in an old chest.
It ain't like you to get worked up over
nothin'."

Elizabeth bit her lip. What made her
feel this way about a harmless old box?
It was ridiculous! And yet, try as she
would, she could not even look at it now.
When she had bent over it and put her
hand on its cold, wet surface, when she had
heard those strange flapping and scratching sounds within, a wave of intense, if
unaccountable, fear and repulsion had
passed through her. Now trembling little
patches of gooseflesh stood out on her
brown arms. This was absurd. She must
have caught cold. Or perhaps she just had
a touch of malaria.

"I think I'll go back to the house, Captain Ben," she said at last. "I feel cold."

"You don't look very hearty today,
missy, and that's a fact. You'd better
change yer shoes and stockin's, I reckon.
But what will I do with the box?"

"Bring it up to the house, Captain Ben.
You can leave it on the back stoop."

"Aye aye, missy. I'll tote it up in a
wheelbarrow. Mebbe there's some likely
sized fish in this here chest. They seem
lively enough. And a good crab ain't to
be sneezed at, neither, if it's cooked
proper."

## CHAPTER II

### A CLAIMANT FOR THE CHEST

MR. WILKINSON greeted his daughter as she mounted the veranda. He
was a stout, middle-aged man with a
sallow complexion, dull, prominent eyes
and a predilection for a quiet, uneventful
life. The one excitement which he allowed
himself was an occasional flyer in Wall
Street. He was proverbially lucky in such
speculations. The considerable fortune,
which his father had left him, had never
taken wings—on the contrary, like a snow-
ball rolling down-hill, it had gathered to itself many lesser fortunes. But this success
without effort had given him no flicker of
joy.

Each year his complexion had grown
sallower, his eyes duller, his muscles flab-
bier. The boredom which must necessarily
attend a smooth existence, was smothering
the manhood in the financier. Beneath a
mountain of down, he was snoring his life
away.

Now he rose ponderously, and laid a
plump, moist hand on his daughter's shoulder. "I've got a surprise for you, Bessie,"
he said in a slow, heavy voice.

"A surprise, dad! What is it?"

Mr. Wilkinson smiled sleepily. He had
intended teasing her, but now lacked the
vitality. "The surprise is upstairs, shav-
ing," he said, sinking back into the easy-
chair like a large stuffed doll.

Elizabeth flushed. In an instant she forgot all about the wooden box and her dread
of its flapping, scratching contents. "You
don't mean that the surprise is Jay, dad,
do you?"

Mr. Wilkinson nodded and smiled,
"Yes," he murmured. "Dropped into my

office just after he got off the boat. Didn't wire—wanted to make it a surprise. But here he is to tell you about it himself."

At this moment a tall, athletic young man opened the screened door, and, seeing Elizabeth, hurried forward and took her in a bearlike hug. Jay had never been a gentle lover, but she liked him all the better for that.

"Well, old girl," he said at last, holding her off at arm's length and regarding her attentively with his steady gray eyes, "you're looking pretty fit. You didn't expect me home so soon, eh?"

"No, I didn't," she murmured. "You wrote me that you intended doing Europe with the rest of the team."

He smiled a trifle shamefacedly. "I intended to," he said. "I thought that you'd think all the more of me if I stayed away a little longer. After we beat the Englishmen that deciding game, the team broke up. Larry and Martin dropped in on Paris; Henry and I were going to do Scotland and Ireland, but at the last moment I quit. I had to do some explaining. Henry was as sore as a boil." He paused and stroked the cleft in his prominent chin meditatively. "Well, here I am," he finished, "and willing to step up to the altar most any time."

"Wait till somebody asks you, sir," she said with a sudden flash of color. "Do you still think that polo is the most important thing in life?"

The young man shook his head. "No, but it's exciting; and I crave excitement."

Elizabeth experienced the disquieting sensation at her fiancé's words which is common enough to most girls when they are brought face to face with their great enemy —that priestess of adventure which beckons the swift and the strong. It is the instinct of feminine love to be everything, and it must content itself with so little.

After a moment she said a trifle bitterly: "At one moment, Jay, you talk of settling down, of becoming thoroughly domesticated; at the next, you sigh for speed and thrills. Which side of you am I to believe? I like excitement, but I don't put it above everything else in the world."

"You're a girl," her fiancé answered calmly, "and with a girl it's different. But a fellow has to be doing strenuous things or else—" He paused and shrugged.

"Haskin' pardon, lady and gentlemen," said a strange, husky voice which sounded like the scraping together of two rusty iron bars, "a chap down at the beach says as 'ow you 'ad picked up a old chest."

All three turned their heads in surprise. There, standing on the lower step of the veranda, swinging a mildewed, canvas cap between finger and thumb, was one of the strangest figures Elizabeth had ever seen.

Above medium height, but so bent that his back rounded out like a drawn bow; his long legs wide apart as though balancing himself against the shock of the sea; his head, with its great bulbous nose and close-set black eyes, cocked on one side shrewdly like a bird about to take flight—he resembled some scarecrow posturing in a cornfield. And yet, on the second glance, one felt the humanness of the man. It was in his crafty, thin-lipped mouth, in the swing of his lantern jaws, in the twitching of his corded, brown fists, which resembled two sea-spiders. All in all, from his tangle of straw-colored hair to his shining boots, he looked as out of place on Mr. Wilkinson's broad, sun-swept veranda as one of the pirates in "Treasure Island."

"The chap as I spoke to," the man continued, "said as 'ow 'e 'ad brought the chest up 'ere a few minutes back. Now could I once lay my eyes on it, lady and gentlemen, I'd know it fast enough by some 'oles I drilled in its side."

"I think he must mean the box I picked out of the surf," Elizabeth said, turning toward her father. "There was some holes in that, I remember."

"Was there, lady, was there?" cried the man in evident excitement. "The Lord love yer, lady! That's news to warm a poor sailor's soul! Now did these 'oles form a kind of a 'eart, lady—a 'eart like yer see on this 'ere arm of mine?"

He rolled up his sleeve, disclosing a sunburnt arm on which was tattooed in gay coloring a three-masted schooner; two lovers sitting under a dark blue tree; a queen of spades; and, lastly, a mermaid reclining on a cliff and pulling up, hand over hand, a large scarlet heart, on which was inscribed in minute lettering, "Caught again! September 15, 1935."

"You're well decorated, my man," said Mr. Wilkinson with a flicker of an eyelash in Jay's direction. "Who was the artist?"

"It's a tasty bit of work, ain't it?" said the sailor in evident pleasure. "That's what I halways says—*tasty!* Black Tom did 'em hall—'im who was my shipmate aboard the Sea King. Lord, 'e was a hartist-born, was Tom! Liked nothin' better than to get a poor chap in front of 'im like a bloody blackboard to draw purty pictures on. 'E did this 'ere when we was shipwrecked together on a coral island in the China Seas. 'E never got off that island neither, did Black Tom."

"Never got off it!" Elizabeth cried. "Did he die there?"

"Now I wouldn't say so much as that, gal. Leastwise, I ain't. 'E went off and left me sudden one mornin' and 'e never showed up no more. They catched 'im, I guess."

"*Who* caught him?" Jay broke in.

The sailor half-closed his eyes till they were mere pin-points. "*They,*" he muttered. "Them things what live on coral islands in the China Seas."

"He means *whimpus,*" said Captain Ben, who had at that moment hobbled up.

"Right you are, matey," said the man. "The whimpus got Black Tom, soul and body. 'E was uncommon fond of gals, was Tom."

At this point Mr. Wilkinson rose impatiently to his feet. "Now what can we do for you?" he said rather sharply. "If you've come up here to tell us lies about mermaids you're wasting your time. We've got a first-class liar here as it is." He gave Captain Ben a significant stare.

"There's more things afloat, Mr. Wilkinson, than you ever heard tell of," Captain Ben began in a plaintive, asthmatic whine. "This man here is right when he speaks of whimpus. I heard tell of 'em afore."

But the sailor cut him short. "Look here, lady and gentlemen," he said, stepping forward, "I come peaceful enough for my property, and I'm bound I'll 'ave it!"

"My daughter picked the box out of the water. Well, according to law, it now belongs to her. If you want it back, you'll have to pay salvage," said Mr. Wilkinson.

Now the sailor turned toward Elizabeth. "I'll pay salvage, lady," he whined. "Now would a ten-pound note be agreeable? Say the word, lady." He began to fumble in his pocket.

"Don't take it, Bessie," Mr. Wilkinson advised, enjoying the affair as a child enjoys a new kind of game. "Take an old business man's advice. He offers fifty dollars— well, it must be worth a good deal more."

"Lord love yer, no, lady! There ain't nothin' in that old chest but a few keepsakes and trinkets. Pictures of gals and the likes of that. I wouldn't give no ten pounds if my 'eart wasn't kinder set on 'em."

Elizabeth bit her lip to repress a laugh. The sailor was lying so poorly that a child would not have been deceived. But what could be in the chest? Something alive— she had heard it move—something which this man considered to be worth more than fifty dollars. It was worth finding out.

"It couldn't be your box I found," she said at last.

"And why ain't it, lady? Ain't there no 'eart cut in it?"

"Yes, I believe there is a heart."

"Well, ain't that proof enough, lady, that it's Bill Farley's chest right enough?"

"Is your name Bill Farley?"

"Aye, aye, ma'am. And you'll find a *B* and a *F* on the tother end, burnt there with a red-hot poker—rough, I grant you; but plain to see in the sunlight."

"That's all very well, Mr. Farley," said Elizabeth very sweetly. "You seem to know what the outside of the box looks like. But that isn't enough. I believe you said that there were a few trinkets inside?"

"Yes, ma'am."

"Well, that isn't so, Mr. Farley. There's something alive in that box."

For a moment there was a disconcerting silence. The sailor's crafty eyes wandered here, there, and everywhere: Mr. Wilkinson's round face indicated surprise; Jay began stroking his amber-colored mustache thoughtfully. At last Captain Ben spoke up.

"It's no use, Bill Farley, or whatever your name may be," he said. "You've gone and steered yourself into a fog. None of us here will rest easy till we've had a peep into that chest of yourn. You've lied yourself into a heap more trouble than ten pounds will buy yer out of."

Suddenly Elizabeth uttered a little cry of horror. "Have you a baby in that box?" she asked excitedly.

"Perhaps he's a kidnaper," Jay suggested. "They're quite common."

"He's got a bad face," Captain Ben muttered, casting a suspicious look at the cowering Bill Farley. "When a Britisher *is* bad, he's most uncommon bad."

Mr. Wilkinson took a step forward with the air of a stern judge. "What *have* you got in the box?" he demanded harshly.

The sailor looked from right to left, as though contemplating escape, and then into the faces of his persecutors. Tiny beads of perspiration had gathered on his forehead; his eyes looked like those of a trapped animal.

"I got—" He paused for breath and swallowed several times.

"What?" they demanded almost in unison.

"I got a whimpus in that there chest," Bill Farley said a trifle wearily.

## CHAPTER III

### A CHINESE MERMAID

FOR several moments there was a dead silence. All regarded the sailor with open-eyed amazement. Mr. Wilkinson was the first to speak.

"You've got a *what?*" he asked.

"I got a whimpus," Bill Farley repeated stubbornly. "It's a Chinese mermaid fish, common enough on that coral island where me and Tom was cast away."

Jay allowed himself an incredulous smile. "Where did you put that box, Captain Ben?" he asked.

"It's on the back porch, sir. Will I get it?"

"Yes," Mr. Wilkinson broke in, "get it. This man must be drunk or mad. A whimpus—a mermaid—whoever heard of such nonsense?"

Captain Ben turned away with a shake of his head. "I told you more times than once, sir, that there be strange creatures in the sea what you never heard tell of," he mumbled.

Bill Farley stared sullenly at his boots with the air of an abused man. "What's the odds whether a chap lies or tells the Gospel truth?" he muttered. "'E ain't believed neither way."

"A whimpus!" Mr. Wilkinson continued irritably. "And perhaps you'll be kind enough to tell us how you happened to catch your mermaid?"

"I will that," said Bill Farley. "It 'appened this way: I rigged up a kind of dragnet while I was on that there coral island, and put it out each mornin' to catch gay-colored fish of which there was aplenty. One mornin' I pulls the net in and finds 'er lyin' there as snug as a bug in a rug. She give me a start, lookin' at me most like a gal with 'er big blue eyes kinder smilin' in 'er 'ead. 'Lord, Bill,' I says to myself, 'you've 'ad a touch of sun, my poor lad!' "

"Here comes Captain Ben with the box, dad," Elizabeth broke in.

As she spoke her eyes were fixed on the chest which the old fisherman carried; and once again that wave of incomprehensible fear passed through her.

"Why open it, dad?" she murmured. "Let the man have it."

It is doubtful if Mr. Wilkinson heard her. At that moment he and Jay were bending over the box. Captain Ben had placed it on the veranda in a stream of sunshine. In this bright light the small, drilled holes, so arranged that they formed the outline of a human heart and the blurred *B* and *F* were plainly to be seen. Several knotted cords encircled the chest.

Jay, with the impatience of a small boy on Christmas morning, pulled out a penknife and severed them. Mr. Wilkinson began to lift the lid.

"'Ave a care!" Bill Farley warned him. "She's got a most uncommon nasty temper with strangers. You're like to lose a finger if you don't watch your 'and!"

Mr. Wilkinson, in spite of his incredulous smile, raised the lid slowly and cautiously. A shaft of sunlight stole into the chest. At the next moment he uttered an ejaculation of amazement, which was echoed by Jay. Captain Ben hobbled up and bent forward in his turn.

"It's a whimpus, sure enough!" he cried, a shrill note of triumph ringing through his voice like the clanging of an old, cracked bell. "What did I tell you, Mr. Wilkinson? Do yer see that fish's tail, and them claws, and them long, pointed teeth? And she has yaller hair, too, same as that feller said what had his finger bit off by one of 'em. But look at them gal's eyes! Ain't they purty, though—blue as seashells, yet with a sparkle to 'em! Aye, aye, Mr. Wilkinson, this sure is a whimpus."

"Well, I'm hanged if I ever saw anything like it before!" Jay muttered under his breath.

Even the financier's rather irritating common sense was shattered for the moment. He stared down at the contents of the sailor's chest in blank amazement. His pursed lips seemed on the point of emitting a long-drawn "Oh!" of astonishment.

"Well, now that you 'ave taken a squint at my whimpus," Bill Farley said sullenly, "perhaps you'll be so kind as to return a poor man's property and let 'im be off about his business."

The sailor's words seemed to restore a measure of Mr. Wilkinson's presence of mind. "Not so fast," said he, straightening his back. "You've got a most peculiar freak of nature here; I'll grant you that. The only one in existence, I imagine."

"There's 'undreds and 'undreds of 'em

on Whimpus Island," Bill Farley said composedly.

Once more an incredulous smile flitted across Mr. Wilkinson's face. "I doubt that very much," said he. "However, let's come to terms. You've got a freak in the fish world here—something which will cause considerable comment. What did you intend doing with it?"

A sly, secretive smile played for a moment beneath the sailor's bulbous nose, creasing his face till it resembled a walnut-shell. "This 'ere whimpus is worth money," he muttered. "I was thinkin' of sellin' 'er to a zoo."

"That won't be necessary. I'll buy it myself. How would a hundred dollars strike you?"

"A 'undred dollars—twenty pounds! Gawd, governor!" Bill Farley's face took on an expresion of lively disgust. "This whimpus is worth 'er weight in diamonds. I wouldn't take a thousand pounds for 'er, and that's a fact."

Mr. Wilkinson nodded briskly. "Very well, my man. I'm afraid we can't do business. Good afternoon."

The sailor seemed greatly relieved. Passing the back of his hand across his forehead, he bent down awkwardly and laid hold of the chest. "Come on 'ome with Bill, Lizzie," he muttered. "We've 'ad a mighty tough day of it, old gal."

"Hold on, there!" Mr. Wilkinson called sharply. "What are you about? You can't have that fish until you pay salvage. You said it was worth its weight in diamonds, that you wouldn't take a thousand pounds for it—well, that should make the salvage pretty high."

"Gawd! Ain't you 'ard on a poor chap, gove'nor?" Bill Farley released his hold on the chest and straightend himself. His face drew up into knots of anxiety and grief. "I cawn't pay no 'igh salvage 'cause I ain't got no more than thirty pounds in all the world! This here whimpus is mighty nigh my entire fortune!"

"Now, why not tell us the truth, Farley?" the financier said in a kindlier tone. "It's no use lying—you've got something up your sleeve. Why do you think this fish is worth so much? Tell us the whole story, and I give you my word we'll deal squarely by you."

Bill Farley hesitated and shifted uneasily on his feet. "You 'ave me, gove'nor," he said with a new note of respect in his tone. "Whichever way I turn, you 'ave me. A poor seafarin' chap ain't got a Dutchman's chance with a far-seein' gentleman like you. But I got a question to ask afore I spins my yarn. Is that craft, lyin' so snug in the cove, your yacht, gove'nor?"

"The Adventurer? Yes, she belongs to me."

"That's good news, gove'nor. Now, 'as the young lady 'ere a bit of a ring, a bracelet, or somethin' kinder shiny which she would lend a poor seafarin' chap for the sake of a test?"

Elizabeth nodded. Drawing a thin band of gold from her finger, she presented it to the sailor.

"Thank yer kindly, ma'am," said he. "Now, gove'nor, lady, and gentlemen, will yer take a little walk down to that pier yonder, and I'll show you what Lizzie 'ere can do once she's sot her mind on it."

"What are you driving at?" Mr. Wilkinson asked with some asperity.

"Never you mind, gove'nor. Just you step along with old Bill, and 'ell show you what's what. You ain't afeared, gove'nor?"

Jay burst out into a laugh. "What do you know about that?" he said. "He thinks we're afraid of his mermaid. Let's see what he's got to show us down on the pier."

"Very well," said Mr. Wilkinson, with an uneasy look at the water-soaked box. "Are you coming with us, Bessie?"

Elizabeth shook her head. "Not if you're going to take that creature with you."

"Surely you're not afraid of a fish, Bessie?" Jay broke in. "Why, you haven't even looked at it yet!"

"It isn't fear exactly. I don't know how to explain it. It's the same feeling I have for a mouse—only a thousand times worse. I've had a horror of it from the very first. If I looked at it, I know I'd scream."

"Poor old Lizzie!" Bill Farley muttered, picking the box up in his arms. "You ain't very popular with the gals, are yer, Lizzie? Well, gove'nor, lead the way."

The four men descended the steps of the veranda and started across the lawn toward the pier which stretched out like a wooden arm over the sea. Mr. Wilkinson and Jay led, Captain Ben and Bill Farley brought up the rear.

Elizabeth watched them receding in the distance with a wildly beating heart. Her natural curiosity was battling with that strange repulsion for which she was unable to account. At one moment she wished she had accompanied them; at the next, she was glad that she had remained where she was.

The pier was several hundred yards from the house. Elizabeth, although she strained her eyes, was unable to ascertain what the men were about. By this time they had reached their destination. Looking very small and toylike, they were bending forward as though examining something.

An involuntary shudder passed through the girl's frame. They were now opening the box and examining that horrible creature which Captain Ben had described as having long yellow hair and eyes like a girl's—that must be what they were about. How could they do it? Men were callous. Perhaps they would even touch it. Perhaps Jay, her Jay, might fondle it, might run his fingers through its hair, might—

Something very near akin to jealous rage made Elizabeth rise and hurry toward them. But before she had traversed more than a quarter of the distance, she encountered Captain Ben, who had detached himself from the group on the pier and was hobbling across the front lawn.

"I was comin' up to tell yer all about it, missy," he said, smothering a yawn with a huge fist. "You missed it. It's too late now—they've put the whimpus back in her box."

"What happened, Captain Ben?" she asked breathlessly.

The old man once more paused to open his mouth in a cavernous yawn before he answered. "Funny how sleepy I feel!" he muttered.

"What happened?" Elizabeth repeated impatiently.

"Why, when we got down to the pier, that there sailor opened the box, grabbed the whimpus quick by the neck, and jerked her out. She begin to scratch at him with her claws and gnash her teeth—but it weren't no use, for Farley had her safe by the neck all the time. Well, missy, he had a piece of fishin' line in his trouser-pocket. No sooner did she stop her antics than he made it fast about her. It was curious the easy way he handled the critter."

"What did he do then?" Elizabeth asked.

"Why, then he took that ring that you give him and chucked it into the sea. That made me howlin' mad, I can tell yer. I never expected to see it no more. 'Have yer taken leave of yer senses?' I says, steppin' forward with the thought of layin' my fist on that ugly jaw of his. But he just kinder smiles superior and throws his whimpus overboard, not forgettin' to hold on to the other end of the line. 'Watch my Lizzie,' he says, very proud. 'She's no end of a gal when it comes to findin' valuables.' "

"And then what happened, Captain Ben?"

"Why, we all watched that there fishin' line goin' out farther and farther. Then, all of a sudden, it stopped dead; and Farley begun to pull it in, hand over hand. Pretty soon that whimpus pops out of the water. And what do you think, missy—there was your ring, gripped tight in her claws."

"It picked my ring up?"

"Yes, missy. And Farley let her keep it for a while, sayin' them bright things made the poor gal happy. She's got it along with her now in her box, and she's hummin' like a thousand tops goin' at once."

"Humming?"

"Aye, aye, missy. She hums when she's content, Farley says. And it's a soothin' sound—a most soothin' sound." The old man broke off, and once more displayed his gums in a prodigious yawn.

## CHAPTER IV

### MOONSHINE AND MADNESS

"WELL, now, as I 'ave showed yer what my Lizzie could do, let us talk business, gove'nor."

It was Bill Farley who spoke. Leaning back comfortably in one of Mr. Wilkinson's easy chairs, a corpulent Havana cigar between his yellow teeth, he surveyed the others with a strange air of mingled civility and triumph. The financier, his face still mirroring astonishment and a measure of expectancy, crossed his plump legs and lit a match. Elizabeth and Jay interchanged glances, but remained silent. Captain Ben had taken up a trowel, and was making a pretense at weeding the flower-bed in the shadow of the veranda; while, in reality, he was straining his old ears to catch any scattered fragments of the conversation.

"I don't see how your fish's accomplishments alter the case," Mr. Wilkinson said finally. "It recovered my daughter's ring, certainly; but my daughter recovered it. In a word, the more valuable you make your fish appear, Farley, the higher salvage may be demanded."

"But you ain't got me right, gove'nor," the sailor cried. "Lizzie is a valuable possession—not because she ain't known in these parts, not because she can pick up a gold ring occasional, but because she 'as a fortune of all 'er own. She's a capitalist, that's what my Lizzie is."

"I'm sure I don't know what you're driving at," Mr. Wilkinson broke in.

"Look 'ere, gove'nor—I'll explain." Bill Farley leaned forward and knocked the ash of his cigar off on the toe of his boot. "There's a coral island in the China Seas where there's 'undreds and 'undreds of Lizzies. Them mermaid fish is all alike. They're the same as gals—a diamond or a gold ring, anythin' kinder dazzlin', tickles 'em to death. Now, down on the bottom of the sea there's loads and loads of such things lyin' kinder careless about. Think of the ships what's foundered off the China coast, gove'nor, in them ragin' typhoons; ships loaded down with gold and precious stones, and the like of that. What do yer think them whimpus 'as been doin' these thousands of years? Get my drift, gove'nor?"

"You mean that they've been storing up treasure-trove from wrecked vessels?" Mr. Wilkinson asked, sitting up very straight in his chair.

Jay drew his breath in through his teeth with a hissing sound. "Oh-ho, what an idea!" he muttered.

"That's what I'm a tellin' yer," Bill Farley continued patiently. "Them whimpus 'ave been stealin' from foundered ships since the world was new. There's undreamed-of wealth for the chap what finds their cave, gove'nor. Captain Kidd's treasure wouldn't be a ante in that game. Now, suppose I knowed the whereabouts of that island, gove'nor, and suppose Lizzie 'ere could do the rest?"

Mr. Wilkinson rose and began to pace the veranda. "Of course, all this is just foolishness," he muttered. "And yet—"

"You 'ave a tidy little yacht in the 'arbor," Bill Farley said hopefully. "Just you say the word, gove'nor, and I'll pilot yer to Whimpus Island. We'll split the pot—all 'ands what sails. There'll be enough treasure to spare, or sink me for a Dutchman!"

Mr. Wilkinson came to a sudden halt in front of the sailor. "I want to hear all about this," he said querulously. "How did you happen to get hold of this fish? It'll pay you to stick to the truth."

"Gawd blast me if I lie, gove'nor! It 'appened this way: I was aboard the Sea King what went down in a tornado just off the China coast. Me and Black Tom rigged up a raft. Two days and two nights we drifted, and then we touched ground on one of them coral islands, which is as thick as flees on a mangy dog in them parts. Lucky for us there was a big, 'ollowed-out place in the center of the island which 'ad

caught a deal of rain-water. For food we 'ad the fish, which was all colors of the rainbow, and sweet-tastin' enough."

"Was that Whimpus Island?"

"Aye, aye, gove'nor. We didn't see 'ide nor 'air of 'em for the first few days. Only we 'eard a low 'ummin' sometimes which would put Black Tom and me to sleep like we was kids. One day Black Tom catches one sunnin' 'erself. 'E come runnin' to me, 'oldin' 'er in a bit of fish-net.

"'Just look 'ere, Bill!' 'e says, swallowin' 'ard. 'Look what this gal 'as in 'er fist!'

"Well, I gives 'er a stare; and she stares back at me, as bold as you please, through the 'oles in the net. Pretty soon I see somethin' shinin' in 'er claws. Gawd! I give my eyes a rub, but it weren't no use! That there shinin' stone in 'er fist was a diamond as big as a robin's egg.

"'We're rich men, Tom,' I says joyful.

"But 'e gives a shake of 'is 'ead, bein' a gloomy, sorrowful chap mostly. 'We might be bloody millionaires, Bill,' says 'e; 'but what good would it do us on this blawsted gridiron?'

"Well, for all that, Black Tom took the diamond out of the whimpus's fist—though 'e 'ad to treat 'er a bit rough first, she bein' havaricious, as are most females. Then 'e made a pet of 'er, feedin' 'er bits of fish, and now and then givin' 'er a swim on the end of a cord. And it was a most unnatural thing to see, that there fish and Black Tom sleepin' alongside one another each night—she with 'er 'ead on 'is breast, 'er golden 'air brushin' 'is cheek. Lord, it give me the creeps—the way she 'ad of lookin' at 'im like a lovesick gal on 'er 'oneymoon! And it made me feel kinder lonesome, too. I began to wish I 'ad a whimpus of my own.

"One day I was all alone, sunnin' myself on a bit of rock. Black Tom was out walkin' with 'is whimpus—though 'e did all the walkin', wadin' about the island while she swum alongside. Pretty soon I 'ears a great 'ullabaloo; and 'ere comes Black Tom, runnin' fit to bust, 'is lady friend under 'is arm.

" 'What's the row?' says I. 'Row?' says 'e. 'We're the richest men in the world, Bill! And it's all because of this little gal 'ere.' Then 'e gives 'is whimpus a squeeze which makes 'er cock one blue eye at me kinder coy.

" ' 'Ave you found another diamond?' I asked.

" 'A diamond, Bill!' says 'e kinder scornful. 'Where I just come from they're as thick as pebbles on the beach.'

"Then 'e went on to tell me as 'ow the whimpus 'ad took 'im into a cave while they was walkin', and pretty soon they come to a strip of sand where there was a pile of rubies and diamonds and gold pieces. And there was bones, too—human bones, white as chalk—and bits of junk which weren't no use to nobody.

" 'You come away in a hurry,' says I.

" 'I did that,' says 'e, blinkin' 'is eyes at me solemn. 'There was some skulls sittin' on them piles of precious stones, and they give me the creeps. 'Owsomever, I'm goin' back now and take another squint.'

" 'I'll go with yer,' says I.

" 'No, yer won't,' says 'e, givin' me a nasty look. 'Two's company, three's a crowd.' 'E give a little 'itch to 'is knife which I knew meant trouble. 'Dolly and me 'll treat yer square, Bill,' 'e says, 'but we don't want yer nosin' around in there.'

"With that 'e starts back again with a ugly grin at me over 'is shoulder and 'is 'and on the 'aft of 'is knife. Now, bein' a peaceful man myself, 'avin' sung in the church choir in my youth, I let 'im 'ave 'is way—more especial as 'e was a wicked chap to cross and as tall as a steeple. Pretty soon I lost sight of 'im and 'is whimpus behind a bit of rock. And I never laid eyes on either of 'em since that day, gove'nor."

Bill Farley paused to light his cigar, which had gone out. Elizabeth glanced at Jay, and saw that his eyes were flashing brightly, and that there was a hectic splash of color in each cheek. She glanced at her father, and saw that he, also, showed marked signs of excitement. The sailor's box stood near the railing. A low, intermittent buzzing sound came from it.

"How is it that you never saw him again?" Mr. Wilkinson asked.

"I dunno, gove'nor. That there cave 'e told me about must 'ave swallowed 'im like the whale swallowed Jonah. 'E never come out alive—nor dead neither, I reckon."

"Did you discover the entrance of the cave?" Jay asked suddenly.

"Not me, sir," Bill Farley answered with a weak smile. "Black Tom would 'ave skinned me alive 'ad I followed 'im. 'E was a mean man when crossed. But Lizzie, she knows where that cave is, right enough."

"How did you happen to catch your whimpus?" Mr. Wilkinson asked.

"I catched 'er with a bit of net when I was fishin' off the rocks. But I wasn't takin' no chances at explorin' caves with no one 'andy in case of trouble. I put Lizzie in my old sea-chest, and a day or so later I got picked up by a tramp steamer bound for New York. Natural enough, I didn't tell them what I knowed. There was too many 'ands aboard. 'When I gets to New York,' I says to myself, 'I'll find some skipper I can trust, and then—' "

"But how did the chest happen to be in the water?" Jay broke in.

Bill Farley moved his feet uneasily, and a guilty flush spread over his face. "That tramp steamer went aground off Wishbone Point," he muttered. "Them custom officers might 'ave made things 'ot for Lizzie and me, so I took French leave in one of the life-boats when none of the crew was lookin'. Pretty soon a squall comes up, and the boat capsizes. Lizzie come aground 'ere, but I swam to shore half a mile farther up. Gawd, I was near out of my 'ead till that old chap told me 'e 'ad seen my chest."

"That's a very strange tale," said Mr. Wilkinson, chewing savagely on his cigar. "If you're lying, you do it very well."

Bill Farley's heavily wrinkled face took on a grieved expression. "So 'elp me, I ain't spinnin' a yarn, gove'nor! This 'ere is Gospel truth. You've a sizable yacht in the cove. What do yer say if we go treasure-'untin'?"

"This is all moonshine and madness," Mr. Wilkinson muttered. "Still, I was thinking of taking a cruise; and it might as well be the China Seas as anywhere else."

"I'm all for it!" Jay cried enthusiastically. "This is the kind of thing which makes life worth while."

Suddenly a long, solemn face appeared over the railing of the veranda. It was Captain Ben's. "What have I always told yer, Mr. Wilkinson?" he said. "There's more strange critters and strange adventures out there"—he pointed unsteadily toward the surging stretch of sea—"than you ever heard tell of. Can't I go along, sir? I ain't so spry as I was, but I'm a deep thinker and all."

"You can go, Captain Ben!" cried Mr. Wilkinson with a strange note of boyish enthusiasm in his voice. "How about you, Bessie?"

Elizabeth nodded her head. "I'll go, too, dad," she murmured. "Perhaps I might be able to help some way. There might be something that—"

Suddenly she broke off. A dozen feet from her, from the interior of the sailor's chest, a strange flapping, scratching sound could be heard.

"Never you mind 'er, ma'am," said Bill Farley, with an embarrassed smile. "Lizzie 'as tantrums when she ain't fed regular. Poor gal, she's 'ad a 'ard day."

## CHAPTER V

### ANCHORS AWEIGH

FOR the next few days Maple Ridge, as Mr. Wilkinson's country place was called, was humming with activity. The preparations for the extended voyage went on apace, and the obese financier attended to the work with unusual animation.

Captain Ben and Farley slept together in the fisherman's cottage. They kept the sailor's chest in the same room with them. Often, and especially while the moon was full, the whimpus would emit that strange humming sound so peculiar to it, and at these times the men's snores would grow in volume till the tiny apartment seemed the interior of some huge beehive.

But Elizabeth, unlike the others, did not view the contemplated cruise for treasure with sparkling eyes and flushed cheeks. No; on the contrary, an involuntary tremor passed through her when she thought of it. During these days a shadow dogged her footsteps. And because this shadow was so vague in outline, so incomprehensible, it was doubly terrifying.

"What am I afraid of?" she would ask herself. "Am I afraid of a trip by sea to the China coast?"

"No," an inner voice would answer. "You are afraid of arriving safely at an island where there will be hundreds and hundreds of creatures like that creature which is now in the sailor's box."

"Perhaps. But why should I fear these creatures. I did not even see the one in the box."

"Very true," the voice would answer with terrifying calmness; "but you have a feminine intuition which tells you that there are worse things than death—an intuition which has shown you the meaning of such creatures in your dreams. Beware the whimpus! Was it not chanted over your cradle by another woman who, in her turn, heard it almost at dawn of thought? The whimpus, that intangible something which robs women of husbands and homes—the whimpus, that destroyer of our faith in those we hold close to our breasts, that breaker of men's destinies, that flapping, scratching creature of guile —beware the whimpus!"

And Elizabeth could not rid herself of that shadow. She saw it reflected in her father's kindling eyes and flushed cheeks; she saw it written in the curve of Jay's prominent chin; and she noted that even the aged Captain Ben, bore its dread echo in his shrill voice as the rusted antique bugle holds the echo of war somewhere in its dry throat. Like a relentless Medusa, it was turning to stone all those kindlier, gentler traits of man. Somewhere in the distance—on a coral island in the China

Seas—strange, flapping, scratching creatures were beckoning to them. The men heard their call. They were going, even as Bill Farley had gone, even as all men had gone through all centuries. It was destiny—destiny sad for women to look upon. She was alone, and they were many; she went unprotected, and they were armed with all the hidden guile of the infinite. What was waiting for her on Whimpus Island?

At last came that never-to-be-forgotten day when the *Adventurer*, who had not earned her name till then, weighed anchor and swept majestically out of the harbor into the open sea. Elizabeth, from the upper deck, watched the shore slip past and finally disappear like a cloud of smoke. Several gulls followed the yacht, emitting shrill, plaintive cries. The wind had freshened, and a sprinkling of spray was borne against her face. The waves, in a long slanting procession, marched gaily forward against the prow of the *Adventurer*, only to be disemboweled and cast aside. They seemed an army seeking suicide. Each perished with a little gasp. A few somber clouds rode the heavens. They looked down on the bright tumult beneath like elderly, corpulent generals who watch the battle from afar.

"Well, ma'am, 'ow's it feel to go sailin' arter treasure?"

It was Bill Farley who spoke. He and Captain Ben had sauntered over to the rail, within arm's reach of Elizabeth's chair. They both wore a grin, now that they were safe at sea.

"Of course, I feel very excited," Elizabeth murmured. "What have you done with your fish, Mr. Farley?"

"Who? Lizzie, ma'am? She's as safe as a bug in a rug. I 'ave 'er alongside my 'ammock. I wouldn't take 'alf a chance with Lizzie."

"I'll miss the sound of her to-night, Bill," Captain Ben broke in. "That there whimpus has a soothin' sound when a feller's sleepy—a most soothin' sound."

"So I 'ave took notice, matey," Bill Farley muttered reflectively. "She's dif-ferent than most gals there—beggin' your pardon, ma'am. I 'ad a wife in Singapore once. Gawd, that gal wouldn't lull yer off to sleep none, not 'er! She was hall for talk. She 'ad a tongue like a tin knife beatin' on a fryin'-pan. Give me Lizzie in a 'urricane to 'er."

The yacht had weighed anchor in the late afternoon. Now night began to settle down over the waste of tossing waters. The lips of foam, which rode each wave, seemed encrusted with tiny sparks of living fire. The wake was a flaming phosphorescent streak. Very gradually, very timidly, the stars appeared and looked down vacantly on the sea. The moon rose grinning from a patch of clouds far ahead. It had an air of jovial hospitality about it. "I'm glad you've come," it seemed to be saying through its wide, toothless mouth. "Step this way, won't you? I've got a surprise for you on the other side of the world."

Elizabeth rose with a little shiver. Night had suddenly reached out and gripped the *Adventurer* in her huge shadowy palm. Mystery and adventure were all about in those charging waves, in that somber sky, in that surge and sweep, in that power and passion of the sea.

## CHAPTER VI

### AN IRON WHIRLWIND

IT WAS a calm day. Not a breath of air ruffled the placid surface of the sea which stretched out like some solid, luminous substance. The *Adventurer* plowed her way forward unconcernedly, casting a foam-capped furrow on either side.

"Aye, aye, governor," Bill Farley said in reply to a question of Mr. Wilkinson's, "we should sight Whimpus Island to-morrow night. And a very fine cruise we 'ad of it, weather as though served to order and no sea to speak of."

"We ain't there yet," Captain Ben broke in with a pessimistic shake of his grizzled head. It's a treacherous sea at this time of the year. Them iron whirlwinds pops up as sudden as a devil out of hell!"

"An iron whirlwind?" Jay asked.

" 'E means a typhoon, gov'nor," Bill Farley explained. "They calls 'em iron whirlwinds 'ereabouts."

At that moment Elizabeth mounted the companionway and joined the four men. "Isn't it warm?" she murmured.

"Aye, aye, it's 'ot," Bill Farley replied.

"It is," said Captain Ben. "I recollect that it was on a day like this that—"

"Hello!" Mr. Wilkinson broke in. "Here comes the skipper! I wonder what he wants?"

The tall, lean figure of the captain of the *Adventurer* came striding toward them. His usually placid countenance wore a lugubrious expression.

"Well, what is it, Masters?" Mr. Wilkinson asked.

"The barometer has been falling for the last hour, sir. I think we're due a bit of rough weather."

Bill Farley drew in his breath sharply. "That looks bad 'ereabouts," he muttered.

"Bad signs both," said Captain Ben. "Take an old sailor's advice and don't let a iron whirlwind sneak up behind yer when you're not lookin'. Listen! What's that I hear?"

Far away across the calm expanse of water to the east a faint moaning could be heard. It was as though a grieving human soul were wandering in that vast amphitheater between sea and sky. Now other voices joined it in a melancholy chorus. The pack was coming from all sides—that pack of wind-wolves which would soon be down on them with a rush and a roar.

"What is it?" Mr. Wilkinson asked in a bewildered tone.

"There's a typhoon comin' up, gov'nor," said Bill Farley, tightening his leather belt. "There'll be 'ell presently. Take a squint at the sky, gov'nor."

Even as he spoke great black clouds, like knights fully caparisoned for the lists, rode swiftly into the pale-blue sky. They had appeared with startling suddenness as though they had been created in an instant by some malevolent magician of the infinite; and, with their coming, the whole

face of the heavens was altered. A soft glow suffused the heights above. The sky glowed ruby red in spots as though it were a glass door against which gigantic tongues of flame were pushing forward. At any moment one expected to see it come crashing down in red-hot fragments.

Suddenly the mournful wailing ceased. It was followed by a silence so profound that the ticking of Captain Ben's large silver watch was distinctly audible to all. There was something awe-inspiring in this silence. One felt that all about in that sullen sky, in that motionless sea now shot with fiery corrugations, in those swiftly gathering clouds, a relentless force was creeping forward noiselessly on hands and knees.

A solid white wall had risen up from the sea a mile or so away. For an instant it hovered there, a mound of snow against a murky background, and then it swept toward them with a sullen roar.

"Hurry, missy, hurry!" cried Captain Ben in a high falsetto.

Seizing Elizabeth's hand, he half led and half dragged her toward her cabin. Scarcely had they stumbled down to comparative safety before a huge wave tossed the *Adventurer* up on her beam-ends as though she were a toy; and a frantic, tearing wind, like a mad old woman, screaming, chuckling, roaring, circled about overhead, raking the yacht from stem to stern.

The sudden wild bound of the *Adventurer* skyward threw Elizabeth on the floor of her cabin, and Captain Ben, head first, against the wall. Both were stunned. For a long time they lay there, unconscious of the progress of the typhoon.

When Elizabeth opened her eyes again, night had fallen. But what a strange night it was!—a luminous night which enveloped the raging sea with a pall of fire. Through the doorway she caught a glimpse of a blood-red heaven. Indeed the sea and the sky had apparently become as one—a fiery brotherhood, inseparable on the horizon's edge.

The typhoon had not abated in fury since those first few blinding moments.

On the contrary, the ocean had been so lashed by that terrific and luminous wind that it had risen up in wild revolt, threatening the very sky. Great billows, with fiery locks, charged down on the *Adventurer* and tossed her heavenward in derision. Each instant it seemed that she must perish in those glowing chasms ahead; but she fought her way through them somehow and rose up gamely on the other side, salt incrusted from her keel to her smoke-stacks.

Elizabeth was too weak to move. She lay there, a blinding pain creasing her forehead, staring about her like a terror-stricken child. There was no light in the cabin except those strange, vivid flashes which stole in through the doorway and which served to illumine objects in a fragmentary fashion. Now Captain Ben's face could be seen. He lay within arm's-reach of Elizabeth, huddled up against the wall. She wondered if he were dead.

But now something happened which made her forget Captain Ben entirely. Suddenly the roaring of the wind died down as though by magic—it was as though nature were holding her breath—and she heard strange flapping, scratching sounds in the cabin where the steps led up to the main deck. Whatever it was, it was coming closer.

A great, numbing fear enveloped Elizabeth like a coverlet of snow. Only too well she knew those flapping, scratching sounds. She tried to scream, but her voice was frozen in her throat; she tried to rise, but her limbs refused their office. And now even the luminous light from the sea failed her. An inky blackness succeeded it which draped all things in impenetrable shadow.

But the flapping, scratching sounds continued. They were not more than two feet away—now less than a foot—now— Suddenly she felt something cold and sharp touch her outstretched palm.

"Lizzie!" a hoarse voice shouted. "Lizzie! Where 'ave yer got to, Lizzie?"

Bill Farley's dark figure blocked the cabin door. Striking a match, he peered about him anxiously. At this moment Captain Ben sat up and rubbed his head.

"Who's that?" he called weakly.

"It's Bill Farley, matey. 'Ave yer seen my Lizzy 'ereabouts? That there iron whirlwind smashed my chest ag'in' the wall; and Lizzie took it into 'er 'ead to skedaddle."

Captain Ben drew an electric flash-light from his pocket and touched the button. As the cabin became illumined, Bill Farley uttered a cry of joy.

"There she is!" he shouted jubilantly. "Lizzie, old gal, don't you go for to desert Bill. Come out from under that bed afore I go arter yer. Bli'me, if this ain't luck!"

BEFORE dawn the typhoon wore itself out. All night the *Adventurer* had been running before the hurricane like a chip in a mill-race; now she was able to pursue her course unmolested. The wind had died down to a gentle breeze; and, although the waves still rode mountain high, their crests were no longer flecked with foam. Soon the sun rose and looked down reassuringly on a wind-scarred sea.

The passengers of the yacht, looking much the worse for the night's rough usage, gathered under the awning on the afterdeck.

"Here comes Captain Masters," said Elizabeth suddenly. "He seems to be rather excited."

"Perhaps the old tub's sprung a leak," Bill Farley suggested. "These pleasure-boats ain't built for seas like we was ridin' all of last night."

By now Captain Masters had drawn up alongside the owner of the *Adventurer*. "There's land off our port bow," he said, raising his hat. "A coral island, I believe, sir."

"You don't say so!" Mr. Wilkinson began to fumble with his case of binoculars. "I think I'll take a look at it, Masters."

Bill Farley silently went aft, reappearing a moment later with a long, brass telescope. "I can see it now," Jay said, shielding his eyes with the palm of his hand. "There was a curtain of mist hiding it, but it's rising."

Bill Farley raised the telescope to his eye and gazed long and attentively. Suddenly it began to shake oddly. "Gawd!" he muttered, "if it ain't Whimpus Island!"

"There must be some mistake!" Mr. Wilkinson cried. "We couldn't have run into it by accident like this!"

"Nary a mistake, gov'nor. There she is just as I seen her last, shaped like a 'orse-shoe and all. And there's that bit of flag-pole what me and my mate rigged up with Black Tom's red flannel drawers still flappin' there, or what's left of 'em."

Jay took the telescope from his hand. "He's right, Mr. Wilkinson," he said at length. "At least I can see the pole and something red flying from it."

"Run in closer, Masters," Mr. Wilkinson ordered.

The *Adventurer* ran slowly forward. It came to a halt along the coral shores which glowed like molten metal in the sun. A great splash of foam told that the anchor had been lowered.

"What's that?" Jay cried suddenly. "I thought I saw something dive off that ledge of coral into the water."

"It was a whimpus, gove'nor," said Bill Farley composedly. "I saw 'er myself. There's 'undreds 'ere—'undreds."

"When shall we begin searchin' for the treasure?" Captain Ben asked, moving his nutcracker jaws as though he were chewing a delectable morsel. "I'm most too tired to go skinnin' my shins on diamonds till I've had a few winks of sleep."

"And me too, matey," Bill Farley agreed. "My 'ead's swimmin' around, I'm that wore out. Let's us 'ave our beauty sleep, governor, afore we tackle treasure-'untin'."

"I'd like to start right now," Jay cried impatiently. "We've got all the rest of our lives to sleep."

But Mr. Wilkinson shook his head. "No, no Jay. Captain Ben and Farley are right. We want to start at this thing when we can do our best. Let's turn in now, and in the afternoon we can land and look over the ground."

"Right you are, gove'nor!" Bill Farley cried with alacrity. "I'm off to my 'am-mock this minute. Sweet dreams to one and all." With a smile which was half a grimace and a bow which bent him double, the sailor turned and made off toward his quarters.

"I don't fancy that fellow's manners," Jay said with a flush. "He's entirely too free and easy. What he needs is a strenuous toe-application on the right spot."

"Never mind, Jay," Mr. Wilkinson said. "We can teach him his place after he's found the treasure for us. But speaking about place, mine should be in a downy couch this minute. How about you, Bessie?"

"I'm awfully tired, dad. I'm going to turn in."

"Every one is goin' to take a snooze," Captain Ben said. "Even the crew. Captain Masters has give orders to that effect. Well, they deserve it, the poor lads." Smothering a yawn, he turned and hobbled off.

Fifteen minutes later Elizabeth lay on her berth in the cabin sound asleep.

Almost immediately she heard the muffled sound of oars working smoothly in well-oiled oarlocks.

When the girl awoke the red rays of the setting sun streamed through the porthole.

Conscious that some one was pounding on the door, she sat up and rubbed her eyes.

"Who is it?" she called softly.

"It's Jay," said a voice which shook with anger. "I came to wake you. What do you think happened while we were all asleep?"

"I haven't an idea. What?" the girl asked.

"Why, that Cockney sailor sneaked off to Whimpus Island in one of our life-boats and he hasn't come back."

"What of it? Probably he's taking a little row. He'll be back for supper," she said.

A bitter, incredulous laugh rasped through the keyhole. "I fancy not," Jay said calmly. "He's taken his whimpus with him."

## CHAPTER VII

### "AYE, AYE, SIR—JUST FISH"

ELIZABETH dressed quickly and hurried on deck. In spite of Jay's disappointment, she felt relieved at the disappearance of the sailor and his whimpus. She had great difficulty in hiding her real feelings from the group of excited, angry men whom she encountered near the empty davits where the missing life-boat had reposed.

"This is a pretty kettle of fish, missy!" Captain Ben cried in his high treble. "But I never liked that Britisher from the first."

"I can't see his game," Mr. Wilkinson said irritably. "How can he double-cross us? We've got the yacht; and, without that, all the treasure in the world wouldn't do him any good."

"He's got something up his sleeve," Jay muttered.

"Funny we can't see him on the island," Mr. Wilkinson said thoughtfully. "He's probably hiding on the other side of that mound."

"Or in the treasure-cave," Captain Ben suggested. "That's where he's at—fillin' his pockets with diamonds, I wouldn't wonder."

Elizabeth shaded her eyes and gazed over the now calm stretch of water toward Whimpus Island. To the west, a red sullen sun swam on the horizon. It colored the coral with a last faint glow before it sank beneath the surface of the sea. The wind had died away. Not a breath of air ruffled the placid surface; and the red rags, which had once served as a part of Black Tom's wardrobe, hung disconsolately from the flagpole.

Suddenly the girl uttered a shrill cry. "Why, there's the boat now!" she said. "No, two of them—one right behind the other!"

Mr. Wilkinson raised the binoculars to his eyes in some excitement. After a moment he lowered them with an exclamation of disgust. "It's only Masters," he told his daughter. "We sent him to look for Farley in the other life-boat."

"Yes, but there are two boats coming this way."

"Masters has Farley's boat in tow. He probably found it on the island."

"Well, the man can't dodge us!" Jay cried. "He'll stay on the island till we say the word. I think we've got him where we want him."

"Perhaps he drownded," Captain Ben suggested. "A lot of them sailors can't swim. I recollect one time off Gibraltar there was just such another feller—"

But Mr. Wilkinson interrupted the old fisherman with scant ceremony. Raising his voice to a bellow, he hailed Captain Masters who was not more than a stone's throw from the *Adventurer*.

"Is Farley on the island?"

"He must be there, sir," Captain Masters answered through his speaking-trumpet. "We found his boat pulled up on the shore."

"Hiding in the cave," Mr. Wilkinson muttered. "Well, we'll starve him out. But I don't see his little game."

"Nor I," Jay agreed. "He stands to win nothing by acting this way. But don't you think we could find the cave without him or his whimpus?"

"Not me," said Captain Ben. "It's like lookin' for a needle in a haystack. That there island is hollowed out with caves, thousands and thousands of 'em. We ain't got no chance without a whimpus."

For the next few days a cloud of despondency hung over the *Adventurer*. In vain the coral island was kept under strict surveillance, not a vestige of Bill Farley was to be seen; in vain exploring parties ransacked it from end to end, no cave in any way resembling Black Tom's description was to be found. At the end of the week, even Jay had given up hope. Undoubtedly Bill Farley and his secret had died together.

On the following Monday Mr. Wilkinson made known his intention of quitting the island and starting home. "We're just wasting our time here," he told Jay. "If Bill Farley were still alive, we'd have heard from him before this."

"I suppose so," the young man muttered. "He must have fallen into some hole and broken his neck. But it seems a shame to turn back without getting a glimpse of the treasure."

Mr. Wilkinson nodded solemnly. "I know. But what's to be done? I've told Masters to weigh anchor to-morrow."

At this moment Captain Ben's decrepit figure was seen approaching across the deck at a strange ambling trot. He was waving his arms about like a windmill; his long white hair was flying in the wind.

"Well, what is it?" Mr. Wilkinson asked.

The old man moistened his lips and launched out into speech. "I've been fishin' for the last few days while you all have been searchin' this island. There's some most curious fish in these parts—gay-colored, with tails most like a lady's fan and pop eyes like a frog. But they're tasty, too, when cooked with plenty of butter."

"Is that all you've got to tell us about—*fish?*" Jay cried impatiently. "I thought that perhaps you'd discovered something. "So it's just fish, eh?"

"Aye, aye, sir—just fish," said Captain Ben, a sly smile creeping under his nose. "Well?"

"Well, Mr. Wilkinson, this mornin' I lost my sinker; and, havin' nothin' handy but a gold goat which my sister's son give me for a watch-charm, I hitched it on my line till I could find somethin' better and threw it overboard. Now I didn't get a bite for nearly ten minutes; then, all of a sudden, somethin' gives that line a awful jerk. 'What's this?' I says to myself, for the coral fish don't pull near so hard. 'Perhaps a young shark has laid hold.' Well, I pulled that fish up on deck, although I had a sweatin' time of it, and what do you think it was gentlemen?"

"I'm sure I don't know," said Jay.

"Was it a shark?" Mr. Wilkinson asked.

Captain Ben surveyed his employer with an air of triumph. "Not so you could notice!" said he. "That there fish was nothin' more nor less than a whimpus."

"A whimpus!" cried Mr. Wilkinson.

"Yes, sir. As like to Bill's Lizzie as two peas. Just as ugly natured, too. She had laid hold of that gold goat; and, when I tried to pry it free, she begins bubblin' like a tea-pot and gnashin' her teeth. Well, I tied her up in a net and give her the goat to play with for a spell."

"Where is she now?" Mr. Wilkinson asked.

"Down in my quarters, sir. She's safe enough."

"If this is true," Jay cried with flashing eyes, "if Captain Ben has actually caught another whimpus, we don't need Bill Farley at all. We can take that whimpus on shore and let it lead us to its cave. We'll tie a string to its claw, eh?"

"Let's land on the island the first thing to-morrow morning," Mr. Wilkinson said. "Not one or two of us, but every man on board. And we'll go armed. Whatever is in that cave must have finished Bill Farley off."

"Probably," Jay agreed. "But lead us to your whimpus, Captain Ben."

THE life-boat was lowered carefully into the sea. One by one the men, each armed with a revolver, climbed down the rope ladder and seated themselves. Captain Ben, Jay, and Mr. Wilkinson were the last to leave the deck. They all turned to Elizabeth for a final word of leave-taking.

"We'll be home in time for lunch," Jay said. "Do you see this, Bessie?" He held a large canvas bag aloft. "I brought it along so that I could bring back the diamonds and gold."

"Don't look so downhearted, Bessie," Mr. Wilkinson said good-humoredly. "I'd take you along if we didn't have a lot of climbing and wading in front of us. Too rough work for a girl, eh, Captain Ben?"

"True enough, sir."

"Have you got the whimpus safely aboard?"

"That I have, sir. I got her in a bird-cage one of the men had. These whimpus can cut up rough."

"What will I do if anything should happen to you, dad?" Elizabeth asked.

"What could happen to *us?*" Mr. Wilkinson said reassuringly. "We're eight strong and all armed to the teeth. Don't worry, Bessie—we'll be back for lunch."

"All aboard!" cried Jay. "The sooner we start the sooner we'll be back with the booty."

But Captain Ben lingered for an instant after the other two had clambered down into the boat. "Don't you fret, missy," he said, giving her shoulder a furtive pat. "We'll make out all right. I've got a wise head on my shoulders."

But in spite of these reassuring words, Elizabeth felt a lump rising in her throat when she saw the life-boat push off and the oars flash in the early sunlight. Ever since the preceding afternoon, when the second whimpus had been caught and she had learned of the intended expedition, the girl had been the prey of wild fancies. All night, dark forebodings of she knew not what had haunted her pillow. And now a settled despondency enveloped her optimism like a wet blanket.

For some time she stood at the rail, watching the progress of the life-boat. Finally, after it had disappeared around one of the curving arms of Whimpus Island, she turned away with a sigh and entered her cabin.

Elizabeth glanced about in search of some refuge from herself. She saw a book lying on the table within arm's reach. Picking it up hurriedly, she opened it at random and began to read. Unfortunately for her peace of mind, the book happened to be a volume of Poe's verses. The particular poem she turned to was *The Bells* and those lines which run:

> They are neither man nor woman—
> They are neither brute nor human—
> They are Ghouls—

She dropped the volume with a cry of disgust and hurried up to the main deck. It was well past noon. A blazing sun rode the sky, casting its rays on Whimpus Island which seemed to be wavering in the intense heat. Elizabeth gazed long in that direction, but she could see no vestige of humanity on the shimmering shore.

"'It's nearly one o'clock," the girl murmured. "I've half a mind to go and see what's happened to them."

There was a small skiff on the after-deck which she had often used when at home. To-day the sea was so calm that a canoe could have ridden it with perfect safety. Acting on a sudden impulse, she lowered the skiff into the water and, in a moment more, was seated in the stern, paddling swiftly toward Whimpus Island.

In less than fifteen minutes the skiff grounded on the shore and Elizabeth began her search.

Whimpus Island extended for nearly three miles. In breadth, however, it rarely exceeded two hundred yards. The walking was very rough. There were all manner of hummocks, which rose up like bumps on a bald head, and fissures in the coral which had to be taken into account.

Elizabeth was a strong, active girl, but she was nearly worn-out before she had circled the island. Every now and then she stopped to rest. At these times she called aloud, whereupon her voice would be caught up by every cave and echoed back hollowly. But no human voice answered hers; no human figure met her eye in all that weary tramp. Indeed, a blight seemed to rest on the island. Unlike any other which she had ever seen, no sea-gulls whined about its cliff and no grasses grew even where there was a stretch of solid soil.

"They must still be in the cave," Elizabeth murmured in a vain effort to fight off growing depression. "It won't do any good hunting for them. I'll go back to the boat and wait there."

When she came to this decision, she was standing on the hummock from which Black Tom's gaudy nether garments fluttered brazenly in the wind. The girl, tired in both body and mind, seated herself for an instant beneath this barbaric emblem and rested her chin in her hands. Several paces from her, a long red fissure in the coral seemed to grin at her as though it were a human mouth.

Suddenly she heard a strange sound

which made her start and look up. It was a dull droning like the humming of innumerable bees, not unmusical and rather soothing except for an occasional loud snort which broke into it like a peremptory command. These sounds evidently issued from the fissure already alluded to.

"What can it be?" Elizabeth wondered. She walked over to the fissure and tried to peer down.

Now the dull buzzing sounds grew louder. Suddenly there came such a loud snort from the shadowy depths that Elizabeth involuntarily recoiled.

"Sea-lions!" she murmured. "I've heard them snort just like that in the zoo. The buzzing sound must be water running into some cave. No doubt the tide rises and falls."

At last she retraced her steps to where she had left the skiff, and, with a heavy heart, paddled back to the *Adventurer*. As she neared the yacht, hope rose up in her. Perhaps they had returned while she had been out of sight on the other side of the island; perhaps they were safe on board, laughing at her fears.

Making the skiff fast, she clambered aboard the *Adventurer* and was greeted by silence and shadows. A glance at the empty davits where the life-boat usually reposed, blighted her hopes. She experienced a moment of complete weakness. Sinking down on the hard deck, she began to sob.

Night was slowly falling. A gray mist stole up silently from the water, enveloping Whimpus Island in an impenetrable curtain of mystery. The sun sank with startling suddenness as though its fiery light had been extinguished by the touch of that calm, luminous sea. A legion of languid shadows stole about the hysterical girl on noiseless feet. They bent backward and forward like flowers fondled by the breeze; they pointed at Whimpus Island with ghostly fingers; they were like embodied dreams which seek release.

But Elizabeth wept on, quite unheeding their silent supplications; wept on, while the stars opened timidly like frightened eyes; wept on, while the moon, grinning,

rose up triumphantly as though to say: "Well, what did I tell you? Here we are on the other side of the world. Look where I am looking, and you will see something very strange. Come, this is a surprise!"

## CHAPTER VIII

### A WOMAN AND A WHIMPUS

THE hours which followed the disappearance of the treasure-hunters, seemed like so many years to Elizabeth. All alone on the *Adventurer*, a prisoner in a floating prison, she experienced a thousand and one terrors which threatened her very reason.

At one moment, she would abandon herself to despair; at the next, a sudden sound—the swishing of water against the ship's side, the creaking of an overtaxed beam—would make her leap to her feet in a frenzy of hope.

A hundred times during that first terrible night, she thought she heard the squeaking of oar-locks. Then she would hurry up on deck, her heart beating wildly, expecting to see the life-boat pull up alongside. At each disappointment, her spirits would sink again into the darkest depths of despondency.

The next morning she paddled her skiff to shore and searched the island from end to end. She returned sadly to the ship.

On the third day all hope deserted her. Straining her eyes across the silver-shod sea, she saw the island like a sinister red question-mark standing out against a pale blue page. Not a vestige of life was stirring there. Black Tom's tattered garments—how dear, how human a symbol after all!—waved in melancholy triumph over a hot, blistering waste of coral.

Perhaps it was this still vivid remnant of a brave man who had gone to his everlasting rest, perhaps it was a fine frenzy of despair, but certain it is that Elizabeth took her courage in both hands and went out alone to battle against the whimpus.

Very calmly, though with a wildly beating heart, she went down to Captain Ben's quarters, ransacked his belongings and returned on deck with a strong fishing-line. Her next problem was to bait the hook properly. She examined her trinkets, one by one, and finally decided on the ring which Jay had given her on the day of their engagement. Why did she choose this ring among all the others? Was it because she loved it best; or, perhaps, because it symbolized her love which was as keen and brave as a sword?

Elizabeth lowered her bait carefully over the side. Bending forward, she saw it slip into the water, which was as clear as crystal; saw it sink down slowly into the depths, saw a host of flaming darts shooting this way and that—coral fish, which were all colors of the rainbow—and finally saw it resting on a strip of snow-white sand. For several minutes she stood there, immovable, staring down; and then she uttered a low exultant cry.

Several dark gliding shapes began to approach the glittering bait. They formed about it in a solemn circle as though deciding. Elizabeth caught a glimpse of slowly moving tails, beneath a long, silky substance which trailed out behind and which glimmered dully. Surely these were whimpus. She even caught a glimpse of an outstretched, avaricious claw. What was in that held them back? Why didn't they bite?

She leaned forward further still and saw the answer to her question mirrored on the placid water. Her own face looked back at her. Yes, evidently the whimpus had seen her. Now they were pointing upward with their clawlike fingers, now they were stealing off in a stately procession. Soon they had disappeared.

"Perhaps they are as afraid of me as I was afraid of them," Elizabeth told herself.

This thought gave her a new confidence and a new idea. Pulling the line up, hand over hand, she hurried into her cabin, and, opening one of the port-holes wide, threw her bait out into the sea. Then she seated herself and waited.

In her present position she could not be seen from the water. If they had not gone too far away, perhaps they would return and nibble, now that she had disappeared. At any rate, it was just possible.

For five minutes, ten minutes, Elizabeth sat as silent as a statue, with a white face and flashing eyes; and then, just as she was about to pull the line in and cast again, she felt a violent jerk which nearly pulled her to her feet. The line had suddenly grown taut and it took all her strength to hold it.

And then the struggle began. Elizabeth was an athletic girl. Her muscles served her well that day. Little by little, with gasping breath and straining arms, she fought it out. Often she gained a yard, only to lose it again. But now her fighting blood was up; she knew no weakness or fear.

Gradually, inch by inch, the girl drew the whimpus to the surface of the water and then above it. Now it was dangling in the air; now it shot through the porthole like an arrow and fell, flapping and scratching, to the floor.

Then, at last, the whimpus relinquished its frenzied hold on the glittering bait. Moving its small, round head from side to side, it clawed its tangle of golden hair from its face and stared at Elizabeth. Slowly the large blue eyes became dilated with fear, the large loose-lipped mouth fell open, disclosing sharp yellow fangs, the tail flapped wildly, and both claws were raised on high like terror-stricken hands.

And Elizabeth looked at this monster concocted in the laboratories of the sea—at this creature, half fish and half vampire; at this composition of scales and flesh—with horror, it is true, but without fear. Her imagination had long ago pictured it. She had seen it so often in her dreams, that now the reality was not so difficult to view.

And thus it was that a woman and a whimpus faced each other for the first time since the world began—while the clock in the cabin ticked on contentedly; while the chairs presented their stolid wicker backs like disinterested strangers; while the sea, as though amused at what it saw, tickled the yacht's sides, and, laughing merrily, sped by.

## CHAPTER IX

### TREASURE TROVE

ELIZABETH was the first to act. A colossal calmness had descended upon her which had crystallized her every thought, her every sensation, into a well-formulated plan. She must not fail now. She realized with a perfect clarity of vision that all her hopes of ultimate happiness, her life and the lives of her dear ones, depended on an immediate exertion of her mental and physical powers. She loathed this abysmal monster on the floor with both a fleshly and spiritual loathing, but she must not falter in her self-appointed task.

There was a large wicker lunch-basket on the chair beside her. Picking it up, she raised the lid and took a step forward.

And the whimpus, which, up to this, had been in an attitude of frozen horror, its clawlike hands raised above its head—now seemed to read its adversary's intent. Hissing faintly, its fishy eyes covered by a gray film of fear, it squirmed backward as Elizabeth advanced till finally its flapping tail touched the wall. There it paused and, with gnashing teeth and extended nails, awaited the attack.

But the girl did not hesitate. Stepping bravely forward, she bent down and attempted to force the creature into the lunch-basket. Hissing, it squirmed to one side and escaped. Once more she essayed her task; and this time the whimpus's sharp teeth were embedded for a moment in her arm.

Now a blind fury drove Elizabeth on. As she felt the sudden pain, her left hand found the monster's throat and tightened there till it relinquished its hold to gasp for breath, till its tongue protruded like a scarlet streamer, till its eyes were nearly popping from its head. And then she lifted it from the floor; lifted it and held it at arm's length. Her fingers, like steel rings, still encircled its slender throat.

But as the whimpus's pale, leprous face turned scarlet, as its blood-shot eyes rolled upward till nothing was visible of them but their crimson-threaded whites, she relaxed her hold. It would never do to kill it outright. It must serve her first; it must guide her to her loved ones.

The whimpus squirmed only very feebly now. Elizabeth had no difficulty in placing it in the lunch-basket, where it lay flapping faintly. Her next task was to tie the fishing-line securely about its waist, where the fish's tail joined the woman's body. Now it could not escape, but its swimming powers would remain unimpeded.

She then closed the lid on her prisoner, secured it, and carried the lunch-basket up on deck.

She tied a handkerchief about the wound, and climbed down the ladder, still holding the lunch-basket, and into the skiff. Slipping the oars into place, she bent her strong, supple back to the task and was soon propelling the boat swiftly toward the island.

When the skiff was finally grounded on the shore, she sprang out with all the eagerness of one who goes willingly to battle.

Elizabeth opened the lunch-basket and drew out the whimpus. The monster by this time had regained some of its strength. As she held it suspended in mid air on the end of the fishing-line, it squirmed frantically, gnashed its teeth, and emitted a strange hissing sound.

For a moment she swung it back and forth to see that the line held; then she threw it from her into the sea.

At first the whimpus swam straight out with incredible swiftness—so fast, indeed, that she was put to it to give it free play —but after it had traversed a hundred yards or so, it turned and began to creep back further down the shore. Fortunately the fishing-line was very long; but, at that, she was soon forced to follow it along the beach.

In this way Elizabeth half circled the island. At last she came to a tangle of salt grass which grew in profusion against one of the coral cliffs. To her amazement the fishing-line passed through this tangle as if the creature on the other end had clambered back on shore. And yet this seemed impossible, for the shoulder of the island at this point was precipitous.

As she paused before the green, swaying door of salt grass, there came another tug on the line which showed her that the whimpus was still in active flight. Pushing the nodding sea-foliage aside with her left hand, she uttered an ejaculation of surprise.

There, in the coral wall, was a cave hollowed out as though by human hands. Undoubtedly this subterranean passageway led into the very heart of the island. Perhaps the whimpus was leading her into the treasure-chamber where, dead or alive, she might find the missing passengers of the *Adventurer*.

Elizabeth, with a wild beating heart, stepped through the dark portal and was immediately swallowed up in the gloom. Not a light glimmered; soon the opening in the cave was lost to view. Walking in pitch blackness, a stream of running water above her ankles, the taut line leading her forward as a blind man is guided by holding to the leash of some intelligent dog, she stumbled on for a hundred yards or more. Suddenly a strange sound came to her out of the darkness far ahead.

Elizabeth paused and listened, in spite of a sudden angry tug on her wrist. There it was again—only louder now. A drowsy, humming sound it was, followed almost immediately by a loud snort.

It is no telling whether Elizabeth could have mustered up enough courage to go further had not the whimpus at that moment given the line such a frenzied jerk that she was carried forward a step in spite of herself. This step was the deciding one. There was no use turning back now. Behind her lay loneliness, starvation, death; before her? Well, that might be quicker, at any rate.

The frightened girl waded onward through the blackness, while the strange sounds grew louder and louder. Now a gray shaft of light stole around a bend in the passage. She reached it; she turned an abrupt shoulder of rock and uttered a cry which echoed through the vault. She was destined never to forget the sight which met her eyes.

The passageway here terminated in a spacious hall. Through a fissure in the ceiling, javelins of flaming sunlight poured down on a strip of shimmering sand which barely raised its head above the shallow water. And on this sand, piled up in a glittering heap and indiscriminately mingled, were precious stones, pieces of colored glass, yellow bars of gold, brass door-knobs, a child's toy sword, several helmets which the soldiers of Cæsar might have worn, rattles with colored beads, a crown set with gigantic emeralds which might have adorned some fair Egyptian's brow. But one and all caught the shafts of sunlight and reflected them, casting a luminous light on the dark, dripping walls and on the pale sheet of water.

It was not the sight of these precious stones and glittering gewgaws which wrung the cry from Elizabeth. No, it was the group which sat about this treasure in a solemn circle—these men, with their chins resting on their breasts; these skeletons from whom hung in tatters the clothing of an earlier age; these gleaming skulls and moldy thigh-bones, more aged relics still, which time had crumbled into little powdery heaps beneath the weight of its relentless hand. And also it was that outer ring of custodians which guarded both—that swimming ring of whimpus, whirling round and round in a magic circle and emitting that strange, unearthly humming sound as they went—those singular creatures that were neither brute nor human, their large blue eyes fixed with a glassy stare on what rested on that strip of sand, their long, golden hair floating behind them in a filmy gauze.

Scarcely had Elizabeth's cry echoed through the chamber than a change took place. The humming died away as though by magic. Now a hundred pairs of terror-stricken eyes were turned on her, a hundred pairs of terror-stricken clawlike hands were raised on high, a hundred scaly tails churned the water into foam. Once, twice, the whimpus sped around the strip of sand

and then straight toward her and the passageway.

She floundered to one side; the fishing-line dropped from her nerveless hand. The next instant they were past her, gliding by swiftly and out into the passageway. Leaving a trail of foam, they vanished in the gloom. She was left entirely alone with the dead.

But, ah, no, they were not all dead! What was that? Surely it was a human snore—a snore so awe-inspiring, so sonorous, that from a distance it had seemed the snorting of an animal in pain.

Elizabeth stepped cautiously forward. The light reflected from the heap of treasure was blinding. She shaded her eyes with her hand.

Could it be? Yes, it was. There was no doubt about it. The snorer was Captain Ben! There he sat, his cavernous mouth gaping, his hairy fists doubled on his knees. And next to him, his head resting on his shoulder, a strang expression of physical loathing on his face, sat—Jay! Surely there was her father on his right, sleeping soundly, his chin resting on his breast! And the other sleepers were the crew of the *Adventurer*. None were dead as yet—thank God! —not one.

Elizabeth put her hand on Captain Ben's shoulder and shook him. "Wake up!" she cried. "Wake up!"

The old man's stentorian snore ceased on the instant. He raised his face and Elizabeth saw that it was bedewed with perpiration. "Don't you touch me!" he muttered. "Can't you see I'm an old man? I—I—"

"It's Bessie!" the girl cried. "Don't you know me?"

Suddenly the light of recognition flared up in the old fisherman's eyes. "Oh, missy," he said feebly, like a frightened child, "take me out of here. I want to go home, missy."

But Elizabeth was shaking Jay. "Wake up! Wake up!"

The young man opened his gray eyes. "Oh!" he cried. "Get me out of here! Oh, Bessie, dearest girl, it's you! You don't know what a horrible dream I've had!"

But Elizabeth had turned to her father. "Wake up, dad!" she cried.

"What do you want?" the financier muttered. "Oh, Dolly, Dolly, shameful Dolly!"

"Wake up, dad!"

And then Mr. Wilkinson opened his eyes and stared solemnly at his daughter. "I've had a nightmare, Bessie," he said. "Get me out of here if you can. I'm about all in!"

But Elizabeth woke the others first. Captain Masters and his crew. Last of all, she came to Bill Farley. He was sitting beside a skeleton which still wore a tattered sailorsuit. The cockney had a sentimental smile playing beneath his bulbous nose. One of his arms were buried to the elbow in a heap of precious stones; the other clasped the body of a dead whimpus to his breast. His eyes were swallowed in cavernous hollows; his lips were a chalky white.

"Wake up!" Elizabeth cried bravely, although the man's face frightened her. "Wake up!"

Bill Farley was silent. But his smile broadened and twitched his upper lip above two yellow fangs.

"Wake up!" she cried again, shaking him violently.

The sailor did not move, but his eyes flickered open for an instant. "I 'ears you, ma'am," he said very faintly. "Call louder, ma'am. A girl such as you can pull a chap outer 'ell, if she tries real 'ard. Call louder, ma'am."

Once more Elizabeth's voice echoed through the chamber. "Wake up!" she cried. "It's time we went home!"

Again Bill Farley's white lips moved. "It ain't a bit of use, ma'am. I'm goin' 'ome, but not with you. Black Tom 'ere is more my kind. 'E and me—them whimpus 'as got us, soul and body. Lizzie, 'ere, she kept on singin' to me on the *Adventurer*. It weren't me that double-crossed yer, ma'am, it was 'er. Gawd! What was a poor sailor-man to do? She 'ad a 'old on me most as strong as a gal; and she was all for gettin' 'ome. I guess I—"

The muffled voice died away; the long, lean head rolled over on one shoulder; a frozen, sentimental smile was still stamped on the chalky lips.

"It ain't no use, missy," Captain Ben said, touching her on the arm. "That feller's dead. Let us clear outer here afore them things come back. I had a horrid dream, missy!"

## CHAPTER X

### THREE WEEKS LATER

THE *Adventurer*, her engine beating rhythmically like a human heart, plowed through the shadowy sea. To the west a last faint, crimson streak in the sky showed where the sun had struggled for the mastery and died. Now night ruled the world.

Elizabeth, Captain Ben, Mr. Wilkinson, and Jay, sat on the after deck. A silence had fallen between them which was broken only by the faint gurgling of the fisherman's ancient pipe as he inhaled silver threads of smoke into his lungs. The girl was the first to speak.

"You haven't told me how you happened to fall asleep there," she said with some asperity. "That would be the last thing I'd do after finding all those precious stones."

Captain Ben cleared his throat; Mr. Wilkinson rose and walked to the rail; Jay seemed engrossed in a silent contemplation of the stars.

"Well, aren't any of you going to tell me?"

Captain Ben took the pipe out of his mouth and yawned. "Yes, missy," he said, "I'll spin you the yarn. But remember you're a gal, and there's lots of things gals can't seem to get into their heads."

"I wouldn't be so sure of that, Captain Ben."

"Well, it's as true as gospel, missy. Just you take them whimpus for instance. They couldn't do you no harm 'cause you're a gal and they ain't got no power over gals. You was stronger than they was, and they know'd it. There ain't a whimpus livin'

what can hold her own against a decent gal like you, missy. They're common critters, mostly."

"But I want to know how you happened to fall asleep in that cave."

"Aye, aye, missy, I'll tell yer. The whimpus what had us in tow led us into that cave as pretty as you please. When we seen all them diamonds and things, we didn't stop for nothin'—just waded through them swimmin' whimpus and climbed up on the sand and begin to play with the jewels like we was babies. Even the skeletons didn't scare us none—though Bill Farley give me kind of a start when I seen that silly grin on his mug. Well, you know the sound them whimpus made while they was swimmin'?"

"Yes," said Elizabeth. "It got on my nerves. It was a most unpleasant sound."

Captain Ben shook his aged head. "It might have sounded unpleasant to you, missy, 'cause you're a gal; but it didn't to us. Lord, no! It was a soothin' sound—a most soothin' sound! Well, pretty soon I give up countin' diamonds and take a look about me. What do you think I saw, missy? Why, there was your pop, Mr. Jay, and them sailors, all fast asleep! They had kinder silly grins on their faces—leastwise, so I thought."

"You old liar!" cried Jay with some heat. "I heard that snore of yours before I even closed my eyes."

"And I, too," Mr. Wilkinson muttered. "He was asleep before any of us."

But Captain Ben went on as though he had not heard them. "Well, I kinder wondered why they should all go off to sleep like that. But pretty soon that hummin' sound grew louder and crept into my head —the same as gas does when some dentist feller goes to yank yer tooth. I tried to fight it, missy, but it weren't possible. Pretty soon, before I realized it, I slipped off into a dream."

"A dream? What kind of a dream? That's what I want to find out. When you woke up, you all said that you had had such horrible dreams."

The three men exchanged covert

glances. Captain Ben rose and knocked the ashes out of his pipe. "You ask your pop, missy," he said. "He's a whole lot better at tellin' things than me."

Mr. Wilkinson frowned. "I don't remember anything about it," he muttered, "not a thing. But I think I'll go up and ask Masters where we are. He said we might sight Fire Island Light before the moon rose."

"I'll go with yer, sir," said Captain Ben, hobbling after his employer. "It takes the young fellers to remember them dreams right. Mr. Jay, I reckon, can tell about his'n like it was a story outer one of them books you're always readin', missy."

"What *was* your dream, Jay?" Elizabeth asked after the two elder men had gone.

The young man's eyes avoided hers.

"I can't tell you, Bessie," he said. "That dream was too much a part of myself to share it with another. There come such dreams in a man's life—dreams, distorted and terrible, which one must keep always in the dark closet of one's mind. Women should be satisfied with realities— a man's dreams must always be his own."

"I suppose you're right. But it must have been horrible dreams which drove you all out of the cave without the treasure."

"They *were* horrible dreams, Bessie—at least, mine was." Jay paused and stroked his chin meditatively. "But it cured me, Bessie."

"Cured you?" the girl asked in surprise. "What did it cure you of?"

"It cured me of that wild craving for adventure which used to drag me from place to place as a kitten drags a mouse. This time I've absorbed enough excitement for the rest of my life. You'll find that when I get my feet on dry ground I'll turn out to be the most thoroughly domesticated husband in the world."

"I'll be so glad of that," Elizabeth said earnestly. "If that happens, I will never ask you about your dream; if that happens, I shall know that I have really conquered the whimpus."

There was a moment's silence; and then, from the bow of the *Adventurer*, came a hail which brought them to their feet. It was Captain Ben shouting through Masters's speaking-trumpet.

"Land, ho!" the old man cried in a shrill falsetto. "Land ho, missy!"

And so now Karpen sat in the death chamber while the gas fumes swirled around him

# Karpen the Jew

Around the great table in that impregnable room were gathered the ambassadors of the four magnificoes of the world—and with them, unseen, sat the envoy of an even Greater One

## By ROBERT NEAL LEATH

AFTERWARDS, the newspapers screamed that John Albertson, president of Consolidated American Steel, accidentally had fallen to his death from a window of his suite on the sixth floor of the Mark Hopkins Hotel, San Francisco. Four monstrously important diplomats swore to it.

I was there. Karpen was there also. It didn't happen like that. Probably the diplomats believed what they said and they looked at me with amazement afterwards and called me a liar. They said they had never seen me before. Okay. Select the truth for yourself. But I'm telling it my way because Brenda, she of the gardenia skin and the deeply exciting eyes, had a baby this morning and I fear to watch that baby grow, for it is also the child of Karpen the Jew and I wonder how very long it might live.

I met Karpen through Silverstein, the third night before Christmas Eve. Silverstein was violently shivering, although the fog was not particularly cold that night. I let him in and he sat down, shivering, holding his hat between his knees, and said, "Have you got a drink, Jack?"

"Why, yes. Of course."

I gave him the bottle and he chose a water glass and drank whisky from it. I thought a slug that size would knock him cold, he shook so badly, but it didn't.

"You read the newspapers?" Silverstein asked. He was state executioner at San Quentin, the guy who operated the lethal gas chamber, and I'd met him in a beer joint. I will meet anybody, provided he is not fighting ugly from drink, and I'll listen to anybody, if he will talk, particularly in beer joints. I had known Silverstein thirteen months.

"I do read 'em," I said coldly, because Silverstein certainly couldn't have forgotten I was a newspaperman.

He said, "This morning we tried to execute Karpen," and looked at me with the dark brown eyes of his race almost starting from his head.

His words had had a shock punch behind them, and I'd felt it.

*"Tried?"*

Suddenly Silverstein let his head fall forward where his hands could hold it, and he began to sob. "I tell you!" he said with a gasp. "We tried at ten A.M. on the dot. The lever did not fail. You know how the chamber works? I trip this little lever, see, and a cyanide egg drops into sulphuric acid, and that makes the gas. But within a few seconds I knew there was something wrong. Karpen failed to squirm. He didn't choke nor gasp, the horrible way they do," Silverstein said. "Nothing happened whatever. And there the gas was, rising round him—"

I TOLD Silverstein to take more whisky, and when he realized what I was talking about, he did. He gulped the whisky from the water glass and it didn't hit him. It only made him hold on to himself a little.

Silverstein said, "I watched the indicators, I tell you! Enough gas to kill a herd of elephants. We blew the chamber out and Karpen smiled. We put a white rat in there with him and dropped another cyanide egg and the rat ran about, frantic, squeaking, and went into convulsions and died. But Karpen kept on smiling. After twenty minutes they took Karpen back to his cell. I—I went to see him there."

Abruptly Silverstein's voice was a horrified whisper. "I hadn't really looked at Karpen in the death chamber, but I looked at him now and—so help me!—I remembered him from some time long, long ago! I had never seen him during all my life, but I remembered him. From some time long, long ago," Silverstein whispered. "They were going to try again at ten o'clock tonight. But"—and here his voice rose to an almost uncontrolled screech— "they didn't."

I looked at my clock. Twelve minutes past ten P.M. My reason told me that Silverstein could not possibly know whether the execution had been attempted a second time, or not; because you can't cross the bay from San Quentin to San Francisco in anything even close to twelve minutes. Karpen, I knew, was a murderer, condemned to death for the apparently unprovoked slaying of an international banker.

"Why not?" I said.

"Because—I let Karpen out," Silverstein said. "I—I *remembered* Karpen the Jew from some time long, long ago. I tell you I remembered Karpen the Jew!" the man screamed.

I said, "Excuse me," and started out into the hall where I had a telephone. I figured he was nuts. I figured I could shut the door into the hall and call some help. You never know what a nut might do— especially a nut who has been earning a living as an executioner. Nobody, I thought, can "let" a condemned murderer out of San Quentin, except a court or the California governor.

"Don't telephone," Silverstein said dully. "It's not what you think. I've got my right mind."

I don't know why I believed him. I came back and stood in the middle of my living room.

"Why do you come, now, to me, Silverstein?"

"Because you are my friend," he said, "the only one I have."

From his manner I guessed there was something else. He was holding something back.

"What else?"

"Because Karpen said your name," Silverstein strangely replied, lifting his head. "Karpen is waiting outside in the hall. Can he come in?"

WELL, that was something, all right. Perhaps you know that feeling when your spine seems suddenly to chill and the hairs rise on the back of your neck and between your shoulder blades. A condemned killer, fugitive from a death house, waiting outside in my hall. Wanting to come in. A killer whom I'd never seen in the flesh although I knew his features quite well from pictures—but who could have been acquainted with my own name only through some circumstance unknown to me. *Can he come in?*

"Has he got a gun?" I said.

"Why no. No, of course not," Silverstein said, and queerly added: "I think he does not need a gun."

I did. I needed a gun and I had one. I got it out of my desk and put it in my right coat pocket. I said, "Open the door."

Silverstein obeyed and Karpen the Jew came in.

He was wearing an old, dark suit that needed pressing. He was tall, well over six feet. He was gaunt, with wide shoulders and long arms and the slightest trace of a stoop, although he held his head erect. His head was entirely bald; no single hair was on it. His skin was very dark and his face was wide across the cheek bones and rather flat, as though his blood had been peasant's blood some time long ago.

He looked in the vigorous middle of life, although I could not then, nor did I ever, determine his precise age. But despite all the extraordinary qualities of his appearance I thought most striking of all was the extraordinary, deep sadness in his eyes.

There were a couple of severe wrinkles down his cheeks, a couple more across his forehead, but he had a complete absence of small wrinkles. I thought, without being able to put my finger on my reason, that he looked somehow unlike any other man I'd ever seen. He took the poorest chair and sat down, clasping his knobby hands together on his lap.

"Would you like a drink?" I said. "Whisky?"

"Please," he said.

What else could you say, what else could you do for a man who had just skipped a date with death—save offer him a drink? "I haven't much time," I said. I wanted to get out of there. "I'm taking a plane for New York."

Karpen said, "You don't mean Washington?"

I stared at him.

No, I very carefully had not meant, nor said, Washington. But I'd been lying. Washington was correct. I had a tip on the strangest story any newspaperman could hope to get. I had the address of a Washington house—a palace, really. I probably wouldn't be able to get inside that house, but merely to try was worth a hop across a whole continent.

"Don't bother," Karpen softly said. Then he added in a swift monotonous tone, as though parroting from memory: "You've got a tip, Jack Murphy, on the strangest story that could ever come a newspaperman's way."

He wasn't reading my mind. Nobody can read your mind, my reason told me. But—I strangely questioned—*can* nobody? I felt sweat coming out of my skin.

"How do you know that?"

Karpen smiled.

"Don't bother," he repeated. "Their plans have been changed. I need some money. Let's take a walk."

My brain was whirling like an off-centered top.

"Whose plans?" I demanded savagely.

KARPEN put one big hand out, palm upward, and ticked the names off with his fingers.

"The plans of five men. John Albertson. Prince Taguchi. Bahkmeteff. Callieri. Sturmer. They won't meet in Washington. Taguchi was delayed."

I said, "Taguchi arrived here yesterday morning on the *President Cleveland*. He started east immediately."

"No. Taguchi's brother arrived, using the name of the Prince. For purposes of dissimulation. Prince Taguchi is coming on the *Asama Maru* and the *Asama Maru* survived a slight collision with a barge in Tokio harbor, Nevertheless the ship was delayed sixty hours."

"I'll check that," I said, and stood up.

"The other four men are coming west to meet Taguchi, using a special train. They left Washington yesterday morning. Not by plane. In the air you must keep moving forward to keep on living. Truly important men may invest in the air but they themselves travel on the surface of the ground and the sea. The four will meet Taguchi in the Mark Hopkins Hotel on Christmas Eve."

"I'll check that special train, too," I said.

Silverstein had no idea what it was all about but he said with strained conviction, "You will find Karpen is right."

On my way to the telephone I looked in a mirror. My face was blotched, whitish. Karpen the Jew, within the realm of normal possibility, could not conceivably have known about that scheduled Washington conference. In addition to myself, only a very few other persons in the world were supposed to know. One was a woman.

John Albertson, in secret, sometimes went haywire and blew his top off with drink. He drank with his mistress—a blond and strange and generous girl I'd loved some years ago, during college. Never mind her name. She's still around. Maybe some day she will get on long-distance again and send me another tip, because she still has some affection for me and understands I've got to move up in this newspaper racket and I can't do it without a lot of very special information. She wasn't Brenda. Brenda, you remember, is handsomely dark.

Yes, the office said, it was true that the *Asama Maru* had sustained a minor collision in Tokio harbor. The boat would reach San Francisco Christmas Eve. The office did not, of course, possess the passenger list of the ship. Even had the office had it, the list wouldn't have done any good. Checking Karpen's statement about the special train took more time. More than an hour—and a big telephone bill. I called our Washington staff man and he called me back.

"There's nothing but a rumor," he said. "A special train probably did pull out of here. You may be right. You named four guys. Not one of them can be located in Washington any place he ought to be."

"Thanks," I said.

I returned to my living room. Karpen looked up.

"Let's go out and walk around," he suggested again.

I WENT with him. I was—temporarily, as usual—managing editor of the *Clarion*, but the shop didn't expect me back till the shop saw me coming. My tip had been too important, and I'd decided to run it down myself. But something must have gone screwy with my reflexes and reactions that night. It's the only way I can figure it now.

Yet at the time it seemed perfectly normal that I should go with Karpen instead of doing a lot of other things. There was nothing screwy about the working of my brain, I feel sure. I realized with perfect clarity that Karpen's freedom was itself a spectacular yarn which I should have hopped on with both feet. But perhaps you yourself have had some such experience—a time when, for no reason you can afterwards adequately isolate, your accustomed manner of acting simply does not seem important, and you act differently.

Well, Karpen was there when he should have been in San Quentin or dead; I knew he was Karpen all right because I'd okayed plenty of his pictures for Page One; and I should have hopped on it fast, trying to discover how he had escaped, and perhaps myself recapturing him.

Instead, Karpen insisted and we went for a walk. Silverstein mumbled that he had to get back to the prison and he left us, moving away hastily with a queer motion as though his legs were just recovering from some sort of paralysis.

There were pinpoints of water hanging in the night air and filling it—not rain, exactly, or San Francisco fog, but something between the two. Round every street light a nimbus glowed and the occasional lighted windows in apartment houses and residential hotels looked cheerful and warm and secure against the night and against all the warped things that walk by night, against all dark violence brooding in the strange minds of men.

We came to Powell street and turned into the brighter city and there were late people upon the sidewalks, buttoned and furred, some few desperate homeless men who wanted fifteen cents each for beds and who would want it again tomorrow night and always. People with comfortable slugs of alcohol inside them going home and a few drunks. A ruddy cop named Percival said hello to me and didn't look at Karpen and strolled on. I wanted to find out why Karpen had done the killing.

"Why was it, really?" I said. "Why did you kill Franklin?"

Franklin had been the banker—a gambling thief who had stolen the savings, the security and food, of a hundred thousand men and women and children, yet had not gone to jail.

"I?"

A look of surprise wrinkled Karpen's face.

He said patiently, "I didn't. Franklin was dead already. Jack, you would have said he was insane, if you could have seen clearly the inside of his mind, but my word for it was dead. Franklin had that peculiar cunning insanity which can defeat any scientific test. I merely executed a fiend, a mind in a body which, soulless, stalked the earth. Merely executed a walking, ruthless greed before it could do any further damage."

I stopped where I was, because my own mind burned suddenly with a group of words I'd not brought up from my memory in many a year. "Vengeance is mine—saith the Lord."

"Who do you think you are?" I snarled, frightened. "God?"

"No," Karpen replied softly, humbly. "Only one, particular, servant of—the Son."

"I'll see you later," I said. Courage greater than mine was required here, in panic I told myself. But somehow I didn't flee. Perhaps because Karpen had his bald, hatted head cocked to one side, as though he listened to some directing clear sweet distant voice. "I need some money," he was repeating, and then: "Let's turn up here."

WE LEFT Market and walked, I think, about two blocks. This street was darker than most; standing on our right was a skinny brick building where I remembered a speakeasy used to be, and Karpen hesitated and again he seemed to listen.

"It ought to be here," he said, peering about on the sidewalk. We couldn't see very well but within a few seconds Karpen stooped and rose with a wallet. The wallet was full of money—$357—it had three one-hundred-dollar bills in it, four tens and seventeen ones.

Karpen took the money out as though he had known all the time he would find it there. He put the money in his pants and tossed the excellent wallet and the rest of its contents into the gutter.

"What about the guy who lost all that?" I said.

"He won't be hurt," Karpen replied. "You and I have three nights and two days to pass. How about beer?"

I wanted to get away from Karpen the Jew more than ever, then, but the midnight *Examiner* was on the street and when we returned to Market I bought a copy and looked at the headlines across the top and then I could not leave Karpen at all. The line of black type screamed:

### KARPEN EXECUTED IN SECOND TRY

Now I am not a religious man and I
know no more than any other what may
be the awful abilities of the human spirit,
nor to what special terrific power one
particular human mind might attain, given
time enough for development. In our day,
men do claim they do not believe anything save those matters which exude evi-
dences of their reality in laboratories—
upon ammeters and in test tubes, through
spectroscopes and chemical stains.

Yet such a claim is patently smug and
false, since that thing which is most completely real, life in its strange inexplicable
arrival and residence and departure, cannot be identified in any such way that
a scientist may say, "See, this is life.
This is the mainspring which makes this
body tick."

And all the days of any man's earthly
life are spent in further confusion. Be-
lieving himself armed with test tubes,
millions of him nevertheless swarm the
churches each Sunday, there to listen to
splendid words, splendid meanings which
make no recordings whatever on scientific
instruments.

A girl's eyes are only a couple of eyes,
two ingenious spheroids of fluid and veins
and muscles set in a skull, yet if she
loves you you can´see her spirit shining
deep behind her eyes, and you recognize
its reality so well that you are willing to
blend with her spirit all that you have,
your own life—willing to give into her
keeping your own unprovable spirit which
you do not understand. . . .

### KARPEN EXECUTED IN SECOND TRY

On its front page the *Examiner* had a
picture, too. A picture of the man who
even then walked Market Street at my
left elbow. Karpen's picture. The paper
said Karpen had been gassed to death
yet here he was, walking.

I put a hand out and gripped his arm
hard and it was a real arm, all right,
the flesh firm and muscular under the
worn cloth of his coat, and my reason
was wildly crying out that this entire

happening could not be true yet it *was*
true. It was blackest magic, yet there is
no magic upon the face of the earth and
everything has a natural explanation if you
can only find it. Abruptly I found my
wild reason wondering how much one
man might learn of exotic but scientific
arts such as hypnotism, if he had the
time. A great deal, I thought—if!

So much learning that he might walk
out of a death house, leaving the witnesses
to watch an execution and even a burial
which did not really occur.

If!

If he had the time!

If he had centuries. Of time—of life.
Centuries, to study.

BUT no normal man does live for centuries. No—I thought—and then
told myself with a reasonableness I still
do not understand, that Karpen the Jew
was no normal or ordinary man. Already
tonight he had used up his earthly time
yet here he was alive and walking at my
side.

My heart was wildly pounding and we
came to a beer joint, a rather tough place
patronized considerably by sailors. There
were girls, some of them temporarily without male companions, but we didn't do
anything about the girls. Karpen had a
tormented look. His eyes glowed with tor-
ment and he kept his hat on.

I said, "You don't want beer. You've
got to see your wife."

His sigh was almost a groan and he
moved his great shoulders forward.

"It will not be considerate," he said.
"Cruel. But you're right. Come on."

"Me?" I said, surprised.

"Yes. You must stay with me three
days," Karpen said. "You must stay with
me till the ambassadors of the great ones
have met and you must see what happens
then. Nobody will believe you but you
must write it down."

Well, the great ones planned to start
the killing again. Coldly, deliberately, as
all wars are started. That had been my
monstrous tip, telephoned by John Albert-

son's mistress. The ambassadors of the great ones would meet, fix a schedule of dates, determine last details of an agreement which doubtless had been in process of formulation for months. Write it down? You could bet your living lungs I would write the story down, if I could only get it.

Karpen said, "Machiavelli was quite a guy."

I was startled. I said, "Sure."

"Machiavelli once remarked," Karpen said, "that if a prince, a dictator, a despot of any sort felt himself tottering, the only certain way to restore the power of his despotism was foreign war. Arouse the patriotism of stupid men in any unworthy and needless cause. Wave the flag and beat the drums."

A new feeling of even greater strangeness surged through me. Not from Karpen's meaning, but from the arrangement of his words. And I heard my strained voice asking, "Did you get that out of a book, Karpen?"

"Why, no," he said. "No . . ."

Machiavelli. A Florentine philosopher, a writer, an adviser to potentates—who had lived in the fifteenth and sixteenth centuries. A cold-blooded priest of violence and subjection. How would you, living, know what such a man had said, unless you did get it from a book? *Or unless*—my mind cried out—*unless that long-dead man had spoken to you directly— in person—before he died!*

"You knew Machiavelli?" I ridiculously stammered. And then I leaned on our table and said quickly, loudly: "Who are you, Karpen?"

BUT he didn't reply, and I was glad he didn't because I felt with abrupt terror that I already and certainly knew who he was. I remembered an age-old, persistent, never-explained legend from human history. The tale of how a tormented Man once struggled along a grievous dusty road bearing his Cross, and sought to pause and rest a moment upon the doorstep of a mean hut but was

denied any pause, and of how He uttered a calm and terrible judgment upon the Jewish laborer dwelling there. A curse that the Jew also must never rest, not even in death, but must wander the living earth forever, immune from death, unkillable.

And a waiter who had been staring came to our table and said to me, "You better go home now, buddy. When a guy starts talkin' into his beer he better go home."

The waiter didn't look at Karpen. I think now he didn't know he was there, couldn't see him at all. Probably the waiter thought I was tight, but I was not. I'd had nothing alcoholic in twenty-four hours except that one half-finished glass of beer.

We went out and a taxi took us to an apartment house in Taylor Street. Brenda opened her own door. She was Karpen's young wife and she spoke not a word, she only moved within the circle of his arms and I felt acutely embarrassed, so complete was their kiss. Her great love for Karpen, her entire sweet and passionate and scientifically-unprovable spirit came up into her eyes as she stepped into his arms.

It wasn't till many days later, when everything was over, that I remembered she subsequently asked no questions, no explanation of the bewildering fact of his freedom. Although obviously she had been weeping, I think now she never believed Karpen the killer had really died, nor would die, no matter what was said.

She took us into her rooms and sat down. She folded her small, capable feminine hands in her lap and she looked at Karpen as though she could never stop looking, her eyes big and soft and shining and a little wet. And I knew that if any man can make a girl love him like that, mister, he's got something—but particularly if the girl is like Brenda.

She was completely and astonishingly beautiful. Skin like gardenia petals, as I've said. Large, long eyes so brown they were almost black. Sleek, intensely black, soft hair.

But it was the composition of her features that made a click in my mind. I'm nuts about museums. Give me a museum and I can wander there a long time, happily and oddly excited by these collected tangible inheritances from ancient peoples who were human the same as we are human, but who thought, acted, believed differently; who perhaps possessed strange knowledges which we will never possess again.

Therefore I knew Brenda Karpen at once. I had seen those features—not precisely the same ones, but the same unmistakable type—many times before, carved in stone and copied from death masks of queens of the Nile, of Assyria, Babylon. Features strong yet delicate, the nose straight, the proportions beautifully classic.

And Brenda's possession of them might have been rare among women, but it was certainly not unique. Look around you. The races are mixed now, and confused, but the flawless features of the ancient queens have never died. The girls are generally Syrian, Jewish, Armenian—but you can find them anywhere, among Mexican Indians, in France, Spain, Russia, Park Avenue or the slums of Boston.

"How long has this been going on?" I said.

Karpen lifted his eyelids and I thought a spark was there.

"How long do you think?"

My spine was ice again but I said, "Two thousand years. You will have many wives waiting for you, Karpen, and each will be a copy of the others."

He said with a deep sadness, "I—hope they do not wait. I've instructed Brenda she must—not."

She smiled. It was sweet, enigmatic, secret. The nearest thing to the Mona Lisa smile I'd ever seen. "What little time you've had for me, Karpen, will be always in my heart," she said. "I'm going to have a child of yours."

"It won't be like me," he said. "The child will die when his time has come."

"Listen!" I screamed, because now I felt that I had to know. *"Who are you?"*

He stared at me and replied dully. "Why, merely Karpen. A Jew."

I STAYED there till Christmas Eve. I slept on a couch and thought not once of the office. My spirit was filled with a mounting, swelling dread. Not for Brenda. She, I discovered immediately, was not rich but she had an income which would support her, and any child, in comfort, no matter what happened to Karpen himself. But dread of what he might do when the ambassadors assembled.

We left Brenda's apartment only once during that period, and then to visit an exclusive men's store. There Karpen outfitted himself from head to foot in the finest evening clothes the place could supply, and insisted that I purchase similar gear for myself. The salesman who attended to our wants scarcely opened his mouth. His air was one of fascination, and his face was white and troubled, as though he ought to remember Karpen but could not.

And indeed, the fact that such a strange dark man with the build and rugged countenance of a laborer, the bald head and the wide knobby brow of a wise and ancient spirit, should require the formal tails of highest society, doubtless was enough to silence any salesman. And if he failed to lose his troubled look even when we departed—well, I suppose very few persons would remember and identify any convict, not having known him personally, after newspapers had declared him officially dead.

"Just why are we doing this?" I had growled when the man left us alone a moment.

Karpen replied slowly, with an odd dignity, "I, too, shall be an ambassador of a Great One, and we must do Him honor. We must not appear less well provisioned —than the others."

Afterward, when I had written it down and thought it over, it sounded unnatural, stilted, a trifle absurd. But I wrote it down the way he said it and that was it. "I, too, shall be the ambassador of a Great One," Karpen said.

Afraid? I was plenty afraid. Each meal time, food and wine would appear on Brenda's table. She refused to permit any contribution from me, and Karpen offered none, and then Christmas Eve had arrived and we set forth—tail-coated, top-hatted, caped, gloved. Just Karpen and I. All day Brenda had been very gay, then inexpressibly sad, by turn. She kissed Karpen goodbye, a kiss even more intense than that first one I had unwillingly witnessed, and held him off by his shoulders looking into his eyes.

"You won't be back, Karpen?"

Miserably he shook his great head. "I have—so much to do."

We walked. The night was crisp, clear, chill. The stars shone bright and a slivver of moon hung in the night sky and we did not hasten.

Karpen asked suddenly, "How old are you?"

"Thirty-five. You know that."

He nodded. He counted back, on his fingers. "The last one ended in 1918. You were—"

"Fourteen."

"A Boy Scout?"

"Yeah," I said. "I sold Liberty Bonds going from one office to the next. I had a Boy Scout uniform, I was a runt for my age, I had a lot of badges, an Eagle badge, and I sold plenty of bonds."

"YOU don't know how it was, then," Karpen said and his voice was a sword, steel, bitterly slashing. "The next men never remember, never know till they see new killing, themselves. A few of their fellows turn into animals, ruthless, themselves safe, slavering with power-lust. The few start the bands, the flags. Wave the flags, blow the trumpets, beat the drums. A few start the new men, the next crop who don't remember, again into the killing. No, you're a new one and you don't remember. Nothing of the hush hospitals, where bodies which are only hunks of living meat still do live in this day, souvenirs of violence which the new men are not permitted to see. Nothing of the dawn, and young men whimpering or savage in mud and filth and vermin, hungry, afraid, awaiting zero. Awaiting the dreadful top tick of a watch, then scrambling up, slipping and scrambling in mud, the air screaming and bursting, themselves quiet, only the rifles blasting, themselves moving to death, to dreadful torn flesh and shattered bone. Themselves become animals when they ought to be at home, safe, working, loving their lovely young women, children and dogs in front of a fire. Music and warmth and peace and wine and sunlight, all gone."

"What are you going to do, Karpen?" I muttered urgently. "Your grammar is punk."

He didn't reply. The Mark Hopkins. We entered an elevator, ourselves the only passengers that trip, and Karpen said, "Sixth floor."

The boy stopped the car in front of a blank wall. "You can't go there, sir," he said. "You must have made a mistake."

Karpen's eyes seemed to glow. His chin was a rock. "No mistake," he said.

The frightened boy let us out at the sixth floor. The corridors contained perhaps two dozen men of assorted nationalities. Well-dressed; but tough and hard-eyed men, for all that. Secret police, I thought.

To my astonishment we walked directly through the swarming guards and not one let his glance stop on us, not one attempted to block us. We might have been invisible. I—think we were.

Karpen took a key from one of his pockets and opened a door. I followed him through one room empty even of rugs and furniture and into a second. The second room was long, big. At a long table the conference of the ambassadors was already in session.

Karpen and I selected two chairs against the nearest wall and sat down. Nobody turned a head. Nobody, in fact, seemed even to be aware of our presence till Karpen acted, hours later.

Right now John Albertson was speaking. Later the others spoke, sweated, bargained, approached exhaustion and refused it, spoke again. I think my mouth soon must have dropped open, and stayed that way, because afterward I needed a lot of water.

Bahkmeteff was there, representative of the new dictator of the Union of Socialist Soviet Republics. Callieri was there, from Italy. Prince Taguchi, from Japan. Sturmer, a tall German with a monocle, a horse face, and utterly blank blue eyes. Each man acting not for his people, but for his master.

There was no single dictator in the United States; only a dictating group, an oligarchy. Given continued peace, the United States eventually might overwhelm its oligarchy and become truly democratic. Therefore John Albertson was there also, representing not the President nor the people of the United States, but himself and his group—cunning men who understood the waving of flags and the beating of drums, for profit and personal power.

They used English, in the cultured and conversational tones of gentlemen. So it wasn't their tones that dropped my mouth open. It was the things they said, their terrible calm meanings.

OF COURSE I had known that no modern major conflict ever occurs unprecedented by definite agreements between all powers which may be affected. Later any conflict may get out of hand, but its beginning is always a matter of premeditation and not of passion.

Yet I had never watched the machinery mesh. The ambassadors of the great abhor newspapermen whom they cannot control. Yet there I was, beside Karpen the Jew, and the ambassadors in cultured voices were calmly and cunningly trading in violence, in the lands, the wealth, the human lives and blood of other nations. They calmly estimated how many of their own men would be slaughtered upon the various fronts of attack.

The presence of Bahkmeteff, of course, had amazed me most. Callieri and Taguchi and Sturmer—fanatic fascists. In the next world war the fascists must inevitably fight all the rest of the world but mainly the communists, as they fought so long and horribly in Spain. And yet here, in this hotel room, these fascist leaders were making parley with the enemy.

For peace?

I must have been quite unsophisticated that night, to have felt even that one tingling thrill of hope.

Because these men had assembled not to avoid blood and death, but to cause them and agree upon the details of their manufacture.

"As you know, gentlemen," Bahkmeteff said suavely, "war, to the Russian dictator, is an immediate necessity." Lately, he reminded them, handwriting had appeared upon the wall. Lately the Russian people had demanded that no more foodstuffs be exported from the Soviet Union. A demand which had risen after two decades of cruel, animal-like labor, raising tremendous crops only to watch those crops dumped into foreign world markets at ruinous prices in exchange for machinery which the Russians might use but certainly could not eat. A demand so ugly that wisely it had been granted, at least for the present. But war would lift the minds of the Russians off their bellies —and only war.

Mussolini and Hitler, too, were tottering. The Ethiopian burlesque was past and Italy long ago had seized that luckless African land for its oil. (Since warships burn oil and there is no oil under Italy.) And Czechoslovakia was Hitler's but he needed flames round the earth before he moved to regain Germany's lost and more distant colonies.

And Japan was invading all the markets of the world with manufactured goods and underselling all competitors but going bankrupt doing it, and now particularly needful of further war to keep her people whipped up to the proper frenzy of obedience.

And in America all the business men were desperate from taxes and the insane spending of the government, but America still had no dictator; yet John Albertson thought that war might create a dictatorship and in any event war would bring monstrous profits to the steel industry.

Sturmer and John Albertson, Callieri and Bahkmeteff agreed. Prince Taguchi mentioned a date when Japanese fishing boats would attempt to blow up the U. S. Pacific Fleet and block the Panama Canal, and Japanese warships would shell Manila and Alaska. The Germans were interested, Sturmer said, primarily in France, Belgium, and Southern Africa, but would attack Russia as a matter of form, not really concentrating any force there.

Oh, the ambassadors, personally, and John Albertson, were safe enough in their planning. Not one of them, not one of the dictators for whom the ambassadors spoke, ever would see an actual firing line. They were as impersonal as though they were playing chess. War-is always impersonal to those who start it. It becomes personal only to those hundreds of thousands of younger men who get the bullets in their guts; and then John Albertson was speaking again.

THE bands and the flags were ready, he said. Geniuses of publicity ready also. Nothing would be simpler, to trained propagandists using an oligarchic press, to orators and politicians, than hurling the United States into war—on either side.

Karpen bent toward me and his face was stiff.

"You have heard," he said. "We look now upon one man who is already dead. All here are drunk with power, with ambition, but only John Albertson has already died, a greed-torn dead man who must sell bullets and armor plate."

Fascinated, I watched Karpen rise from his chair. Fascinated, I saw the startled bewildered faces of the diplomats turn to Karpen as though wondering how in the name of highest heaven any man save themselves could be here in this room— a room now guarded by secret police and secret strongarm men from each of their separate nations.

I watched Karpen slowly. stalk to John Albertson and I saw Karpen's great hands deliberately close round Albertson's throat, while I myself and the other four men in the room stared in stunned horror.

There was a small stifled scream from Albertson, president of Consolidated American Steel. Then he was off his chair, his legs wriggling and attempting to brace themselves, his hands viciously and desperately clawing at those other great hands which had his throat. John Albertson was moving across the thick carpet toward a window and when Karpen the Jew had brought him there, Karpen deliberately withdrew one strangling hand and got the window open.

Then he looked down upon Albertson, sadly, and—I thought—compassionately. With the deliberation of an automaton Karpen lifted John Albertson high, held him squirming and screaming thus a short moment, and flung him into space.

Albertson's screams diminished and then, abruptly, sickeningly, ceased.

Karpen turned and faced the ambassadors. His rugged face was gray now.

He spoke in a voice more cultured, tremendously more gentle than any of theirs had been. He said, "Gentlemen, I give you a promise. Each of you is powerful. Not so powerful as the great dictators whom you represent, but still each of you wields colossal influence in his own land. I promise you that if the wars occur which you have agreed upon tonight, each of you shall die in ways far more horrible than the way you have seen John Albertson die. I say to you, ye shall not kill!—and in your own bodies yourselves remain secure! Take my message also to your masters. Should this war occur, *to each great dictator I also shall find my way. And I shall come,*" Karpen said, "*to kill!*" He turned and left, without haste.

I went out following Karpen and that was the way it had happened. If the ambassadors afterward called Albertson's plunge merely a tragic accident—well, perhaps they really do not remember what they saw Karpen do and say, at least not in their conscious minds. But each of those four ambassadors, I notice, has retired now to a private and sedentary life.

And as Karpen reached the street, the paved hill-top where the Mark Hopkins sits, it didn't even occur to me to warn him that for this latest crime he now must surely die. For I understood he would never die, so long as men lived upon the earth. A lethal gas chamber? Probably that had been his last forlorn *hope* of death. . . .

THE street throbbed with excitement, of course, and police and an ambulance were here. But we walked unimpeded past the police, past the broken mashed object that had been John Albertson, and went down into the town. Freshly dressed, quiet people were going into the churches on that Christmas Sunday morning, and there were tollings of bells.

"I can do so little," Karpen said.

"You've done plenty lately," I said.

"One man—in all the world. Why don't the others help?"

"Some of them do."

There was nothing mystic, nothing supernormal in the sardonic glance which this living Jew turned on me then. Nor in his hard, practical words. "Hear me!" Karpen said. "This is the United States of America. I've been here many times. You have a Constitution, the highest law of the land. Adopt an amendment. Say that each member of the Congress who votes for any war or who fails to vote against it, shall upon formal declaration of such war automatically lose his office. That immediately he shall be compelled, re-gardless of age or physical competence, to become an infantry private, ineligible for promotion, ineligible for furlough even if wounded, and assigned to front line combat until dead or until the war ends. Send also to the front any President who signs a declaration of war. Adopt that one simple basic law. Challenge other nations into providing likewise for their own leaders. And then," said Karpen the Jew, "you wouldn't have very many more wars."

He halted without warning, and added: "But the nations will not be permitted to do it. The great rulers are never the ones who fight."

He was looking at me, but his eyes became strangely opaque. Perhaps he wasn't seeing me any longer. His head cocked to one side and again I had that curious impression that he was listening to some voice which I myself could not hear. Within a few seconds, however, his pupils cleared. Hastily and with a queer formality he shook my hand, murmured, "I have so little time!" said goodbye, and was gone.

So little time! All eternity he had—yet Karpen the Jew was pressed and had to hurry. And Brenda's son was born today —Karpen's son—and although Karpen had assured her the child would not be like himself, I cannot help wondering. I pray it will not, because Karpen, the last I saw of him, was walking away in Christmas sunlight while bells tolled, repeating that another child, a Christ had been born; walking down a city sidewalk, through the moving crowds in their fine new clothing, stalking the world, himself one symbol of his entire deep and peaceful and homeless race. One lonely man accursed forever to the choking task of all mankind's salvation.

# The Girl
# in the Golden Atom

## By RAY CUMMINGS

**The super-magnifier showed that there was a whole world within the Chemist's ring, and he meant to find out what went on in it**

## CHAPTER I

### A UNIVERSE IN AN ATOM

"THEN you mean to say there is no such thing as the *smallest* particle of matter?" asked the Very Young man.

"You can put it that way if you like," the Chemist replied. "In other words, what I believe is that things can be infinitely small just as well as they can be infinitely large. Astronomers tell us of the immensity of space. I have tried to imagine space as finite. It is impossible. How can you conceive the edge of space? Something must be beyond—something or nothing, and even that would be more space."

The Chemist resumed, smiling a little. "Now, if it seems probable that there is no limit to the immensity of space, why should we make its smallness finite? How can you say that the atom cannot be divided? As a matter of fact, it already has been. The most powerful microscope will show you realms of smallness to which you can penetrate no other way. Multiply that power a thousand times, or ten thousand times, and who shall say what you will see?"

The Chemist paused, and looked at the intent little group around him.

He was a youngish man, with large features and horn-rimmed glasses, his rough English-cut clothes hanging loosely over his broad, spare frame. The Banker drained his glass and rang for the waiter.

"Very interesting," he remarked.

"Don't be silly, George," said the Big Business Man. "Just because you don't understand, doesn't mean there is no sense to it."

The Doctor crossed under the light and took an easier chair. "You intimated you had discovered something unusual in these realms of the infinitely small," he suggested, sinking back luxuriously. "Will you tell us about it?"

"Yes, if you like," said the Chemist, turning from one to the other. A nod of assent followed his glance, as each settled himself more comfortably.

"Well, gentlemen, when you say I have discovered something unusual in another world—in the world of the infinitely small —you are right in a way. I have seen something and lost it. You won't believe me probably," he glanced at the Banker an instant, "but that is not important. I am going to tell you what happened."

The Big Business Man filled up the glasses all around, and the Chemist resumed:

"To begin with, I succeeded some time ago in having a microscope made which was more powerful than any known to science even up to the present moment.

"I can recall now my feelings when it arrived. I was about to see into another world, to behold what no man had ever looked on before. What would I see? What new realms was I, first of all our human race, to enter? With furiously beating heart, I sat down before the huge instrument and adjusted the eye-piece.

"Then I glanced around for some object to examine. On my finger I had a ring, my mother's wedding ring, and I decided to use that. I have it here." He took a plain gold band from his little finger and laid it on the table.

"You will see a slight mark on the outside. That is the place into which I looked."

His friends crowded around the table and examined a scratch on one side of the band.

"What did you see?" asked the Very Young Man eagerly.

"Gentlemen," resumed the Chemist, "what I saw staggered even my own imagination. With trembling hands I put the ring in place, looking directly down into that scratch. For a moment I saw nothing. I was like a person coming suddenly out of the sunlight into a darkened room. I knew there was something visible in my view, but my eyes did not seem able to receive the impressions. I realize now they were not yet adjusted to the new form of light. Gradually, as I looked, objects of definite shape began to emerge from the blackness.

"Gentlemen, I want to make clear to you now—as clear as I can—the peculiar aspect of everything that I saw under this microscope. I seemed to be inside an immense cave. One side, near at hand, I could now make out quite clearly. The walls were extraordinarily rough and indented, with a peculiar phosphorescent light on the projections and blackness in the hollows. I say phosphorescent light, for that is the nearest word I can find to describe it—a curious radiation, quite different from the reflected light to which we are accustomed.

"I said that the hollows inside of the cave were blackness. But not blackness—the absence of light—as we know it. It was a blackness that seemed also to radiate light, if you can imagine such a condition; a blackness that seemed not empty, but merely withholding its contents just beyond my vision.

"Except for a dim suggestion of roof over the cave, and its floor, I could distinguish nothing. After a moment this floor became clearer. It seemed to be—well, perhaps I might call it black marble—smooth, glossy, yet somewhat translucent. In the foreground the floor was apparently liquid. In no way did it differ in appearance from the solid part, except that its surface seemed to be in motion.

"Another curious thing was the outlines of all the shapes in view. I noticed that no outline held steady when I looked at it directly; it seemed to quiver. You see something like it when looking at an object through water—only, of course, there was no distortion. It was also like looking at something with the radiation of heat between.

"Of the back and other side of the cave, I could see nothing, except in one place, where a narrow effulgence of light drifted out into the immensity of the distance behind.

"I do not know how long I sat looking at this scene; it may have been several hours. Although I was obviously in a cave, I never felt shut in—never got the impression of being in a narrow, confined space.

"On the contrary, after a time I seemed to feel the vast immensity of the blackness before me. I think perhaps it may have been that path of light stretching out into the distance. As I looked it seemed like the reversed tail of a comet, or the dim glow of the Milky Way, and penetrating to equally remote realms of space.

"Perhaps I fell asleep, or at least there was an interval of time during which I was so absorbed in my own thoughts I was hardly conscious of the scene before me.

"Then I became aware of a dim shape in the foreground—a shape merged with the outlines surrounding it. And as I looked, it gradually assumed form, and I saw it was the figure of a young girl, sitting beside the liquid pool. Except for the same waviness of outline and phosphorescent glow, she had quite the normal aspect of a human being of our own world. She was beautiful, according to our own standards of beauty; her long braided hair a glowing black, her face, delicate of feature and winsome in expression. Her lips were a deep red, although I felt rather than saw the color.

"She was dressed only in a short tunic of a substance I might describe as gray opaque glass, and the pearly whiteness of her skin gleamed with iridescence.

"She seemed to be singing, although I heard no sound. Once she bent over the pool and plunged her hand into it, laughing gaily.

"Gentlemen, I cannot make you appreciate my emotions, when all at once I remembered I was looking through a microscope. I had forgotten entirely my situation, absorbed in the scene before me. And then, all at once, a great realization came upon me—the realization that everything I saw was inside that ring. I was unnerved for the moment at the importance of my discovery.

"When I looked again, after the few moments my eye took to become accustomed to the new form of light, the scene showed itself as before, except that the girl had gone.

"For over a week, each night at the same time I watched that cave. The girl came always, and sat by the pool as I had first seen her. Once she danced with the wild grace of a wood nymph, whirling in and out of the shadows, and falling at last in a little heap beside the pool.

"It was on the tenth night after I had first seen her that the accident happened. I had been watching, I remember, an unusually long time before she appeared, gliding out of the shadows. She seemed in a different mood, pensive and sad, as she bent down over the pool, staring into it intently. Suddenly there was a tremendous cracking sound, sharp as an explosion, and I was thrown backward upon the floor.

"When I recovered consciousness—I must have struck my head on something—I found the microscope in ruins. Upon examination I saw that its larger lens had exploded— flown into fragments scattered around the room. Why I was not killed I do not understand. The ring I picked up from the floor; it was unharmed and unchanged.

"Can I make you understand how I felt at this loss? Because of the great expense I knew I could never rebuild my lens—for many years, at any rate. And then, gentlemen, came the most terrible feeling of all; I knew at last that the scientific achievement I had made and lost counted for little with me. It was the girl. I realized then that the only being I ever could care for was living out her life with her world, and, indeed, her whole universe, in an atom of that ring."

The Chemist stopped talking and looked from one to the other of the tense faces of his companions.

"It's almost too big an idea to grasp," murmured the Doctor.

"What caused the explosion?" asked the Very Young Man.

"I do not know." The Chemist addressed his reply to the Doctor, as the most understanding of the group. "I can appreciate, though, that through that lens I was magnifying tremendously those peculiar light-radiations that I have described. I believe the molecules of the lens were shattered by them—I had exposed it longer to them that evening than any of the others."

The Doctor nodded his comprehension of this theory.

Impressed in spite of himself, the Banker took another drink and leaned forward in his chair. "Then you really think that there is a girl now inside the gold of that ring?" he asked.

"He didn't say that necessarily," interrupted the Big Business Man.

"Yes, he did."

"As a matter of fact, I do believe that to be the case," said the Chemist earnestly. "I believe that every particle of matter in our universe contains within it an equally complex and complete a universe, which to its inhabitants seem as large as ours. I think, also, that the whole realm of our interplanetary space, our solar system and all the remote stars of the heavens are contained within the atom of some other universe as gigantic to us as we are to the universe in that ring."

"Gosh!" said the Very Young Man.

"It doesn't make one feel very important in the scheme of things, does it?" remarked the Big Business Man dryly.

The Chemist smiled. "The existence of no individual, no nation, no world, nor any one universe is of the least importance."

"Then it would be possible," said the Doctor, "for this gigantic universe that contains us in one of its atoms, to be itself contained within the atom of another universe, still more gigantic, and so on."

"That is my theory," said the Chemist.

"And in each of the atoms of the rocks of that cave there may be other worlds proportionately minute?"

"I can see no reason to doubt it."

"Well, there is no proof, anyway," said the Banker. "We might as well believe it."

"I intend to get proof," said the Chemist.

"Do you believe all these innumerable universes, both larger and smaller than ours, are inhabited?" asked the Doctor.

"I should think probably most of them are. The existence of life, I believe, is as fundamental as the existence of matter without life."

"How do you suppose that girl got in there?" asked the Very Young Man, coming out of a brown study.

"What puzzled me," resumed the Chemist, ignoring the question, "is why the girl should so resemble our own race. I have thought about it a good deal, and I have reached the conclusion that the inhabitants of any universe in the next smaller or larger plane to ours probably resemble us fairly closely. That ring, you see, is in the same —shall we say—environment as ourselves. The same forces control it that control us. Now, if the ring had been created on Mars, for instance, I believe that the universes within its atoms would be inhabited by beings like the Martians—if Mars has any inhabitants. Of course, in planes beyond those next to ours, either smaller or larger, changes would probably occur, becoming greater as you go in or out from our own universe."

"Good Lord! It makes one dizzy to think of it," said the Big Business Man.

"I wish I knew how that girl got in there," said the Very Young Man, looking at the ring.

"She probably didn't," retorted the Doctor. "Very likely she was created there, the same as you were here."

"I think that is probably so," said the Chemist. "And yet, sometimes I am not at all sure. She was very human." The Very Young Man looked at him sympathetically.

"How are you going to prove your theories?" asked the Banker, in his most irritatingly practical way.

The Chemist picked up the ring and put it on his finger. "Gentlemen," he said, "I have tried to tell you facts, not theories. What I saw through that ultramicroscope was not an unproven theory, but a fact. My theories you have brought out by your questions."

"You are quite right," said the Doctor, "but you did mention yourself that you hoped to provide proof."

The Chemist hesitated a moment, then made his decision. "I will tell you the rest," he said.

"After the destruction of the microscope, I was quite at a loss how to proceed. I thought about the problem for many weeks. Finally I decided to work along another altogether different line—a theory about which I am surprised you have not already questioned me."

He paused, but no one spoke.

"I am hardly ready with proof to-night," he resumed after a moment. "Will you all take dinner with me here at the club one week from to-night?" He read affirmation in the glance of each.

"Good. That's settled," he said, rising. "At seven, then."

"But what was the theory you expected us to question you about?" asked the Very Young Man.

The Chemist leaned on the back of his chair.

"The only solution I could see to the problem," he said slowly, "was to find some way of making myself sufficiently small to be able to enter that other universe. I have found such a way and one week from to-night, gentlemen, with your assistance, I am going to enter the surface of that ring at the point where it is scratched!"

## CHAPTER II

### INTO THE RING

THE cigars were lighted and dinner over before the Doctor broached the subject uppermost in the minds of every member of the party.

"A toast, gentlemen," he said, raising his glass. "To the greatest research Chemist in the world. May he be successful in his adventure to-night."

The Chemist bowed his acknowledgment.

"You have not heard me yet," he said smiling.

"But we want to," said the Very Young Man impulsively.

"And you shall." He settled himself more comfortably in his chair. "Gentlemen, I am going to tell you, first, as simply as possible, just what I have done in the past two years. You must draw your own conclusions from the evidence I give you.

"You will remember that I told you last week of my dilemma after the destruction of the microscope. Its loss and the impossibility of replacing it, led me into still bolder plans than merely the visual examination of this minute world. I reasoned, as I have told you, that because of its physical proximity, its similar environment, so to speak, this outer world should be capable of supporting life identical with our own.

"I saw then but one obstacle standing between me and this other world—the discrepancy of size. The distance separating our world from this other, is infinitely great or infinitely small, according to the viewpoint. In my present size it is only a few feet from here to the ring on that plate. But to an inhabitant of that other world, we are as remote as the faintest stars of the heavens, diminished a thousand times."

He paused a moment, signing the waiter to leave the room.

"This reduction of bodily size, great as it is, involves no deeper principle than does

a light contraction of tissue, except that it must be carried further. The problem, then, was to find a chemical, sufficiently unharmful to life, that would so act upon the body cells as to cause a reduction in bulk, without changing their shape. I had to secure a uniform and also a proportionate rate of contraction of each cell, in order not to have the body shape altered.

"After a comparatively small amount of research work, I encountered an apparently insurmountable obstacle. As you know, gentlemen, our living human bodies are held together by the power of the central intelligence we call the mind. Every instant during your lifetime your subconscious mind is commanding and directing the individual life of each cell that makes up your body. At death this power is withdrawn; each cell is thrown under its own individual command, and dissolution of the body takes place.

"I found, therefore, that I could not act upon the cells separately, so long as they were under control of the mind. On the other hand, I could not withdraw this power of the subconscious mind without causing death.

"I progressed no further than this for several months. Then came the solution. I reasoned that after death the body does not immediately disintegrate; far more time elapses than I expected to need for the cell-contraction. I devoted my time, then, to finding a chemical that would temporarily withhold, during the period of cell-contraction, the power of the subconscious mind, just as the power of the conscious mind is withheld by hypnotism.

"I am not going to weary you by trying to lead you through the maze of chemical experiments into which I plunged.

"I worked on rabbits almost exclusively. After a few weeks I succeeded in completely suspending animation in one of them for several hours. There was no life apparently existing during that period. It was not a trance or coma, but the complete simulation of death. No harmful results followed the revivifying of the animal. The contraction of the cells was far more difficult to accomplish; I finished my last experiment less than six months ago."

"Then you really have been able to make an animal infinitely small?" asked the Big Business Man.

The Chemist smiled. "I sent four rabbits into the unknown last week," he said.

"As I was planning to project myself into this unknown universe and to reach the exact size proportionate to it, I soon realized such a result could not be obtained were I in an unconscious state. Only by successive doses of the drug, or its retardant about which I will tell you later, could I hope to reach the proper size. Another necessity is that I place myself on the exact spot on that ring where I wish to enter and to climb down among its atoms when I have become sufficiently small to do so. Obviously, this would be impossible to one not possessing all his faculties and physical strength."

"And did you solve that problem, too?" asked the Banker. "I'd like to see it done," he added.

The Chemist produced two small paper packages from his wallet. "These drugs are the result of my research," he said. "One of them causes contraction, and the other expansion, by an exact reversal of the process. Taken together, they produce no effect, and a lesser amount of one retards the action of the other." He opened the papers, showing two small vials. "I have made them as you see, in the form of tiny pills, each containing a minute quantity of the drug. It is by taking them successively in unequal amounts that I expect to reach the desired size."

"There's one point that you do not mention," said the Doctor. "Those vials and their contents will have to change size as you do. How are you going to manage that?"

"By experimentation I have found," answered the Chemist, "that any object held in close physical contact with the living body being contracted is contracted itself at an equal rate. I believe that my clothes will be affected also. These vials I will carry strapped under my armpits."

"Suppose you should die, or be killed, would the contraction cease?" asked the Doctor.

"Yes, almost immediately," replied the Chemist. "Apparently, though I am acting through the subconscious mind while its power is held in abeyance, when this power is permanently withdrawn by death, the drug no longer affects the individual cells. The contraction or expansion ceases almost at once."

"Is it your intention to take this stuff yourself to-night?" asked the Big Business Man.

"If you will give me your help, I think so, yes. I have made all arrangements. The club has given us this room in absolute privacy for forty-eight hours. Your meals will be served here when you want them, and I am going to ask you, gentlemen, to take turns watching and guarding the ring during that time. Will you do it?"

"I should say we would," cried the Doctor, and the others nodded assent.

"It is because I wanted you to be convinced of my entire sincerity that I have taken you so thoroughly into my confidence. Are those doors locked?" The Very Young Man locked them.

"Thank you," said the Chemist, starting to disrobe. In a moment he stood before them attired in a woolen bathing-suit of pure white. Over his shoulders was strapped tightly a narrow leather harness, supporting two silken pockets, one under each armpit. Into each of these he placed one of the vials, first laying four pills from one of them upon the table.

At this point the Banker rose from his chair and selected another in the further corner of the room. He sank into it a crumpled heap and wiped the beads of perspiration from his face with a shaking hand.

"I have every expectation," said the Chemist, "that this suit and harness will contract in size uniformly with me. If the harness should not, then I shall have to hold the vials in my hand."

On the table, directly under the light, he spread a large silk handkerchief, upon which he placed the ring. He then produced a teaspoon, which he handed to the Doctor.

"Please listen carefully," he said, "for perhaps the whole success of my adventure, and my life itself, may depend upon your actions during the next few minutes. You will realize, of course, that when I am still large enough to be visible to you I shall be so small that my voice may be inaudible. Therefore, I want you to know, now, just what to expect.

"When I am something under a foot high, I shall step upon that handkerchief, where you will see my white suit plainly against its black surface. When I become less than an inch high, I shall run over to the ring and stand beside it. When I have diminished to about a quarter of an inch, I shall climb upon it, and, as I get smaller, will follow its surface until I come to the scratch.

"I want you to watch me very closely. I may miscalculate the time and wait until I am too small to climb upon the ring. Or I may fall off. In either case, you will place that spoon beside me and I will climb into it. You will then do your best to help me get on the ring. Is all this quite clear?"

The Doctor nodded assent.

"Very well, watch me as long as I remain visible. If I have an accident, I shall take the other drug and endeavor to return to you at once. This you must expect at any moment during the next forty-eight hours. Under all circumstances, if I am alive, I shall return at the expiration of that time.

"And, gentlemen, let me caution you most solemnly, do not allow that ring to be touched until that length of time has expired. Can I depend on you?"

"Yes," they answered breathlessly.

"After I have taken the pills," the Chemist continued, "I shall not speak unless it is absolutely necessary. I do not know what my sensations will be, and I want to follow them as closely as possible." He then turned out all the lights in the room with the exception of the center electrolier, that shone down directly on the handkerchief and ring.

The Chemist looked about him. "Good-by, gentlemen," he said, shaking hands all around. "Wish me luck," and without hesitation he placed the four pills in his mouth and washed them down with a swallow of water.

Silence fell on the group as the Chemist seated himself and covered his face with his hands. For perhaps two minutes the tenseness of the silence was unbroken, save by the heavy breathing of the Banker as he lay huddled in his chair.

"Oh, look, he's really growing smaller!" whispered the Big Business Man in a horrified tone to the Doctor. The Chemist raised his head and smiled at them. Then he stood up, steadying himself against a chair. He was less than four feet high. Steadily he grew smaller before their horrified eyes. Once he made as if to speak, and the Doctor knelt down beside him. "It's all right, good-by," he said in a tiny voice.

Then he stepped upon the handkerchief. The Doctor knelt on the floor beside it, the wooden spoon ready in his hand, while the others, except the Banker, stood behind him. The figure of the Chemist, standing motionless near the edge of the handkerchief, seemed now like a little white wooden toy, hardly more than an inch in height.

Waving his hand and smiling, he suddenly started to walk and then ran swiftly over to the ring. By the time he reached it, somewhat out of breath, he was little more than twice as high as the width of its band. Without pausing, he leaped up, and sat astraddle, leaning over and holding to it tightly with his hands. In another moment he was on his feet, on the upper edge of the ring, walking carefully along its circumference toward the scratch.

The Big Business Man touched the Doctor on the shoulder and tried to smile. "He's making it," he whispered. As if in answer the little figure turned and waved its arms. They could just distinguish its white outline against the gold surface underneath.

"I don't see him," said the Very Young Man in a scared voice.

"He's right near the scratch," answered

the Doctor, bending closer. Then, after a moment, "He's gone." He rose to his feet. "Good Lord! why haven't we a microscope!" he added.

"I never thought of that," said the Big Business Man, "we could have watched him for a long time yet."

"Well, he's gone now," returned the Doctor, "and there is nothing for us to do but wait."

"I hope he finds that girl," sighed the Very Young Man.

## CHAPTER III

### AFTER FORTY-EIGHT HOURS

THE Banker snored stertorously from a davenport in a corner of the room. In an easy-chair near by, with his feet on the table, lay the Very Young Man, sleeping also.

The Doctor and the Big Business Man sat by the handkerchief.

"How long has it been now?" asked the latter.

"Just forty hours," answered the Doctor, "and he said that forty-eight hours was the limit. He should come back at about ten to-night."

"I wonder if he *will* come back," questioned the Big Business Man nervously.

They were silent for a moment, and then he went on: "You'd better try to sleep a while," he said to the Doctor, "you're worn out. I'll watch here."

"I suppose I should," answered the Doctor wearily. "Wake up that kid, he's sleeping most of the time."

"No, I'll watch," repeated the Big Business Man; "you lie down over there."

The Doctor did so while the other settled himself more comfortably on a cushion beside the handkerchief, and prepared for his lonely watching.

The Doctor apparently dropped off to sleep at once, for he did not speak again. The Big Business Man sat staring steadily at the ring, bending nearer to it occasionally. Every ten or fifteen minutes he looked at his watch.

Perhaps an hour passed in this way, when the Very Young Man suddenly sat up and yawned. "Haven't they come back yet?" he asked in a sleepy voice.

The Big Business Man answered in a much lower tone. "What do you mean— they?" he said.

"I dreamed that he brought the girl back with him," said the Very Young Man.

"Well, if he did, they have not arrived," answered the Big Business Man. "You'd better go back to sleep. We've got six or seven hours yet."

The Very Young Man rose and crossed the room. "No, I'll watch a while," he said, seating himself on the floor. "What time is it?"

"Quarter of three."

"He said he'd be back by ten to-night. I'm crazy to see that girl."

The Big Business Man rose and went over to a dinner-tray, standing near the door. "Lord, I'm hungry. I must have forgotten to eat to-day." He lifted up one of the silver covers. What he saw evidently encouraged him, for he drew up a chair and began his lunch.

The Very Young Man lighted a cigarette. "It will be the tragedy of my life," he said, "if he never comes back."

The Big Business Man smiled. "How about *his* life?" he answered, but the Very Young Man had fallen into a reverie and did not reply.

The Big Business Man finished his lunch in silence and was just about to light a cigar when a sharp exclamation brought him hastily to his feet.

"Come here, quick, I see something." The Very Young Man had his face close to the ring and was trembling violently.

The other pushed him back. "Let me see. Where?"

"There by the scratch; he's lying there; I can see him."

The Big Business Man looked and then hurriedly woke the Doctor.

"He's come back," he said briefly; "you can see him there." The Doctor bent down over the ring while the others woke up the Banker.

"He doesn't seem to be getting any bigger," said the Very Young Man; "he's just lying there. Maybe he's dead."

"What shall we do?" asked the Big Business Man, and made as if to pick up the ring. The Doctor shoved him away. "Don't do that!" he said sharply. "Do you want to kill him?"

"He's sitting up," cried the Very Young Man. "He's all right."

"He must have fainted," said the Doctor. "Probably he's taking more of the drug now."

"He's much larger," said the Very Young Man; "look at him!"

The tiny figure was sitting sidewise on the ring, with its feet hanging over the outer edge. It was growing perceptibly larger each instant, and in a moment it slipped down off the ring and sank in a heap on the handkerchief.

"Good Heavens! Look at him!" cried the Big Business Man. "He's all cut and scratched!"

The little figure presented a ghastly sight. As it steadily grew larger they could see and recognize the Chemist's haggard face.

"Look at his feet," whispered the Big Business Man. They were horribly cut and bruised and greatly swollen.

The Doctor bent over and whispered gently, "What can I do to help you?" The Chemist shook his head. His body, lying prone upon the handkerchief, had torn it apart in growing. When he was about twelve inches in length he raised his head. The Doctor bent closer. "Some brandy, please," said a wraith of the Chemist's voice. It was barely audible.

"He wants some brandy," called the Doctor. The Very Young Man looked hastily around, then opened the door and dashed madly out of the room. When he returned, the Chemist had grown to nearly four feet. He was sitting on the floor with his back against the Doctor's knees.

"Here!" cried the Very Young Man, thrusting forth the brandy. The Chemist drank a little of it. Then he sat up, evidently somewhat revived.

"I seem to have stopped growing," he said. "Let's finish it up now. My! how I want to be the right size again," he added fervently.

The Doctor helped him extract the vials from under his arm, and the Chemist touched one of the pills to his tongue. Then he sank back, closing his eyes. "I think that should be about enough," he murmured.

No one spoke for nearly ten minutes. Gradually the Chemist's body grew, the Doctor shifting his position several times as it became larger. It seemed finally to have stopped growing, and was apparently nearly its former size.

"Was it all as you expected?" asked the Banker.

"To a great extent, yes," answered the Chemist. "But I had better tell you just what happened." The Very Young Man nodded his eager agreement.

"When I took those first four pills," began the Chemist in a quiet, even tone, "my immediate sensation was a sudden reeling of the senses, combined with an extreme nausea. This latter feeling passed after a moment." He paused to light a cigar.

"You will remember that I seated myself upon the floor and closed my eyes. When I opened them my head had steadied itself somewhat, but I was oppressed by a curious feeling of drowsiness, impossible to shake off.

"My first mental impression was one of wonderment when I saw you all begin to increase in size. I remember standing up beside that chair, which was then half again its normal size, and you"—indicating the Doctor—"towered beside me as a giant of nine or ten feet high.

"Steadily upward, with a curious crawling motion, grew the room and all its contents. Except for the feeling of sleep that oppressed me, I felt quite my usual self. No change appeared happening to me, but everything else seemed growing to gigantic and terrifying proportions.

"Can you imagine a human being a hundred feet high? That is how you looked to me as I stepped upon that huge expanse of black silk and shouted my last good-by to you!

"Over to my left lay the ring, apparently fifteen or twenty feet away. I started to walk toward it, but although it grew rapidly larger, the distance separating me from it seemed to increase rather than lessen. Then I ran, and by the time I arrived it stood higher than my waist—a beautiful, shaggy, golden pit.

"I jumped upon its rim and clung to it tightly. I could feel it growing beneath me as I sat. After a moment I climbed upon its top surface and started to walk toward the point where I knew the scratch to be.

"I found myself now, as I looked about, walking upon a narrow, though ever broadening, curved path. The ground beneath my feet appeared to be a rough, yellowish quartz. This path grew rougher as I advanced. Below the bulging edges of the path, on both sides, lay a shining black plain, ridged and indented, and with a sunlike sheen on the higher portions of the ridges. On the one hand this black plain stretched in an unbroken expanse to the horizon. On the other, there appeared a circular valley, enclosed by a shining yellow wall.

"The way had now become extraordinarily rough. I bore to the left as I advanced, keeping close to the outer edge. The other edge of the path I could not see. I clambered along hastily, and after a few moments was confronted by a row of rocks and boulders lying directly across my line of progress. I followed their course for a short distance, and finally found a space through which I could pass.

"This transverse ridge was perhaps a hundred feet deep. Behind it and extending in a parallel direction lay a tremendous valley. I knew then I had reached my first objective.

"I sat down upon the brink of the precipice and watched the cavern growing ever wider and deeper. Then I realized that I must begin my descent if ever I was to reach the bottom. For perhaps six hours I climbed steadily downward. It was a fairly easy descent. According to the stature I was when I reached the bottom, I had descended perhaps twelve thousand feet during this time.

"The latter part of this journey found me nearing the bottom of the cañon. Objects around me no longer seemed to increase in size, as had been constantly the case before, and I reasoned that probably my stature was remaining constant.

"I noticed, too, as I advanced, a curious alteration in the form of light around me. The glare from above (the sky showed only as a narrow dull ribbon of blue) barely penetrated to the depths of the cañon's floor. But all about me there was a soft radiance, seeming to emanate from the rocks themselves.

"I have not told you, gentlemen, that at the time I marked the ring I made a deeper indentation in one portion of the scratch and focused the microscope upon that. This indentation I now searched for. Luckily I found it, less than half a mile away—an almost circular pit, perhaps five miles in diameter, with shining walls extending downward into blackness. There seemed no possible way of descending into it.

"The sleepy feeling that had formerly merely oppressed me, combined now with my physical fatigue and the larger dose of the drug I had taken, became almost intolerable. I yielded to it for a moment, lying down on a crag near the edge of the pit. I must have become almost immediately unconscious, and remained so for a considerable time. I can remember a horrible sensation of sliding headlong for what seemed like hours. I felt that I was sliding or falling downward. I tried to rouse but could not. Then came absolute oblivion.

"When I recovered my senses I was lying partly covered by a mass of smooth, shining pebbles. I was bruised and battered from head to foot—in a far worse condition than you first saw me when I returned.

"I sat up and looked around. Beside me, sloped upward at an apparently increasing angle, was a high glossy plane. This extended as far as I could see both to the right and left and upward into the blackness of the sky overhead. It was this plane that had evidently broken my fall, and I had been sliding down it, bringing with me a considerable mass of rocks and boulders.

"The incline down which I had fallen was composed of some smooth substance suggesting black marble. The floor underfoot was quite different—more of a metallic quality with a curious corrugation. Before me, in the dim distance, I could just make out a tiny range of hills.

"I rose, after a time, and started weakly to walk toward these hills.

"There I found what had evidently once been a deep forest, but which now was almost utterly desolated. Only here and there were the trees left standing. For the most part they were lying in a crushed and tangled mass, many of them partially embedded in the ground.

"I cannot express adequately to you, gentlemen, what an evidence of tremendous superhuman power this scene presented. No storm, no lightning, nor any attack of the elements could have produced more than a fraction of the destruction I saw all around me.

"I climbed cautiously upon a fallen tree-trunk, and from this elevation had a much better view of my surroundings. I appeared to be near one end of the desolated area, which extended in a path about half a mile wide and several miles deep. In front, a thousand feet away, perhaps, lay the unbroken forest.

"Descending from the tree-trunk I walked in this direction, reaching the edge of the woods after possibly an hour of the most arduous traveling of my whole journey.

"On one of the fallen tree-trunks I found a sort of vine growing. This vine bore a profusion of small gray berries, much like our huckleberries. They proved similar in taste, and I sat down and ate a quantity.

"When I reached the edge of the forest I felt somewhat stronger. I had seen up to this time no sign of animal life whatever. Now, as I stood silent, I could hear around me all the multitudinous tiny voices of the woods. Insect life stirred underfoot, and

in the trees above an occasional bird flitted to and fro.

"Perhaps I am giving you a picture of our own world. I do not mean to do so. You must remember that above me there was no sky, just blackness. And yet so much light illuminated the scene that I could not believe it was other than what we would call daytime. Objects in the forest were as well lighted—better probably than they would be under similar circumstances in our own world.

"The trees were of huge size compared to my present stature: straight, upstanding trunks, with no branches until very near the top. They were bluish-gray in color, and many of them well covered with the berry-vine I have mentioned. The leaves overhead seemed to be blue—in fact the predominating color of all the vegetation was blue, just as in our world it is green. The ground was covered with dead leaves, mold, and a sort of a gray moss. Fungus of a similar color appeared, but of this I did not eat.

"I had penetrated perhaps two miles into the forest when I came unexpectedly to the bank of a broad, smooth-flowing river, its silver surface seeming to radiate waves of the characteristic phosphorescent light. I found it cold, pure-tasting water, and I drank long and deeply. Then I remember lying down upon the mossy bank, and in a moment, utterly worn out, I again fell asleep."

## CHAPTER IV

### LYLDA

"I WAS awakened by the feel of soft hands upon my head and face. With a start I sat up abruptly; I rubbed my eyes confusedly for a moment, not knowing where I was. When I collected my wits I found myself staring into the face of a girl, who was kneeling on the ground before me. I recognized her at once—she was the girl of the microscope.

"To say I was startled would be to put it mildly, but I read no fear in her expression, only wonderment at my springing so suddenly into life. She was dressed very much as I had seen her before. Her fragile beauty was the same, and at this closer view infinitely more appealing, but I was puzzled to account for her older, more mature look. She seemed to have aged several years since the last evening I had seen her through the microscope. Yet, undeniably, it was the same girl.

"For some moments we sat looking at each other in wonderment. Then she smiled and held out her hand, palm up, speaking a few words as she did so. Her voice was soft and musical, and the words of a peculiar quality that we generally describe as liquid, for want of a better term. What she said was wholly unintelligible, but whether the words were strange or the intonation different from anything I had ever heard, I could not determine.

"The gap separating us, however, was very much less than you would imagine. Strangely enough, though, it was not I who learned to speak her tongue, but she who mastered mine."

The Very Young Man sighed contentedly.

"We became quite friendly after this greeting," resumed the Chemist, "and it was apparent from her manner that she had already conceived her own idea of who and what I was.

"For some time we sat and tried to communicate with each other. My words seemed almost as unintelligible to her as hers to me, except that occasionally she would divine my meaning, clapping her hands in childish delight. I made out that she lived at a considerable distance, and that her name was Lylda. Finally she pulled me by the hand and led me away with a proprietary air that amused, and, I must admit, pleased me tremendously.

"We had progressed through the woods in this way, hardly more than a few hundred yards, when suddenly I found that she was taking me into the mouth of a cave or passageway, sloping downward at an angle of perhaps twenty degrees. I noticed now, more graphically than ever before, a truth that had been gradually forcing itself upon

me. Darkness was impossible in this new world. We were now shut in between narrow walls of crystalline rock, with a roof hardly more than fifty feet above.

"No artificial light of any kind was in evidence, yet the scene was lighted quite brightly. This, I have explained, was caused by the phosphorescent radiation that apparently emanated from every particle of mineral matter in this universe.

"As we advanced, many other tunnels crossed the one we were traveling. And now, occasionally, we passed other people, the men dressed similarly to Lylda, but wearing their hair chopped off just above the shoulder line.

"Later, I found that the men were generally about five and a half feet in stature: lean, muscular, and with a grayer, harder look to their skin than the iridescent quality that characterized the women.

"They were fine-looking chaps, these we encountered. All of them stared curiously at me, and several times we were held up by chattering groups. The intense whiteness of my skin, for it looked in this light the color of chalk, seemed to both awe and amuse them. But they treated me with great deference and respect, which I afterward learned was because of Lylda herself, and also what she told them about me.

"At several of the intersections of the tunnels there were wide open spaces. One of these we now approached. It was a vast amphitheater, so broad its opposite wall was invisible, and it seemed crowded with people. At the side, on a rocky niche in the wall, a speaker harangued the crowd.

"We skirted the edge of this crowd and plunged into another passageway, sloping downward still more steeply. I was so much interested in the strange scenes opening before me that I remarked little of the distance we traveled. Nor did I question Lylda but seldom. I was absorbed in the complete similarity between this and my own world in its general characteristics, and yet its complete strangeness in details.

"I felt not the slightest fear. Indeed the sincerity and kindliness of these people seemed absolutely genuine, and the friendly, naive manner of my little guide put me wholly at my ease. Toward me Lylda's manner was one of childish delight at a new-found possession. Toward those of her own people with whom we talked, I found she preserved a dignity they profoundly respected.

"We had hardly more than entered this last tunnel when I heard the sound of drums and a weird sort of piping music, followed by shouts and cheers. Figures from behind us scurried past, hastening toward the sound. Lylda's clasp on my hand tightened, and she pulled me forward eagerly. As we advanced the crowd became denser, pushing and shoving us about and paying little attention to me.

"In close contact with these people I soon found I was stronger than they, and for a time I had no difficulty in shoving them aside and opening a path for us. They took my rough handling all in good part, in fact, never have I met a more even tempered, good-natured people than these.

"After a time the crowd became so dense we could advance no further. At this Lylda signed me to bear to the side. As we approached the wall of the cavern she suddenly clasped her hands high over her head and shouted something in a clear, commanding voice. Instantly the crowd fell back, and in a moment I found myself being pulled up a narrow flight of stone steps in the wall and out upon a level space some twenty feet above the heads of the people.

"Several dignitaries occupied this platform. Lylda greeted them quietly, and they made place for us beside the parapet. I could see now that we were at the intersection of a transverse passageway, much broader than the one we had been traversing. And now I received the greatest surprise I had had in this new world, for down this latter tunnel was passing a broad line of men who obviously were soldiers.

"The uniformly straight lines they held; the glint of light on the spears they carried upright before them; the weird, but rhythmic, music that passed at intervals, with which they kept step; and, above all,

the cheering enthusiasm of the crowd, all seemed like an echo of my own great world above.

"This martial ardor and what it implied came as a distinct shock. All I had seen before showed the gentle kindliness of a people whose life seemed far removed from the struggle for existence to which our race is subjected. I had come gradually to feel that this new world, at least, had attained the golden age of security, and that fear, hate, and wrong-doing had long since passed away, or had never been born.

"Yet here, before my very eyes, made wholesome by the fires of patriotism, stalked the grim God of War. Knowing nothing yet of the motives that inspired these people, I could feel no enthusiasm, but only disillusionment at this discovery of the omnipotence of strife.

"For some time I must have stood in silence. Lylda, too, seemed to divine my thoughts, for she did not applaud, but pensively watched the cheering throng below. All at once, with an impulsively appealing movement, she pulled me down toward her, and pressed her pretty cheek to mine. It seemed almost as if she was asking me to help.

"The line of marching men seemed now to have passed, and the crowd surged over into the open space and began to disperse. As the men upon the platform with us prepared to leave, Lylda led me over to one of them. He was nearly as tall as I, and dressed in the characteristic tunic that seemed universally worn by both sexes. The upper part of his body was hung with beads, and across his chest was a thin, slightly convex stone plate.

"After a few words of explanation from Lylda, he laid his hands on my shoulders near the base of the neck, smiling with his words of greeting. Then he held one hand before me, palm up, as Lylda had done, and I laid mine in it, which seemed the correct thing to do.

"I repeated this performance with two others who joined us, and then Lylda pulled me away. We descended the steps and turned into the broader tunnel, finding near at hand a sort of sleigh, which Lylda signed me to enter. It was constructed evidently of wood, with a pile of leaves, or similar dead vegetation, for cushions. It was balanced upon a single runner of polished stone, about two feet broad, with a narrow, shorter outrider on each side.

"Harnessed to the shaft were two animals, more resembling our reindeers than anything else, except that they were gray in color and had no horns. An attendant greeted Lylda respectfully as we approached, and mounted a seat in front of us when we were comfortably settled.

"We drove in this curious vehicle for over an hour. The floor of the tunnel was quite smooth, and we glided down its incline with little effort and at a good rate. Our driver preserved the balance of the sleigh by shifting his body from side to side so that only at rare intervals did the side-runners touch the ground.

"Finally, we emerged into the open, and I found myself viewing a scene of almost normal, earthly aspect. We were near the shore of a smooth, shining lake. At the side a broad stretch of rolling country, dotted here and there with trees, was visible. Near at hand, on the lake shore, I saw a collection of houses, most of them low and flat, with one much larger on a promontory near the lake.

"Overhead arched a gray-blue, cloudless sky, faintly star-studded, and reflected in the lake before me I saw that familiar, gleaming trail of star-dust, hanging like a huge straightened rainbow overhead, and ending at my feet."

## CHAPTER V

### THE WORLD IN THE RING

THE Chemist paused and relighted his cigar. "Perhaps you have some questions," he suggested.

The Doctor shifted in his chair.

"Did you have any theory at this time" —he wanted to know—"about the physical conformation of this world? What I mean is, when you came out of this tunnel were you on the inside or the outside of the world?"

"Was it the same sky you saw overhead when you were in the forest?" asked the Big Business Man.

"No, it was what he saw in the microscope, wasn't it?" said the Very Young Man.

"One at a time, gentlemen," laughed the Chemist. "No, I had no particular theory at this time—I had too many other things to think of. But I do remember noticing one thing which gave me the clue to a fairly complete understanding of this universe. From it I formed a definite explanation, which I found was the belief held by the people themselves."

"What was that?" asked the Very Young Man.

"I noticed, as I stood looking over this broad expanse of country before me, one vital thing that made it different from any similar scene I had ever beheld. If you will stop and think a moment, gentlemen, you will realize that in our world here the horizon is caused by a curvature of the earth below the straight line of vision. We are on a convex surface. But as I gazed over this landscape, and even with no appreciable light from the sky, I could see a distance of several miles. I saw at once that quite the reverse was true. I seemed to be standing in the center of a vast shallow bowl. The ground curved upward into the distance. There was no distinct horizon line, only the gradual fading into shadow of the visual landscape. I was standing obviously on a concave surface, on the inside, not the outside of the world.

"The situation, as I now understand it, was this: According to the smallest stature I reached, and calling my height at that time roughly six feet, I had descended into the ring at the time I met Lylda several thousand miles, at least. By the way, where is the ring?"

"Here it is," said the Very Young Man, handing it to him. The Chemist replaced it on his finger. "It's pretty important to me now," he said, smiling.

"You bet!" agreed the Very Young Man.

"You can readily understand how I descended such a distance, if you consider the comparative immensity of my stature during the first few hours I was in the ring. It is my understanding that this country through which I passed is a barren waste—merely the atoms of what we call gold.

"Beyond that I entered the hitherto unexplored regions within the atom. The country at that point where I found the forest, I was told later, is habitable for several hundred miles. Around it on all sides lies a desert, across which no one has ever penetrated.

"This surface is the outside of the Oroid world, for so they call their earth. At this point the shell between the outer and inner surfaces is only a few miles in thickness. The two surfaces do not parallel each other, so that in descending these tunnels we turned hardly more than an eighth of a complete circle.

"At the city of Arite, where Lylda first took me, and where I had my first view of the inner surface, the curvature is slightly greater than that of our own earth, although, as I have said, in the opposite direction."

"And the space within this curvature—the heavens you have mentioned—how great do you estimate it to be?" asked the Doctor.

"Based on the curvature at Arite it would be about six thousand miles in diameter."

"Has this entire inner surface been explored?" asked the Big Business Man.

"No, only a small portion. The Oroids are not an adventurous people. There are only two nations, less than twelve million people all together, on a surface nearly as extensive as our own."

"How about those stars?" suggested the Very Young Man.

"I believe they comprise a complete universe similar to our own solar system. There is a central sun-star, around which many of the others revolve. You must understand, though, that these other worlds are infinitely tiny compared to the Oroids, and, if inhabited, support beings nearly as much smaller than the Oroids, as they are smaller than you."

"Great Cæsar!" ejaculated the Banker. "Don't let's go into that any deeper!"

"Tell us more about Lylda," prompted the Very Young Man.

"You are insatiatable on that point," laughed the Chemist. "Well, when we left the sleigh, Lylda took me directly into the city of Arite. I found it an orderly collection of low houses, seemingly built of uniformly cut, highly polished gray blocks. As we passed through the streets, some of which were paved with similar blocks, I was reminded of nothing so much as the old jingles of Spotless Town. Everything was immaculately, inordinately clean. Indeed, the whole city seemed built of some curious form of opaque glass, newly scrubbed and polished.

"Children crowded from the doorways as we advanced, but Lylda dispersed them with a gentle, though firm, command. As we approached the sort of castle I have mentioned, the reason for Lylda's authoritative manner dawned upon me. She was, I soon learned, daughter of one of the most learned men of the nation and was—handmaiden, do you call it?—to the queen."

"So it was a monarchy?" interrupted the Big Business Man. "I should never have thought that."

"Lylda called their leader a king. In reality he was the president, chosen by the people, for a period of about what we would term twenty years; I learned something about this republic during my stay, but not as much as I would have liked.

"The food was not greatly different from our own, although I found not a single article I could identify. It consisted principally of vegetables and fruits.

"Lylda visited me at intervals, and I learned I was awaiting an audience with the king. During these days she made rapid progress with my language—so rapid that I shortly gave up the idea of mastering hers.

"And now, with the growing intimacy between us and our ability to communicate more readily, I learned the simple, tragic story of her race—new details, of course, but the old, old tale of might against right, and the tragedy of a trusting, kindly people, blindly thinking others as just as themselves.

"For thousands of years, since the master life-giver had come from one of the stars to populate the world, the Oroid nation had dwelt in peace and security. These people cared nothing for adventure. No restless thirst for knowledge led them to explore deeply the limitless land surrounding them. Even from the earliest times no struggle for existence, no doctrine of the survival of the fittest, hung over them as with us. No wild animals harassed them; no savages menaced them. A fertile boundless land, a perfect climate, nurtured them tenderly.

"Under such conditions they developed only the softer, gentler qualities of nature. Many laws among them were unnecessary, for life was so simple, so pleasant to live, and the attainment of all the commonly accepted standards of wealth so easy, that the incentive to wrongdoing was almost non-existent.

"Strangely enough, and fortunately, too, no individuals rose among them with the desire for power. Those in command were respected and loved as true workers for the people, and they accepted their authority in the same spirit with which it was given. Indolence, in its highest sense the wonderful art of doing nothing gracefully, played the greatest part in their life.

"Then, after centuries of ease and peaceful security, came the awakening. Almost without warning another nation had come out of the unknown to attack them.

"With the hurt feeling that comes to a child unjustly treated, they all but succumbed to this first onslaught. The abduction of numbers of their women, for such seemed the principal purpose of the invaders, aroused them sufficiently to repel this first crude attack. Their manhood challenged, their anger as a nation awakened for the first time, they sprang as one man into the horror we call war.

"With the defeat of the Malites came another period of ease and security. They had learned no lesson, but went their in-dolent way, playing through life like the kindly children they were. During this last period some intercourse between them and the Malites took place. The latter people, whose origin was probably nearly opposite them on the inner surface, had by degrees pushed their frontiers closer and closer to the Oroids. Trade between the two was carried on to some extent, but the character of the Malites, their instinctive desire for power, for its own sake, their consideration for themselves as superior beings, caused them to be distrusted and feared by their more simple-minded companion nation.

"You can almost guess the rest, gentlemen. Lylda told me little about the Malites, but the loathing disgust of her manner, her hesitancy, even to bring herself to mention them, spoke more eloquently than words.

"Four years ago, as they measure time, came the second attack, and now, in a huge arc, only a few hundred miles from Arite, hung the opposing armies."

The Chemist paused. "That's the condition I found, gentlemen," he said. "Not a strikingly original or unfamiliar situation, was it?"

"By Jove!" remarked the Doctor thoughtfully, "what a curious thing that the environment of our earth should so effect that world inside the ring. It does make you stop and think, doesn't it, to realize how those infinitesimal creatures are actuated now by the identical motives that inspire us?"

"Yet it does seem very reasonable, I should say," the Big Business Man put in.

"IT was the morning of my third day in the castle," began the Chemist again, "that I was taken by Lylda before the king. We found him seated alone in a little anteroom, overlooking a large courtyard, which we could see was crowded with an expectant, waiting throng. I must explain to you now, that I was considered by Lylda somewhat in the light of a Messiah, come to save her nation from the destruction that threatened it.

"She believed me a supernatural being, which, indeed, if you come to think of it, gentlemen, is exactly what I was. I tried to tell her something of myself and the world I had come from, but the difficulties of language and her smiling insistence and faith in her own conception of me, soon caused me to desist. Thereafter I let her have her own way, and did not attempt any explanation again for some time.

"For several weeks before Lylda found me sleeping by the river's edge, she had made almost a daily pilgrimage to that vicinity. A maidenly premonition, a feeling that had first come to her several years before, told her of my coming, and her father's knowledge and scientific beliefs had led her to the outer surface of the world as the direction in which to look. A curious circumstance, gentlemen, lies in the fact that Lylda clearly remembered the occasion when this first premonition came to her. And in the telling, she described graphically the scene in the cave, where I saw her through the microscope." The Chemist paused an instant and then resumed.

"When we entered the presence of the king, he greeted me quietly, and made me sit by his side, while Lylda knelt on the floor at our feet. The king impressed me as a man about fifty years of age. He was smooth-shaven, with black, wavy hair, reaching his shoulders. He was dressed in the usual tunic, the upper part of his body covered by a quite similar garment, ornamented with a variety of metal objects. His feet were protected with a sort of buckskin; at his side hung a crude-looking metal spear.

"The conversation that followed my entrance, lasted perhaps fifteen minutes. Lylda interpreted for us as well as she could, though I must confess we were all three at times completely at a loss. But Lylda's bright, intelligent little face, and the resourcefulness of her gestures, always managed somehow to convey her meaning. The charm and grace of her manner, all during the talk, her winsomeness, and the almost spiritual kindness and tenderness that characterized her, made me feel that she embodied all those qualities with which we of this earth idealize our own womanhood.

"I found myself falling steadily under the spell of her beauty, until—well, gentlemen, it's childish for me to enlarge upon this side of my adventure, you know; but—Lylda means everything to me now, and I'm going back for her just as soon as I possibly can."

"Bully for you!" cried the Very Young Man. "Why didn't you bring her with you this time?"

"Let him tell it his own way," remonstrated the Doctor. The Very Young Man subsided with a sigh.

"During our talk," resumed the Chemist, "I learned from the king that Lylda had promised him my assistance in overcoming the enemies that threatened his country. He smilingly told me that our charming little interpreter had assured him I would be able to do this. Lylda's blushing face, as she conveyed this meaning to me, was so thoroughly captivating, that before I knew it, and quite without meaning to, I pulled her up toward me and kissed her.

"The king was more surprised by far than Lylda, at this extraordinary behavior. Obviously neither of them had understood what a kiss meant, although Lylda, by her manner, evidently comprehended pretty thoroughly.

"I told them then, as simply as possible to enable Lylda to get my meaning, that I could, and would gladly aid in their war. I explained, then, that I had the power to change my stature, and could make myself grow very large or very small in a short space of time.

"This, as Lylda evidently told it to him, seemed quite beyond the king's understanding. He comprehended finally, or at least he agreed to believe my statement.

"This led to the consideration of practical questions of how I was to proceed in their war. I had not considered any details before, but now they appeared of the utmost simplicity. All I had to do was to make myself a hundred or two hundred feet high, walk out to the battle lines, and scatter the opposing army like a set of small boys' playthings."

"Then like three children we plunged into a discussion of exactly how I was to perform these wonders, the king laughing heartily as we pictured the attack on my tiny enemies.

"He then asked me how I expected to accomplish this change of size, and I very briefly told him of our larger world, and the manner in which I had come from it into his. Then I showed the drugs that I still carried carefully strapped to me. This seemed definitely to convince the king of my sincerity. He rose abruptly to his feet, and strode through a doorway onto a small balcony overlooking the courtyard below.

"As he stepped out into the view of the people, a great cheer arose. He waited quietly for them to stop, and then raised his hand and began speaking. Lylda and I stood hand in hand in the shadow of the doorway, out of sight of the crowd, but with it and the entire courtyard plainly in our view.

"It was a quadrangular enclosure, formed by the four sides of the palace, perhaps three hundred feet across, packed solidly now with people of both sexes, the gleaming whiteness of the upper parts of their bodies, and their upturned faces, making a striking picture.

"For perhaps ten minutes the king spoke steadily, save when he was interrupted by applause. Then he stopped abruptly, and turning, pulled Lylda and me out upon the balcony. The enthusiasm of the crowd doubled at our appearance. I was pushed forward to the balcony rail, where I bowed to the cheering throng.

"Just after I left the king's balcony, I met Lylda's father. He was a kindly faced old gentleman, and took a great interest in me and my story. He it was who told me about the physical conformation of his world, and he seemed to comprehend my explanation of mine.

"That night it rained—a heavy, torrential downpour, such as we have in the tropics. Lylda and I had been talking for some time, and, I must confess, I had been making love to her ardently. I broached now the principal object of my entrance into her world, and, with an eloquence I did not believe I possessed, I pictured the wonders of our own great earth above, begging her to come back with me and live out her life with mine.

"Much of what I said, she probably did not understand, but the main facts were intelligible without question. She listened quietly. When I had finished, and waited for her decision, she reached slowly out and clutched my shoulders, awkwardly making as if to kiss me. In an instant she was in my arms, with a low, happy little cry.

"THE clattering fall of rain brought us to ourselves. Rising to her feet, Lylda pulled me over to the window-opening, and together we stood and looked out into the night. The scene before us was beautiful, with a weirdness almost impossible to describe. It was as bright as I had ever seen this world, for even though heavy clouds hung overhead, the light from the stars was never more than a negligible quantity.

"We were facing the lake—a shining expanse of silver radiation, its surface shifting and crawling, as though a great undulating blanket of silver mist lay upon it. And coming down to meet it from the sky were innumerable lines of silver—a vast curtain of silver cords that broke apart into great strings of pearls when I followed their downward course.

"And then, as I turned to Lylda, I was struck with the extraordinary weirdness of her beauty as never before. The reflected light from the rain had something the quality of our moonlight. Shining on Lylda's body, it tremendously enhanced the iridescence of her skin. And her face, upturned to mine, bore an expression of radiant happiness and peace such as I had never seen before in a woman's countenance."

The Chemist paused, his voice dying

away into silence as he sat lost in thought. Then he pulled himself together with a start. "It was a sight, gentlemen, the memory of which I shall cherish all my life.

"The next day was that set for my entrance into the war. Lylda and I had talked nearly all night, and had decided that she was to return with me to my world. By morning the rain had stopped, and we sat together in the window-opening, silenced with the thrill of the wonderful new joy that had come into our hearts.

"The country before us, under the cloudless, starry sky, stretched gray-blue and beautiful into the quivering obscurity of the distance. At our feet lay the city, just awakening into life. Beyond, over the rolling meadows and fields, wound the road that led out to the battle-front, and coming back over it now, we could see an endless line of vehicles. These, as they passed through the street beneath our window, I found were loaded with soldiers, wounded and dying. I shuddered at the sight of one cart in particular, and Lylda pressed closer to me, pleading with her eyes for my help for her stricken people.

"My exit from the castle was made quite a ceremony. A band of music and a guard of several hundred soldiers ushered me forth, walking beside the king, with Lylda a few paces behind. As we passed through the streets of the city, heading for the open country beyond, we were cheered continually by the people who thronged the streets and crowded upon the housetops to watch us pass.

"Outside Arite I was taken perhaps a mile, where a wide stretch of country gave me the necessary space for my growth. We were standing upon a slight hill, below which, in a vast semicircle, fully a hundred thousand people were watching.

"And now, for the first time, fear overtook me. I realized my situation—saw myself in a detached sort of way—a stranger in this extraordinary world, and only the power of my drug to raise me out of it. This drug you must remember, I had not as yet taken.

"I glanced around. The king stood before me, quietly waiting my pleasure. Then I turned to Lylda. One glance at her proud, happy little face, and my fear left me as suddenly as it had come. I took her in my arms and kissed her there before that multitude. Then I set her down, and signified to the king I was ready.

"I took a minute quantity of one of the drugs, and as I had done before, sat down with my eyes covered. My sensations were fairly similar to those I have already described. When I looked up after a moment, I found the landscape dwindling to tiny proportions in quite as astonishing a way as it had grown before. The king and Lylda stood now hardly above my ankles.

"A great cry arose from the people—a cry wherein horror, fear, and applause seemed equally mixed. I looked down and saw thousands of them running away in terror.

"Still smaller grew everything within my vision, and then, after a moment, the landscape seemed at rest. I kneeled now upon the ground, carefully, to avoid treading on any of the people around me. I located Lylda and the king after a moment; tiny little creatures less than an inch in height. I was then, I estimated from their view-point, about four hundred feet tall.

"I put my hand flat upon the ground near Lylda, and after a moment she climbed into it, two soldiers lifting her up the side of my thumb as it lay upon the ground. In the hollow of my palm, she lay quite securely, and very carefully I raised her up toward my face. Then, seeing that she was frightened, I set her down again.

"At my feet, hardly more than a few steps away, lay the tiny city of Arite and the lake. I could see all around the latter now, and could make out clearly a line of hills on the other side. Off to the left the road wound up out of sight in the distance. As far as I could see, a line of soldiers was passing out along this road—marching four abreast, with carts at intervals, loaded evidently with supplies; only occasionally, now, vehicles passed in the other direction. Can I make it plain to you, gentlemen, my sensations in changing stature? I felt at first as though I were tremendously high in the air, looking down as from a balloon upon the familiar territory beneath me. That feeling passed after a few moments, and I found that my point of view had changed. I no longer felt that I was looking down from a balloon, but felt as a normal person feels. And again I conceived myself but six feet tall, standing above a dainty little toy world. It is all in the view-point, of course, and never, during all my changes, was I for more than a moment able to feel of a different stature than I am at this present instant. It was always everything else that changed.

"According to the directions I had received from the king, I started now to follow the course of the road. I found it difficult walking, for the country was dotted with houses, trees, and cultivated fields, and each footstep was a separate problem.

"I progressed in this manner perhaps two miles, covering what the day before I would have called about a hundred and thirty or forty miles. The country became wilder as I advanced, and now was in places crowded with separate collections of troops.

"I have not mentioned the commotion I made in this walk over the country. My coming must have been told wildly by couriers the night before, to soldiers and peasantry alike, or the sight of me would have caused utter demoralization. As it was, I must have been terrifying to a tremendous degree. I think the careful way in which I picked my course, stepping in the open as much as possible, helped reassure the people. Behind me, whenever I turned, they seemed rather more curious than fearful, and once or twice when I stopped for a few moments they approached my feet closely. One athletic young soldier caught the loose end of the string of one of my buskins, as it hung over my instep close to the ground, and pulled himself up hand over hand, amid the enthusiastic cheers of his comrades.

"I had walked nearly another mile, when almost in front of me, and perhaps a hundred yards away, I saw a remarkable sight that I did not at first understand. The country here was crossed by a winding river running in a general way at right angles to my line of progress. At the right, near at hand, and on the nearer bank of the river, lay a little city, perhaps half the size of Arite, with its back up against a hill.

"What first attracted my attention was that from a dark patch across the river which seemed to be the woods, pebbles appeared to pop up at intervals, traversing a little arc perhaps as high as my knees, and falling into the city. I watched for a moment and then I understood. There was a seige in progress, and the catapults of the Malites were bombarding the city with rocks.

"I went up a few steps closer, and the pebbles stopped coming. I stood now beside the city, and as I bent over it, I could see by the battered houses the havoc the bombardment had caused. Inert little figures lay in the streets, and I bent lower and inserted my thumb and forefinger between a row of houses and picked one up. It was the body of a woman, partly mashed. I set it down again hastily.

"Then as I stood up, I felt a sting on my leg. A pebble had hit me on the shin and dropped at my feet. I picked it up. It was the size of a small walnut—a huge boulder six feet or more in diameter it would have been in Lylda's eyes. At the thought of her I was struck with a sudden fit of anger. I flung the pebble violently down into the wooded patch and leaped over the river in one bound, landing squarely on both feet in the woods. It was like jumping into a patch of ferns.

"I stamped about me for a moment until a large part of the woods was crushed down. Then I bent over and poked around with my finger. Underneath the tangled wreckage of tiny tree trunks, lay numbers of the Malites. I must have trodden upon a thousand or more, as one would stamp upon insects.

"The sight sickened me at first, for after all, I could not look upon them as other than men, even though they were only the length of my thumb-nail. I walked a few steps forward, and in all directions I could see swarms of the little creatures running. Then the memory of my coming departure from this world with Lylda, and my promise to the king to rid his land once for all from these people, made me feel again that they, like vermin, were to be destroyed.

"Without looking directly down, I spent the next two hours stamping over this entire vicinity. Then I ran two or three miles directly toward the country of the Malites, and returning I stamped along the course of the river for a mile or so in both directions. Then I walked back to Arite, again picking my way carefully among crowds of the Oroids, who now feared me so little that I had difficulty in moving without stepping upon them.

"When I had regained my former size, which needed two successive doses of the drug, I found myself surrounded by a crowd of the Oroids, pushing and shoving each other in an effort to get closer to me. The news of my success over their enemy had been divined by them, evidently. Lord knows it must have been obvious enough what I was going to do, when they saw me stride away, a being four hundred feet tall.

"Their enthusiasm and thankfulness now were so mixed with awe and solemn worship of me as a divine being, that when I advanced toward Arite they opened a path immedlately. The king, accompanied by Lylda, met me at the edge of the city. The latter threw herself into my arms at once, crying with relief to find me the proper size once more.

"I need not go into details of the ceremonies of rejoicing that took place this afternoon. These people seemed little given to pomp and public demonstration. The king made a speech from his balcony, telling them all I had done, and the city was given over to festivities and preparations to receive the returning soldiers."

The Chemist pushed his chair back from the table, and moistened his dry lips with a swallow of water. "I tell you, gentlemen," he continued, "I felt pretty happy

that day. It's a wonderful feeling to find yourself the savior of a nation."

At that the Doctor jumped to his feet, overturning his chair, and striking the table a blow with his fist that made the glasses dance.

"You know!" he fairly shouted, "that's just what you can be here to us."

The Banker looked startled, while the Very Young Man pulled the Chemist by the coat in his eagerness to be heard. "A few of these pills," he said in a voice that quivered with excitement, "when you are standing in a country and you can walk over to the next country and kick the houses apart with the toe of your boot." Silence fell in the group as they stared at each other, awed by the possibilities that opened up before them.

## CHAPTER VI

### "I MUST GO BACK"

THE tremendous plan for the salvation of their own suffering world through the Chemist's discovery occupied the five friends for some time. Then laying aside this subject, that now had become of the most vital importance to them all, the Chemist resumed his narrative.

"My last evening in the world of the ring, I spent with Lylda, discussing our future, and making plans for the journey. I must tell you now, gentlemen, that never for a moment during my stay in Arite was I free from an awful dread of this same return trip. I tried to conceive what it would be like, and the more I thought about it, the more hazardous it seemed.

"You must realize, when I was growing smaller, coming in, I was able to climb down, or fall or slide down, into the spaces as they opened up. Going back, I could only imagine the world as closing in upon me, crushing me to death unless I could find a larger space immediately above into which I could climb.

"And as I talked with Lylda about this and tried to make her understand what I hardly understood myself, I gradually was brought to realize the full gravity of the danger confronting us. If only I had made the trip out once before, I could have ventured it with her. But as I looked at her fragile little body, to expose it to the terrible possibilities of such a journey was unthinkable.

"There was another question, too, that troubled me. I had been gone from you nearly a week, and you were only to wait for me two days. I believed firmly that I was living at a faster rate, and that probably my time with you had not expired. But I did not know. And suppose, when I had come out on to the surface of the ring, one of you had had it on his finger walking along the street? No, I did not want Lylda with me in that event.

"And so I told her—made her understand—that she must stay behind, and that I would come back to her. She did not protest. She said nothing—just looked up into my face with wide, staring eyes and a little quiver of her lips. Then she clutched my hand and fell into a low, sobbing cry.

"I held her in my arms for a few moments, so little, so delicate, so human in her sorrow, and yet almost superhuman in her radiant beauty. Soon she stopped crying and smiled up at me bravely.

"Next morning I left. Lylda took me through the tunnels and back into the forest by the river's edge where I had first met her. There we parted. I can see now her pathetic, drooping little figure as she trudged back to the tunnel.

"When she had disappeared, I sat down to plan out my journey. I resolved now to reverse as nearly as possible the steps I had taken coming in. Acting on this decision, I started back to that portion of the forest where I had trampled it down.

"I found the place without difficulty, stopping once on the way to eat a few berries, and some of the food I carried with me. Then I took a small amount of one of the drugs, and in a few moments the forest-trees had dwindled into tiny twigs beneath my feet.

"I started now to find the huge incline down which I had fallen, and when I reached it, after some hours of wandering,

I followed its bottom edge to where a pile of rocks and dirt marked my former landing place. The rocks were much larger than I remembered them, and so I knew I was not so large, now, as when I was here before.

"Remembering the amount of the drug I had taken coming down, I took now twelve of the pills. Then, in a sudden panic, I hastily took two of the others. The result made my head swim most horribly. I sat or lay down, I forget which. When I looked up I saw the hills beyond the river and forest coming toward me, yet dwindling away beneath my feet as they approached. The incline seemed folding up upon itself, like a telescope. As I watched, its upper edge came into view, a curved, luminous line against the blackness above. Every instant it crawled down closer, more sharply curved, and its inclined surface grew steeper.

"All this time, as I stood still, the ground beneath my feet seemed to be moving. It was crawling toward me, and folding up underneath where I was standing. Frequently I had to move to avoid rocks that came at me and passed under my feet into nothingness.

"Then, all at once, I realized that I had been stepping constantly backward, to avoid the incline wall as it shoved itself toward me. I turned to see what was behind, and horror made my flesh creep at what I saw. A black, forbidding wall, much like the incline in front, entirely encircled me. It was hardly more than half a mile away, and towered four or five thousand feet overhead.

"And as I stared in terror, I could see it closing in, the line of its upper edge coming steadily closer and lower. I looked wildly around with an overpowering impulse to run. In every direction towered this rocky wall, inexorably swaying in to crush me.

"I think I fainted. When I came to myself the scene had not greatly changed. I was lying at the bottom and against one wall of a circular pit, now about a thousand feet in diameter and nearly twice as deep.

The wall all around I could see was almost perpendicular, and it seemed impossible to ascend its smooth, shining sides. The action of the drug had evidently worn off, for everything was quite still.

"My fear had now left me, for I remembered this circular pit quite well. I walked over to its center, and looking around and up to its top, I estimated distances carefully. Then I took two more of the pills.

"Immediately the familiar, sickening, crawling sensation began again. As the walls closed in upon me, I kept carefully in the center of the pit. Steadily they crept in. Now only a few hundred feet away! now only a few paces—and then I reached out and touched both sides at once with my hands.

"I tell you, gentlemen, it was a terrifying sensation to stand in that well (as it now seemed), and feel its walls closing up with irresistible force. But now the upper edge was within reach of my fingers. I leaped upward and hung for a moment, then pulled myself up and scrambled out, tumbling in a heap on the ground above. As I recovered myself, I looked again at the hole out of which I had escaped; it was hardly big enough to contain my fist.

"I knew, now, I was at the bottom of the scratch. But how different it looked from before. It seemed this time a long, narrow cañon, hardly more than sixty feet across. I glanced up and saw the blue sky overhead, flooded with light, that I knew was the space of this room above the ring.

"The problem now was quite a different one than getting out of the pit, for I saw that the scratch was so deep in proportion to its width that if I let myself get too big, I would be crushed by its walls before I could jump out. It would be necessary, therefore, to stay comparatively small and climb up its side.

"I selected what appeared to be an especially rough section, and took a portion of another of the pills. Then I started to climb. After an hour the buskins on my feet were torn to fragments, and I was bruised and battered as you saw me. I see, now, how I could have made both the descent into the ring, and my journey back with comparatively little effort, but I did the best I knew at the time.

"When the cañon was about ten feet in width, and I had been climbing arduously for several hours, I found myself hardly more than fifteen or twenty feet above its bottom. And I was still almost that far from the top. With the stature I had then attained, I could have climbed the remaining distance easily, but for the fact that the wall above had grown too smooth to afford foothold. The effects of the drug had again worn off, and I sat down and prepared to take another dose. I did so— the smallest amount I could—and held ready in my hand a pill of the other kind in case of emergency. Steadily the walls closed in.

"A terrible feeling of dizziness now came over me. I clutched the rock beside which I was sitting, and it seemed to melt like ice beneath my grasp. Then I remembered seeing the edge of the cañon within reach above my head, and with my last remaining strength, I pulled myself up, and fell upon the surface of the ring. You know the rest. I took another dose of the powder, and in a few minutes was back among you."

The Chemist stopped speaking, and looked at his friends. "Well," he said, "you've heard it all. What do you think of it?"

"It is a terrible thing to me," sighed the Very Young Man, "that you did not bring Lylda with you."

"It would have been a terrible thing if I had brought her. But I am going back for her."

"When do you plan to go back?" asked the Doctor after a moment.

"As soon as I can—in a day or two," answered the Chemist.

"Before you do your work here? You must not," remonstrated the Big Business Man. "Our nation may need you. You cannot go."

"Lylda needs me, too," returned the Chemist. "I have an obligation toward her now, you know, quite apart from my own feelings. Understand me, gentlemen," he continued earnestly, "I do not mean to place myself and mine before the great fight for democracy and justice which may soon be waged. That would be absurd. But it is not quite that way, actually; I can go back for Lylda and return here in a week.

"Any time that you should take," said the Banker slowly, "might cost this world thousands of lives that you could save. Have you thought of that?"

The Chemist flushed. "I can recognize the salvation of a nation or a cause," he returned hotly, "but if I must choose between the lives of a thousand men who are not dependent on me, and the life or welfare of one woman who is, I shall choose the woman."

"He's right, you know," said the Doctor, and the Very Young Man agreed with him fervently.

Two days later the company met again in the privacy of the club-room. When they had finished dinner, the Chemist began in his usual quiet way:

"I am going to ask you this time, gentlemen, to give me a full week. There are four of you—six hours a day of watching for each. It need not be too great a hardship. You see," he continued, as they nodded in agreement, "I want to spend a longer period in the ring world this time. I may never go back, and I want to learn, in the interest of science, as much about it as I can. I was there such a short time before, and it was all so strange and remarkable, I confess I learned practically nothing.

"I told you all I could of its history. But of its art, its science, and all its sociological and economic questions, I got hardly more than a glimpse. It is a world and a people far less advanced than ours, yet with something we have not, and probably never will have—the universally distributed milk of human kindness. Yes, gentlemen, it is a world well worth studying."

The Banker came out of a brown study. "How about your formulas for these drugs?" he asked abruptly; "where are they?" The Chemist tapped his forehead smilingly. "Well hadn't you better leave them with us?" the Banker pursued. "The hazards of your trip—you can't tell—"

"Don't misunderstand me, gentlemen," broke in the Chemist. "I wouldn't give you those formulas if my life and even Lylda's depended on it. There again you do not differentiate between the individual and the race. I know you four very well. You are my friends, with all the bond that friendship implies. I believe in your integrity—each of you I trust implicitly. With these formulas you could crush nations, or you could, any one of you, rule the world, with all its treasures for your own. These drugs are the most powerful thing for good in the world to-day. But they are equally as powerful for evil. I would stake my life on what you would do, but I will not stake the life of a nation."

"I know what I'd do if I had the formulas," began the Very Young Man.

"Yes, but I don't know what you'd do," laughed the Chemist. "Don't you see I'm right?" They admitted they did, though the Banker acquiesced very grudgingly.

"The time of my departure is at hand. Is there anything else, gentlemen, before I leave you?" asked the Chemist, beginning to disrobe.

"Please tell Lylda I want very much to meet her," said the Very Young Man earnestly, and they all laughed.

When the room was cleared, and the handkerchief and ring in place once more, the Chemist turned to them again. "Good-by, my friends," he said, holding out his hands. "One week from to-night, at most." Then he took the pills.

No unusual incident marked his departure. The last they saw of him he was calmly sitting on the ring near the scratch.

Then passed the slow days of watching, each taking his turn for the allotted six hours.

By the fifth day, they began hourly to expect the Chemist, but it passed through its weary length, and he did not come. The sixth day dragged by, and then came the last—the day he had promised would end their watching. Still he did not come, and in the evening they gathered, and all four watched together, each unwilling to miss the return of the adventurer and his woman from another world.

But the minutes lengthened into hours, and midnight found the white-faced little group, hopeful yet hopeless, with fear tugging at their hearts. A second week passed, and still they watched, explaining with an optimism they could none of them feel, the non-appearance of their friend. At the end of the second week they met again to talk the situation over, a dull feeling of fear and horror possessing them. The Doctor was the first to voice what now each of them was forced to believe. "I guess it's all useless," he said. "He's not coming back."

The Doctor sat for some time in silence, thoughtfully regarding the ring. "My friends," he began finally, "this is too big a thing to deal with in any but the most careful way. I can't imagine what is going on inside that ring, but I do know what is happening in our world, and what our friend's return means to civilization here. Under the circumstances, therefore, I cannot, I will not give him up.

"I am going to put that ring in a museum and pay for having it watched indefinitely. Will you join me?" He turned to the Big Business Man as he spoke.

"Make it a threesome," said the Banker gruffly.

And so to-day, if you like, you may go and see the ring. It lies in the Museum of the American Society for Biological Research. You will find it near the center of the third gallery, lying on its black-silk handkerchief, and covered by a glass bell. The air in the bell is renewed constantly, and near at hand sit two armed guards, watching day and night. And as you stand before it, thinking of the wonderful world within its atoms, you well may shudder at your infinite unimportance as an individual and yet glow with pride at your divine omnipotence as a fragment of human life.

---

The stories appearing in the September-October issue of Famous Fantastic Mysteries have been copyrighted by the Frank A. Munsey Company as follows: The Moon Pool, 1918; Space Station No. 1, 1936; The Whimpus, 1919; Karpen the Jew, 1938; The Girl in the Golden Atom, 1919; The Witch-Makers, 1936; Blind Man's Buff, 1920.

---

"Afraid it's too late.
If he had only come
back an hour sooner—"

# The Witch-Makers

## By DONALD WANDREI

### CHAPTER I

#### FLIGHT

ALWAYS the drums talked in the distance, ceasing neither by night nor day. He had lost track of time. He knew only that open country lay somewhere to the south. Toward it he drove himself by instinct, draining himself of last reserves of energy that should long ago have been exhausted. He fled from the drums and their prophecy of doom, but always they throbbed with a monotonous and maddening beat.

His face was haggard. A wild light shone in his deep-sunken eyes. Beard matted his cheeks, and his hair straggled unkempt. In his blind flight the jungle had tattered his clothing. His sun-baked skin bore the scratches of thorns and the weals of insect bite. Fever consumed him, but not even delirium could end the fear that forced him on to protect the treasure he carried.

He plunged through green nightmare. Only twilight filtered down from the roof of trees and creepers, the tangle of foliage and branches. The vegetation dripped

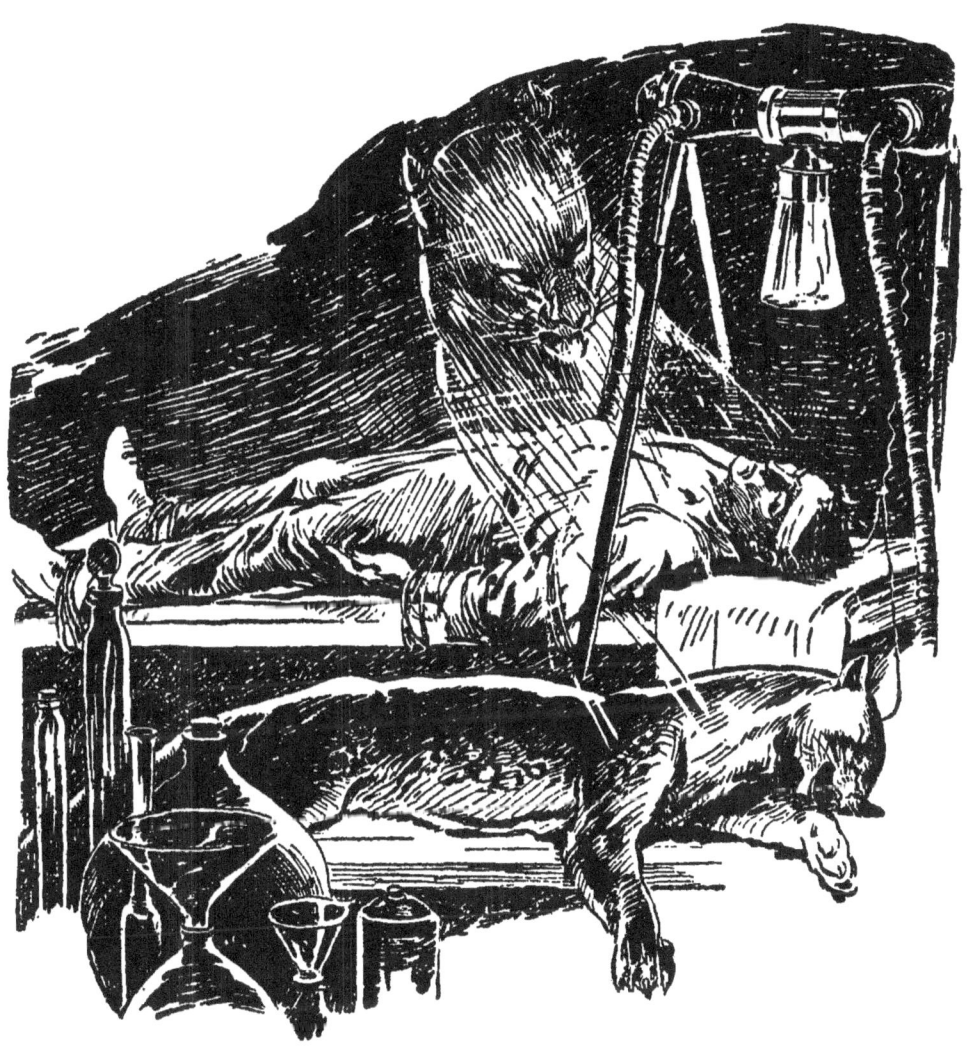

His body was about to die—so they put his mind in
the body of a panther—and turned the panther loose

moisture. His feet squashed sodden, decaying matter. The air steamed like a hothouse, with a wet and musty smell.

Amid the half-light, an evil beauty flourished upon death. Immense orchids, black as ebony or blood-scarlet, striped with golden green, purple, or waxy white, reared their fantastically gorgeous blossoms out of slime and rotting mold. Macaws squawked harshly. Hummingbirds and tanagers made streaks of brilliant color. There were mushrooms two feet tall, and mottled with scabrous pink.

Malaria mosquitoes and carrion flies droned, while now and then the savage scream of a mandril silenced the monkeys.

Crocodiles chased him when he splashed through a murky pool of the stream he was following. Later he floundered across a swamp, waist-deep in ooze. The slime-covered surface rippled. He felt the touch of soft and horrible things that wriggled.

No sane man could have survived so frightful a passage. He should have died a hundred deaths. He should have left his flesh and bones to rot with all that other decaying matter. He reeled onward.

He passed ancient ruins, engulfed by the tide of vegetation, but still preserving a basic outline. Upon colossal blocks of fallen masonry were incised symbols of a language unknown. He had heard legends of lost cities such as this, but he did not stop to investigate. He clambered across mounds and slippery walls.

And always the drums talked, throbbing afar, surrounding him with doom. The heavy revolver lay ever ready in his hand. He expected each moment to feel a poisoned dart or a spear, to meet a ring of painted and grotesquely masked faces. He saw no one.

A tangible foe would have ended the persistent torture of his nerves. His was the terror of expectancy, of inevitable death postponed from minute to minute. He must keep going, keep going, with the stolen witch-charm his prize if he won out. He stumbled on blindly.

## CHAPTER II

### THE WITCH-MAKERS

TWO white men looked down at the cot where the unconscious figure lay bandaged. The younger man, of square build and overweight for his five feet nine, asked in a deep, quiet voice, "What are his chances, Burt?"

"He hasn't any. Oh, the proverbial one in a million at the outside," the older man answered in a dry, rather testy tone. Dr. Ezra L. Burton was a spare and bony scarecrow, his semi-bald head fringed with sandy hair. What was visible of his features looked ruddy, but mostly they were concealed by a black beard of full and alarming proportions. He added, "It's a miracle that the duffer ever got out of the jungle. I've done what I could, but he's dying.

"Travers, I sometimes think that medical science, so-called, is a brutal farce. What was the use of patching him up today so that he can die tomorrow? He's going to die. He should have died days ago, but some silly will to live kept him going until he stumbled into our camp. It would have been better for him if he died in delirium. Now he'll wake up just long enough to know he's dying and to hate himself for it and to hate us for giving him a lease on life just long enough to know he's through."

Travers filled a briar pipe and lighted it.

"There's nothing to identify him except his initials." Burton poked a blunt and gnarled forefinger among the collection removed from the stranger's pockets. It included a bandana, cheap watch, magnifying glass, some coins and gold nuggets, pocket knife, cartridge belt, matches, and the .45, with the initials "L. A." carved on its butt. Amid these items lay a remarkable figurine about six or seven inches tall.

A little less than three inches of it represented a misshapen torso and spindly arms and legs of solid gold. The rest was an enormous emerald for its head. Of rectangular shape, it had been beveled to portray a two-faced monster of inhuman and unearthly attributes, suggesting abysmal antiquity, beyond history. The edges of the jewel had rounded from the wear of countless generations of hands.

Burton lifted the weird figurine. "He would seem to have been an itinerant trader. This idol probably is the key to the mystery. It looks like a fetish, some witch doctor's symbol of power or some tribe's emerald god. I suppose the chap stole it. It isn't exactly the kind of thing you expect stray visitors to carry around with them. As to who he is, my guess would be Leif Abbot, but it's only a guess."

"Leif Abbot?"

"I know of him by hearsay. A Yankee trader with a flair for digging into hidden places. In other words, a complete fool or trail blazer, depending on your point of view. Born in the Mid-west, Minnesota or Wisconsin, as I recall, went to Africa a few years ago, fooled colonial officials, tricked the natives, played both ends against the middle, and became a sort of legend. An imaginative cuss with a heart of gold—fool's gold."

Travers asked, "I wonder if he had anything to do with the drums we heard a while back?"

"I meant to find out about them. I'll see what that black thief Mokoalli has to say."

After Burton stalked out of the tent, Travers dropped into a folding chair.

Growls, snarls, and chattering made an uproar outside the tent. It was always thus at nightfall when the jungle creatures could be heard afar, and the captured animals grew restless. Within the camp enclosure, rows of cages held specimens of the district's life. Lion, jackal, ape, and zebra; python and mamba; buzzard, ostrich, even eels and brightly striped fishes lurked in the tanks and cages.

Travers glanced at the stranger, who was breathing heavily with a rattle in his throat.

IN the same tent, looking oddly out of place, stood modern scientific materials of obscure and specialized purpose. A metal operating table rested beside a curious device that had been assembled from numerous parts. These included a small dynamo, some queerly shaped glass tubes and ovaloids reminiscent of X-ray apparatus, and two tiny plates with a mass of wires hanging from each like fine, golden hair.

Travers reached out and picked up the grotesque idol. He hefted it reflectively, fascinated by its eyes in different colors, and the way glimmers of green flame welled from the heart of the great emerald. There might be fifty or a hundred dollars' worth of gold in the idol, but the jewel must be worth a thousand times as much, and the entire object even more as a curio or museum piece.

He continued to inspect the gem when Burton strode in, his black beard waving, while beads of sweat glistened on his ruddy forehead. "Mokoalli is a liar as well as a thief," Burton announced in the tone of a weather report. "He stole one of my best scalpels which I said he could keep if he told me the truth, whereupon he gave me nothing but the most outrageous lies. He said the drums were talking not because the jungle tribes were tracking the fugitive down, but to warn other tribes to keep out of his way! They thought he was bad medicine, driven by devils, and though he'd made off with a powerful charm they were afraid to touch him till the devils consumed him. They were just keeping an eye on him. That's Mokoalli's story. Moko is a liar. I took the scalpel back."

Travers removed the pipe from his mouth. "Did it occur to you that he might have been telling the truth?"

Burton looked surprised. "Why, no, it didn't."

"I think he earned the scalpel."

"He'll steal it again soon enough."

"The savage mind works in queer ways. The emerald that means a fortune to us wouldn't mean a thing to them except as a fetish or idol. If they were afraid of Abbot, they might well have waited until he died before reclaiming the charm. They might even have expected the emerald god to take vengeance and kill him. Then, when he stumbled toward our camp, the drums stopped."

"That's what Moko said. The natives seem to be pretty much afraid of us by now."

"Do you blame them?" Travers, with a glance at the fugitive, suggested, "Let's break camp as soon as he comes around or passes on. We've got our data. There isn't much more we could accomplish here. Our work's done. Another three months of this and I'll be fit for the booby hatch. Besides, the war zone seems to be creeping up on us. I've seen airplanes in the east twice in the past week. One of these days a bomber may pick us out for target practice or some fancy ground strafing."

Burton tugged at his beard reflectively. He felt the pulse of the patient, listened to his heartbeat, and took his temperature in the course of a careful examination. He shrugged as he turned away. "He's done for. A day or two at most. Even if

he recovers consciousness, which is prob-
lematical, he's too far gone for recovery.
We'll break camp as soon as possible."

"Good."

"But," added Burton with a new note
of decision in his voice, "we will im-
mortalize him by using him as our first
human control."

Travers frowned. "Why? If he's on the
way out? What good would it do?"

"It's his body that's broken down. If
he regains consciousness, his mind and intelligence should be relatively unimpaired.
It's only his life force, his vital spark,
the unit of identity that is his mentality
which we need. And we may be able to
prolong his life somewhat. In any case,
here is an outside chance to obtain data
of immense, I might say priceless importance.

"As you say, we've successfully finished
our work with the animal controls. The
ape-jackal interchange simply corrobo-
rated earlier findings. There is nothing
more to be learned by duplicating previous experiments. We need a human control.
Our next step *must* involve a human control if we are to open up vast new fields
for research.

BURTON'S accents had taken an in-
trospective tone as though he expressed aloud a passionate inner conviction
that drove him. "Thus far, we have only
objective data. The lower vertebrates
couldn't tell us their reactions and experiences in a new environment. Only
man can do that for us. We've already
made revolutionary discoveries, but we
stand on the threshold of a greater miracle
than anything we've yet seen or done.

"We interchanged the lives of a monkey
and a fox. Do you remember how elated
we were with the success of that first experiment? How we watched the fox in
the monkey's body cling to the ground?
How the monkey in the fox's body vainly
tried to swing through the tree tops? We
put the personality of a rhinoceros into
the body of a zebra, and that gentle animal became a driving, tearing Juggernaut

of death, while the great rhino inhabited
by the zebra's spirit fled in fear from the
lion it could have crushed.

"For weeks and months, Travers, we've
torn spirit and flesh asunder. Here in
fifty square miles that contain almost
every kind of the climate and life of Africa, we've learned more about animal
behavior during our three months than
all mankind learned in three thousand
years. We've stolen a march on evolution.
We've knocked the natural selection of
species into a cocked hat.

"Why can't we do the same with the
spirit of man? Maybe we can't, but we
won't know till we've tried. And if we
try and succeed, would you even attempt
to estimate how much we'll enrich man's
imagination and add to his knowledge?
Think of what it would mean if we enabled man to look at the world through
the eyes of his pets, a dog, or a cat, or a
horse! Wouldn't he have a more tender
feeling toward them and a more profound
appreciation of his own capacities? Isn't
it possible that, in course of time, his pets
would acquire a new intelligence of the
order of humanity? Isn't it conceivable
that they could then be trained to speak,
with results in strange, unimaginable new
friendships?

"And after that, Travers—after that—
the transference of intelligence from one
man to another! It's a magnificent and
terrifying thought, isn't it? If we made it
possible, where would it end? In greater
peace for mankind? Would he understand
his fellow men better and comprehend
more fully their weaknesses and follies,
their dreams and nobilities? Would he
spy upon his friends and try to benefit
by what he learned? Would each man
cease to be an individual as he gradually
absorbed the characteristics and peculiari-
ties of other men? Or would he become
more rapacious than ever before, carried
away by the thirst for knowledge, made
drunk by the infinite capacity for un-
limited power?

"I can't answer my own questions,
Travers. They're beyond answer except

in the fateful mold of experience. But we have it within our hands to take the first deliberate step, the step upon which all else hinges. We'll be tampering with the mysteries of life, yes, but it's life that's hopelessly doomed anyway. Abbot, if he is Abbot, can die unconscious and forgotten, or he can have experiences never dreamed of in his last hours. He can die with the certainty of a posthumous immortality that will never fade until earth itself runs its course or man perishes in the eons of the far future."

"You might at least wait till he comes to. He ought to have his say about whether he wants to be a guinea-pig. And there's the little matter of the emerald."

Burton shook his head decisively. His beard jerked like an erratic pendulum. "The emerald? We can donate it to a museum. He won't recover, and as for the experiment, perhaps he *would* object, if he could. I don't suppose he'll thank us for extending his life under altered circumstances. That is too much to expect. And he's apt to suffer a severe shock when and if he awakens, but he'll recover more quickly and adjust himself better than if he approached the experiment with all the fears his imagination could provide."

"Suppose the one chance in a million pulls him through? What if he survives? He could make it pretty hot for us. Society might not approve of our methods or our goals."

"That's why we're here instead of in a nice comfortable laboratory at home. If all experiments were subject to the whims and censorship of society, civilization would still be in the Dark Ages."

"That won't be answer enough if he survives."

"We'll find answers when the need arises. And while I stand here arguing with you, his hold on life grows thinner, and if we don't act immediately our great opportunity will be gone."

Burton walked over to the dynamo and started it. A low hum like the buzz of a persistent mosquito filled the tent. What looked like mist in one of the oddly shaped tubes glowed with a milky light. The mist became rapidly less opaque until only a softly shimmering radiance remained.

He slipped a metal band around his head. The band had a small bulb and reflector in front. He pressed the switch. A beam of light leaped out. He removed the unconscious man from the cot to the operating table, arranged a numer of surgical tools, and pulled rubber gloves over his hands.

Then he left the tent. A few minutes after his return Mokoalli and another native, panting and grunting, brought a cage in. The beast in the cage snarled sullenly.

As the patter of footsteps receded, Burton with a dextrous motion plunged a hypodermic through the bars of the cage. The beast roared and lunged viciously at his arm.

"He almost got you that time," said Travers in a voice of regret.

The guide-light focused on the stranger's head. Burton took a pair of scissors and snipped the hair off the base of his skull.

One by one, the surgical implements grew red. The sound of a man's breathing became harsher, and magnified in the stillness. The air became uncomfortably hot.

The moon rose, and weird noises drifted from the jungle. The animals yowled in their cages. Within the tent, the dynamo droned like a relentless carion fly.

## CHAPTER III

### STRANGE AWAKENING

LEIF ABBOT passed from one fantastic dream to another. In some he was a boy on the Mid-western prairies, chased by monsters foreign to all the continents. In others he wandered endlessly through forests and jungles, alone and hopelessly lost, or accompanied by dead friends and pursued by invisible terrors. There were periods of blankness and periods of skyrocketing flashes. At times he was almost on the verge of knowing that he dreamed, but then he slipped away again into the phantasmagoria of unconsciousness.

Pain entered his dreams. He was running, running, running, with leaden steps that took him forward more slowly than the progress of tortoises. Balanced upon his head was a great cube of gold that for some reason he could neither touch nor dislodge. He was compelled to stagger onward with that intolerable weight while his shadowy pursuers drew nearer with the speed of hawks. Knives flying in all directions impaled him.

Then the nightmare lay behind him. His head throbbed. He felt stifled and breathed unevenly, but he knew that the dream had ended. He lay still, his eyes closed as he half-remembered his last hours of consciousness. Buala, the witch doctor—the emerald god that had passed from tribe to tribe and from father to son through untold ages until it fell into Buala's custody—his days of haggling and cajoling, with Buala adamant in his superstitious faith in the emerald god's magic powers.

Leif Abbot had wanted that treasure. When he couldn't get it by more or less legitimate means, he took it by theft. In spite of his African adventures, however, he had underestimated the emerald's influence and prestige. He awoke one night to find his own carriers attacking him, and to hear the throb of drums. He escaped with the jewel, but his porters and guides deserted him, taking all his supplies.

He could have followed the river, which would have taken him downstream through hostile villages that he now could not pass through and live. He chose the southward course toward the headwaters and open country, where he had heard rumors about two white men whom the natives called "Witch-Makers." Then came the nightmare of his flight through the green hell, the insect hordes, fever, thirst, hunger, and finally delirium. He remembered nothing from that point on.

His thoughts growing clearer each moment, he opened his eyes. A roof lay curiously near, scarcely a yard above his head. He was lying on his side on the floor. Bars interfered with his vision, but he saw two white men in the interior of the tent, and—*lying upon an operating table, his own body!*

Leif Abbot closed his eyes in a daze. He must be dead or in the grip of delirium still. An odd panic filled him, a premonition.

He forced his eyes open again and stared at the figure on the table. He was unquestionably looking at his own emaciated, fever-ridden body, with a metallic gleam showing through bandages on its head!

Suddenly afraid, he strove to rise. Unable to balance on his legs, he toppled crazily and fell with a jarring thud. His head throbbed. A moan of pain came from his lips—*but to his ears it sounded like the whimper of an animal!*

The room reeled around in his vision as he fell. His head lowered, and his stunned gaze fastened upon the padded paws of a beast, and black-furred legs. They seemed part of him. He stretched out a hand, and stared in the hypnotism of horror as a paw scraped the floor where his hand should have been.

FOR a timeless drag of eternity he lay immobile, trying to figure some meaning out of the strange distortion of things. He was not dead, because he was not disembodied, yet he stood apart from his rightful body which lay beyond the bars. The cage inclosed a beast; and he was the beast.

As his thoughts skittered through this new, waking nightmare he became conscious of a voice. It sounded extraordinarily loud and shrill, like a thunderclap. He realized vaguely that he had difficulty understanding the words, and that the room was filled with a multitude of familiar sounds magnified in volume, while other sounds of which he had never before been aware assailed his hearing. His ears had acquired a preternatural sensitivity. In the amplified breathing of the speaker he heard the lungs expand and contract, the heart beat. He heard a fly crawl on the canvas of the tent. When the second man tilted his pipe, he heard fingers rasp on the bowl, and a rustle as of raindrops when some ashes fell to the floor.

"Leif Abbot, if you are Leif Abbot, can you hear me?" asked the booming voice.

The beast in the cage scrambled to all fours and swayed against the bars. Glaring sullenly out, he lowered and raised his head.

Before the speaker could continue, there came a wild interruption. Leif Abbot, looking through the bars, saw his body stiffen on the operating table. The eyes opened with an expression of animal ferocity. Ropes bound the body, but it burst the ropes with a surge of strength that Leif Abbot in all his life had not equaled.

The mouth parted, but from that human throat came a snarl born of the jungle. The body hurtled across the tent in the spring of an animal, teeth bared, arms outstretched like paws ready to rip and gouge. The white men scattered and for seconds a furious battle raged. The white men won, but only because Leif Abbot's body was too exhausted to endure the terrific strain put upon it by the untamed spirit within.

When the struggle ended, the body lay motionless under the influence of an opiate. The taller of the men, the one with the waving black beard, painted their scratches and wounds with iodine.

After he had finished, he turned again toward the cage. "I am Dr. Burton. My colleague is Dr. Travers, a physicist and biochemist. We have been engaged in experiments here for several months. When you staggered half dead into our camp, we were compelled to adopt extreme measures or you would already be dead.

"Do not be alarmed. Whatever seems incredible to you is really very simple. We have discovered how to separate the life-stream or consciousness or whatever you want to call it from the body to which it belongs, and to effect an exchange with some other body. Thus far we have worked only with the lower vertebrates. In your case, your chances for survival as Leif Abbot were so small that we operated upon the six layers of your cerebral cortex and transferred your identity to the body of a strong and healthy black panther. The panther's identity now occupies your own sick and weakened body. By this interchange we hope to strengthen your body sufficiently so that your identity can later be restored to it, with better chances for your recovery and survival.

"In the meantime the door to your cage is open behind you. Go into the jungle, if you like. You probably will be better off there. You have all the intelligence of man, and all the senses and instincts of the big cats. You should be able to avoid any danger and survive any attack."

Leif Abbot attempted to answer, but only a rumbling growl issued from his throat. His new vocal cords either were not capable of speech or would require long practice.

The greenish yellow eyes of the panther glowered his mute hatred. Burton's glib explanation failed to satisfy him. Not for an instant did he believe Blackbeard and his companion. They wanted the emerald god for which he had risked his life. What poorly paid scientist would pass up such an opportunity for easy wealth? They didn't have courage enough to let him die or to kill him. But it would be murder just the same, in a different form, more protracted, and under the guise of science.

Neither Burton nor Travers spoke again They watched him in silence; and he in turn glared balefully from them to the emerald that still lay among his effects, its glitter matched by the smoldering flame in his eyes.

Turbulent emotions swept him. Hatred rankled at the back of his thoughts. He tried to adjust himself to his weird change of state. He plotted a dozen ways of tricking them in order to regain possesion of his treasure, but he hopelessly confused his lost resources as man and his as yet unknown abilities as panther. Forgetting his new form momentarily, he tried to grasp the bars of the cage, but his paws merely slid along the bars. He had no fingers to help him now. He had never before appreciated so fully the infinite utility of hands.

Probably they were merely awaiting his departure into the jungle before killing the panther-spirit that now occupied his real body. And there was absolutely nothing he could do for the present, except take their advice before they changed their minds. He might be doomed to die in the jungle, but while he lived he could scheme ways of vengeance.

He stared for the last time at his captors, then turned and bounded into the darkness outside.

## CHAPTER IV

### THE BLACK MARAUDER

THE rest of the night, all the next day, and the following night the black panther remained away. Burton and Travers watched the body of Leif Abbot, which seemed to grow stronger under the drive of the fierce animal spirit that now dwelt within it.

Toward dawn of the second day, Burton awakened from a fitful sleep to hear a weight dragging on the ground. He sprang up and flashed a light on it. The panther, its right hind leg broken, and bleeding from numerous wounds, dragged itself forward. It did not whimper. Its glazing eyes still burned with sultry hatred and rebellion though death fast approached

"Travers, quick!" Burton shouted. "Turn on the psychotransferometer! Get out adrenalin! Scopolamin!"

He leaped to the dying panther and gathered it in his arms. Its savage heart beat heavily. He carried it to the operating table and laid it beside the shackled body of Leif Abbot.

The hum of the dynamo had already begun. Pale, vaporous light shone in the vacuum tube. Burton fastened the silver plate in the panther's skull and the similar plate in Abbot's cranium to wires connected with the transference apparatus.

It was not a torrid night, but sweat glistened on his face. He watched anxiously, tugging at his beard.

Travers shook his head in doubt. "Afraid it's too late. If he'd only come back an hour sooner—"

As though in mockery at his words, the gleam of animal ferocity suddenly returned to the panther's eyes. For a moment it snarled at them and made an effort to attack. It shuddered, while its eyes filmed more swiftly. The brute thirst faded from the eyes of Leif Abbot as his human identity re-entered his body. A gleam of sanity and intelligence lingered for seconds, gradually to be replaced by an expression of trance-like repose and suspended will-power when the drugs took effect.

Burton heaved a deep sigh. "A close call, that. A few minutes more and our trouble would have gone for nothing. Too bad the panther died, but we have all the notes we need on its behavior while it occupied Leif Abbot's body. And now let's see if he can or will tell us what he did in the part of a black panther."

He bent over and looked into the subject's eyes. They were wide open, but the hypnotic blankness had grown complete.

"Leif Abbot, can you hear me?"

The lips hardly moved, to give a faint answer, "Yes."

"Last night in the body of a panther you left us. You have been gone for two nights and a day. Where did you go? What did you do? What happened to you after you left? How did you receive the wounds?"

SPEAKING as though from a distance, his unblinking eyes exhibiting no change of expression, Leif Abbot said, "When I crept out of the boma, the moon rode high. It was a red moon. It bathed the plain in blood. Black shadows and scarlet moonlight, all the world was strange. I have never seen so strange a world. It was like the landscape of another planet.

"I heard sounds beyond the range of my

normal ears, the wings of night birds, the gliding of a snake, an indescribable chorus of separate sounds around me and drifting from the distant jungle. I heard grass rustle in the faintest of winds. I saw colors that no man has ever watched. They are beyond the spectrum of his eyes, but my panther eyes saw them. I can't tell what they were like, any more than you could describe color to somebody blind from birth. You would have to see those eerie colors for yourselves.

"All my senses were immensely keener. I detected smells of hundreds of different plants, flowers, animals, insects, decaying matter, and other things, where before I had noticed only a sort of general dank mustiness in the air. I was queerly mixed up. As a panther I noticed all these impressions for what they were. As a man I couldn't identify more than a part of them. I had half-memories that didn't quite bridge the gap between my own knowledge and the panther's instincts and habits. Certain odors made me afraid. The panther knew that they came from poisonous plants.

"I didn't know what to do, at first. For a while I strode around, accustoming myself to going on all fours, and to the movements of unfamiliar muscles. Gradually I got a feeling of power, for there was the strength of several men in that long, sleek, and ripplingly muscled body. I tried crouching and leaping, and found that pounces of twenty feet and more came effortlessly.

"I traveled northward, downhill, toward the jungle. I had some vague idea of hunting for Buala and taking vengeance on his tribe. It was a crazy idea because if any vengeance was to be taken it really belonged to him. At the edge of the jungle I stopped. I could see into it better than I could in the daytime with human vision. It was filled with a kind of grayish green light, more ghostly than twilight; the shadows were blackly green; and the patches of moonlight a sort of ghastly red.

"Maybe that's the way the jungle always looks to the great cats by night. I

don't know. That's the way it looked to me and it gave me the creeps. My fears as man carried over into my life as panther. I shied at going into that monstrous tangle.

"Besides, I had an inner pull to travel eastward. I couldn't account for it, unless some latent instinct of the panther was asserting itself. Finally I began to ramble toward the east, keeping at the fringe of the jungle in a long, gliding run that I found easy to maintain.

"I put hours and miles behind me. I followed the instinct that urged me on. While doing so, I became more confident in myself and more sure of my pantherine body.

"Loping through broken, hilly country that was beginning to show a sharp upward rise some hours later, I felt a pull toward the northeast. I turned from my course into the hills and went back to the tangle. I found a dim spoor that lured me on. My surroundings looked as if they ought to be familiar. I almost remembered, but not quite.

"There came a turn in the faint trail I followed. I reached the base of a cluster of rocks. With no intention on my part, a kind of spitting growl broke from my throat. It was instantly answered by a yowl. From a black and cavernous opening that I now noticed, a panther emerged, a female, with a couple of cubs at her heels. I stopped in my tracks.

"For just an instant the creature was on the verge of greeting me home, and I knew that instinct had brought me to the mate of the black panther whose body I had taken possession of. She was deceived only for moments. By whatever subtle or primitive sense, she knew that I was an alien presence, a menace. She came through the air, a snarling fury, with claws raking in an attack that caught me by surprise.

"I suppose I could have put up a battle royal. I didn't. I don't know why. Probably some atavistic feeling of chivalry that was a hangover from my previous life made me turn tail and flee, as if all the devils in hell were yapping at my heels. That female cat was a demon if ever there was one. She ripped a shoulder wide open and took a chunk out of my neck before I got away. Those cursed cubs tumbled around and yowled in glee. I wish I'd knocked the whole litter into kingdom come.

"The sky was turning lighter. I left the denser thickets and ran toward higher ground.

"After that, I decided to go very easy about trusting instincts. I sniffed the air and got wind of a water hole.

"There I drank greedily and shook myself in the tepid water. It soothed the wounds I couldn't reach. There was a rocky ledge beside a trail that animals used in reaching the water hole. I bounded on top of it and lay down to await sunrise.

"While I rested, a deer came mincing along the trail. It was a beautiful creature, a doe. I watched it drink and admired its graceful motions as it frisked away toward the grazing country to the south; and when it was gone I found that I was ravenously hungry and that I had blithely let my dinner skip off.

"My human scruples did not mean a thing in this case. A panther's body supported me and I had to support it in the manner to which it was accustomed. I waited a half hour before I spotted a wild boar. I made short work of it. Eating meat still on the hoof didn't exactly appeal to me, but my substitute palate gorged itself.

"I felt drowsy then. I turned toward the fringe of the jungle in search of a safe nook for a nap. I was looking for a high ledge or a cave, but didn't find anything with suitable protection. I scouted farther away from the water hole, trekking toward thicker jungle. As I was prowling along the trail, a sudden crackle gave me warning, but not warning enough. The ground opened beneath me. I made a vain scramble but felt myself falling. When I hit bottom, the wind was knocked out of me.

# CHAPTER V

### THE PANTHER STRIKES

"THOUGH I didn't fall a great distance, I landed on my neck and shoulders with stunning force. I lay there for perhaps a minute before I grew conscious of a pain in my right hind leg. I tried to get up. It was torture beyond me. I squirmed around, and in the dim light saw that the bottom of the pit held fire-hardened stakes imbedded point up. One of these had pierced the leg. It was only pure luck that others hadn't impaled me. I had fallen into an animal trap.

"A quick, careful jerk of the leg brought agony and freedom. I licked the wound. Looking around then, I estimated my chances of leaping from the pit at exactly zero. The stakes had been cleverly placed and the pit so constructed as to make it impossible for any beast to escape. Yet I escaped.

"How? It was absurdly simple for a creature who could think. I took a stake between my teeth and pulled it out. I turned the sharp point toward the earth wall and pushed it as far in as I could with my jaws. Holding the blunt end in my jaws, and pushing at the same time with two paws grasping the stake, I imbedded it for half its length.

"I removed another stake and drove it in beside the first. I continued the process until I had formed a ladder of stakes in pairs as high as I could reach. It took time, and every second I was desperately afraid that the hunters would come for the kill before I got out.

"My wounded leg hurt badly. I fell several times trying to climb the stakes, but on the fourth try I eased my weight onto the top pair. Then I rose in a swift half-turn on my hind legs. The stakes gave, but I had my forelegs over the edge of the pit and pulled myself out with my hind legs shoving and digging into the wall. The pain was intolerable. After I had regained freedom, I rested for several minutes, my ears listening for footsteps. I would have killed any human being that came in sight, if I could. My rage wore off, and I forgot the wound temporarily, when I thought of a sardonic jest.

"I went to work with a will and a vengeance. Ten minutes later I was crouching on the limb of a tree, hidden by foliage, and with the pit barely visible. The jungle steadily grew hotter as the sun mounted higher.

"I was feeling drowsy again when my ears pricked to the sounds of a party approaching. There were seven of them. I watched intently until the first, a strapping young buck with chest and cheeks cicatrised, came into view carrying a long lance. The only other thing he wore besides a loin cloth was a crude bracelet of some sort twisted tightly around his left arm almost at the shoulder. I don't know what it signified or why he wore it there. I noticed it because his left arm flashed up in a signal and he let out a yell you could have heard a mile off.

"The six others gathered around him, all jabbering at once, and all getting more pop-eyed by the second. I chose that instant to do the best I could on a loud laugh. Even to me the result was weird. They fled like so many rabibts.

"They looked scared silly. My jest had been a complete success. I had scraped a patch of ground smooth. Upon it, using my paw as a pen, I had scrawled, 'Yours Truly, The King of the Panthers,' and under the signature I had drawn the rough outline of a panther's head.

"The natives probably couldn't have read anything in any language, but they knew what writing was. They recognized the panther's head. They saw that there were no human tracks in the vicinity except their own. They saw how the panther had escaped from the trap. For the rest of their lives they'll be talking about the panther god or devil that left his signature.

"I drew back to a crotch in the tree and dozed there.

"The sun stood overhead when distant reports that seemed to come from the east wakened me. They sounded like gunshots. I leaped to the ground and limbered up the injured leg. After a first sharp pain, it became manageable, though it remained stiff and throbbed persistently, forcing me to limp a little.

"I kept to higher ground, where I had good vision in all directions. From time to time I saw small parties of natives. Once I heard and saw a squadron of airplanes to the northeast.

"In a couple of hours or so I reached a region of sheer rock escarpments, hills, deep ravines, and narrow passes. There were patches of dense, semi-tropical jungle around water holes. Elsewhere grew thickets of thorn, stunted trees, and sometimes sparse brown grass. I heard the movements of a considerable force ahead. Guided by the sounds, I struck off at a tangent and hid in the shadow of a large boulder atop a dolomite.

"Over the crest of a hill came native scouts, in advance of a detachment of white infantry and native troops. In all, the raiding party consisted of about two hundred, of whom three-fourths were native troops. They looked like Somalis to me.

"The white men, except for the officers, weren't tanned enough or lean enough to have been hardened by long fighting in the tropics. I judged them to be fairly recent arrivals. All were heavily armed.

"SUDDENLY a rifle cracked, then another. Intermittent shots poured from an ambush ahead. One of the white men fell. A couple of natives staggered when they were hit. The rest was merely efficient slaughter. Two machine guns went into action like magic and peppered the hillside thicket. There were a few answering shots. A few of the black defenders charged into the open. Mowed down by the fusillade, none of them escaped. About a dozen seemed to have been posted in the ambush.

"Red rage seethed inside of me. You have to see things like that in the wild, unknown places of the world to know the seamy side of colonial wars and imperial aggression. Twelve against two hundred—twelve armed with 1876 Springfields and muskets so ancient and rusty that they couldn't tell whether the pin would hit or the cartridge explode when they pulled the trigger—twelve against modern rifles, machine guns and grenades.

"It didn't make any difference that I'd stolen a treasure from Buala when I couldn't get it otherwise. At least I hadn't tried to kick him off of his own land or put a bullet through him when he couldn't see the deal my way. I was mad enough to start a one-man, or rather a one-panther, campaign against the whole detachment. Idiotic? Sure. But here's how it worked out.

"I crept down from the dolomite and detoured ahead until I found a suitable spot for my purposes. At a V-neck that the column must pass and where the legend could not possibly be missed, I scratched on the ground:

WARNING! GO BACK!
The King of the Panthers.

"A quarter-mile beyond the V-neck, I jumped to the top of a great pile of fallen rocks, where I could easily be seen silhouetted against the sky. I had not waited long before the scouts found my message and my tracks. One of them ran back to the main body in great excitement. The others noticed me and stared at me. I stared at them. The moment I saw sunlight gleam on a rifle barrel swinging up, I dropped behind the rocks. Bullets whined past. I took a quick peek and saw a cluster of troops gesticulating and waving over my message.

"The native troops had obviously received a scare and the whites were trying to quiet their fears. It seemed as though they all saw me and turned toward me at once. There was a moment's complete silence, while I looked down toward them. Then I slipped away among the fallen masses of rock and the scrub thorn as more lead hornets buzzed.

"I doubled back by much the same route

until I was well behind the raiders. Then I started catching up with them again.

"I singled out a victim at the very tail of the column. Keeping well to the rear, I took advantage of every possible concealment until the right moment came, when he was temporarily cut off from the rest by a twist in the defile. He saw me just before I hit him. His eyes popped. He didn't have time to squawk. I landed on his shoulders, he slammed against rock, and when his skull hit there came the sharp snap of a neck breaking. I lifted his rifle between my teeth and got back in the brush. Then I let out a terrific screech. I watched just long enough to see several white and native troops rush back. Morale took another blow.

"I had the devil of a time lugging that rifle in a circuitous detour toward the head of the column. I had to stay well covered and at a distance or light gleaming on a barrel would have betrayed me. When I reached a vantage point, my leg was throbbing worse. I was striking for the last time in my one-panther campaign, and I determined to make it a telling shot.

"Beyond the V-neck stretched a valley that lay between rock bluffs. A number of mud-holes extended along the valley like beads on a string, each surrounded by grass, dwarf palms, and scrub. I got wind of a village somewhere ahead but the tribe had either moved on or taken to the hills for the time being. I set up shop, so to speak, on the highest of a series of broken and tumbled masses from the cliffs, a couple of miles from the V-neck.

"The sun was westering and the heat had begun to abate. The valley, at least to my eyes, had acquired a sinister reddish hue. In the quiet air, the sounds of the on-coming force gave an effect like the motions of puppets.

"I had laid the rifle between two rocks so that no gleam would show its presence. The rifle, the shadow, and I blended into one. I was amused to notice the newly acquired caution with which the raiding party advanced. I marked the figure which I hoped was the commanding officer.

"GETTING ready to fire that rifle was one of the hardest jobs I've ever tackled. I had no finger to squeeze the trigger. I could not hold the rifle against my shoulder. I couldn't use the sights. But I'd thought about all the difficulties when I was toting it, and I solved them after a sort. I drew back from the rifle and sighted along the rock groove in which it rested. Then I crawled up to it, shifted its angle, and drew back for another estimate until I had it aimed at a spot below a shoulder-high rock that the column would pass. I made these preparations, of course, before the detachment was in range. Then I lay on my side with the stock against my chest and the nail of a paw hooked around the trigger.

"When the man I had marked stepped into range, I fired. The recoil gave a wallop to my ribs. The officer finished his step, raised a hand toward his ribs, and collapsed. I grabbed the rifle in my teeth and stepped into full view.

"The results were electrical. Silhouetted against the setting sun, I must have presented an awesome appearance. The whole column halted as one, then pandemonium broke out. The Somalis turned retreat into rout. Brave as they were, they couldn't face a panther-devil that wrote warnings and backed them up with deadly marksmanship.

"Shouted commands were ignored. The officers shot down their own men in an effort to stop the panic. They fired at where I had been, but I had ducked.

"For months to come the survivors of that raiding party will, I hope, break into a cold sweat every time they hear a panther howl.

"My lone campaign struck me as a success, but I was weary, my leg ached severely, and night drew near. I decided to return to camp and see what I could do there. Further foraging in my present condition would have been simple suicidal.

"When the sun was ready to drop below the horizon, I had put several miles of the return trip behind me. I traveled clear of the jungle to make better time. Even so, my injured leg hindered me badly. I tried to keep my weight off it by trotting along hippity-hop in a sort of three-legged gait.

"I glanced around when I heard the rush of hooves. A one-horned rhinoceros was charging me like a runaway express train. At the moment of impact it flung its lowered head skyward. Its horn, hooked around me, hurled me high in the air and backward. That terrific heave both saved my life and lost it. I went through the air in an arc and crashed among the branches of a low growing tree. I was knocked unconscious, but out of reach.

"When I opened my eyes, night had fallen. I was draped over a limb. The rhino had departed. Its horn had opened a gash in my side, the branches had cut and bruised me, and my right hind leg which had already taken punishment enough was broken.

"As I jumped to earth I gave a screech that would have brought my friend the rhino back in double-quick time if he had heard it. I couldn't help it, so fierce was the agony. All the rest of the night I spent in hopping and dragging my way back to camp. Only the memory of the emerald drove me on. Growing fainter with every step, and losing blood steadily, it was all I could do not to yield to the temptation to crawl into a thicket and die

"Almost any creature that walked could have beaten me then. The jungle and all its noises, its mysterious life, the strange greenish dusk within it, and the scarlet moonlight filled me with terror. The way back seemed endless. The air smelled sulphurous. I sweltered in that infernal heat. Or perhaps it was only fever that crept over me as I toiled on the long route, fever and the slow finger of death."

In the silence that ensued, Burton, who had taken copious notes on the story, sat brooding for the period in which a man could smoke a pipe. Finally he sighed deeply. "I resent it after a fashion, that he should be first to have so remarkable an experience," he murmured. "By rights you or I should have been elect."

Travers said flatly, "I haven't your skill at surgery. I can't perform the operation and turn you loose, and I won't let you do the job on me."

"I'm afraid you haven't the true instincts of the martyr, Travers. Fame, adventure, pioneering—they mean nothing to you. If I were dependent upon your inclinations, doubtless we might never have passed this milestone on the road of human achievement. It was a stroke of genius, no less, the scientific genius that is today tearing apart the secrets of life, mind, and matter."

"And now that the milestone has been reached?"

"On to the next!" Burton tugged at his beard as he glanced at the sleeper. His expression was curious: a mixture of envy, of regret, and of inhumanly calculating intent.

He rose and began to make preparations.

Travers did not finish the involuntary phrase that came to his lips. "You mean—?"

## CHAPTER VI

### THE END OF THE EMERALD GOD

FROM fever and the slow finger of death, from dreams and memories and lost realities hidden in mists afar, Leif Abbot slowly returned to consciousness. He was afraid to open his eyes through fear of what he would find, through fear that it would not be what he hoped to find.

He recalled Buala, the emerald, flight through jungle. The recollection was mixed up with fever and the impression of a nightmare in which he had somehow been imprisoned in the body of a panther. It had been a harrowing nightmare, too graphic and vivid.

Among his haze of thoughts drifted the faces of two white men who proclaimed themselves scientists but who mastered demoniac arts. Leif Abbot had an uncertain feeling that he had talked to them at considerable length, but he could not imagine what he had talked to them about.

It was all hopelessly involved. He tried vainly to force the pictures into a consecutive sequence.

When he blinked his eyes open and saw his own body still lying upon the operating table, he felt only the dull unhappiness of one who has already been shocked into numbness. Assailed by forebodings, he looked down. His head moved with singularly abrupt and sudden jerks. When he saw the talons, the thin, horny legs, and the feathered body of a bird of prey, he screamed his fury. The result was a croak, harsh and forbidding.

Travers had left the tent. Burton, who was taking the pulse of the body, looked around when the eagle screamed.

"Awake?" he queried, his eyes alight with excitement. "Another triumph, a complete success! Leif Abbot, your body is mending but it still is not out of danger. You fortunately destroyed the black panther by putting its body to excessive strain. You have a very courageous nature, but you let it run away with your better judgment. We have given you a second temporary body. You have wings. You can fly. The skyways are open to you, while the spirit of the eagle is earthbound in your body.

"When you return, I trust that recovery has progressed sufficiently so that the identity of each can be restored to its rightful abode. The cage door is not locked. If you can hear me you are at liberty to open the door and depart. Return when you will, but I would advise you not to remain away for any extended period."

Leif Abbot had an insensate urge to fly straight at that ruddy face, hook his talons in the bushy black beard, and peck at the man's eyes. But out of the turmoil of his emotions, out of the need for radically readjusting himself to his environment, one thought stood clear. An opportunity other than the one specified had been unintentionally given him.

With mental prayers that Burton would not divine his purpose, he used his beak to push the cage door aside. He strutted forth and stretched his wings experimentally to get the feel of them. By the easy response, he knew that the bird's natural motions and habits had carried over.

He struck instantly. A swoop brought him over the emerald figurine that lay among his belongings. He hovered, clutched it in his talons, and sailed for the tent flap. Burton lunged after him, shouting, "Come back here! Drop that, you idiot!"

His wing-tips grazed the canvas and deflected his course. Burton almost caught up with him, but his outstretched hands just missed the eagle's tail feathers.

Then the bird soared.

A bullet buzzed by. Leif Abbot heard a loud report. He squinted earthward. Travers had appeared from nowhere. Running toward the tent, he whipped out his revolver and was emptying it at the flying target. There could be no doubt of his purpose. Only the emerald could have brought such greed to his eyes. He was willing to kill the eagle and the mortal spirit of Leif Abbot if necessary to prevent the loss of that treasure.

LEIF ABBOT swooped, swerved, darted in erratic arcs, mounted suddenly, side-slipped, nose-dived, and straightened out. No ordinary marksman could have hit so crazily veering a target. Only a miracle could have enabled even a superb shot to halt the eagle. Travers was not the marksman, and chance did not provide him the miracle. His bullets went wide of the bird. With his last triumphant glance and a scream of mirthless mockery, Abbot saw Burton struggling to wrest the pistol from Travers, a useless struggle now that the weapon was empty.

The figurine did not weigh enough to prove a hindrance. After the first thrill of flight and escape, he forgot about his prize. He felt a stronger emotion. A rapture gripped him, an ecstasy unlike anything he had yet known.

Many times during his life, when watching the wild ducks fly south on the Mid-Western prairies in autumn, while staring at seagulls as they circled a ship, or admiring the lightning-like speed of hummingbirds as they darted toward honey-flowers, he had envied the birds their winged freedom. He reveled in that freedom now. He rose ever higher, his strong wings beating the way aloft. It took less effort than he had imagined, for his wings slanted automatically to receive the full lifting power of every gust of wind and utilize each upward eddy.

He felt like a spirit liberated from all earthly ties. The jungle became only a dark mass below him. The landscape unfolded toward farther horizons. Trees, rocks, and water holes lost their individuality.

The ground evolved into masses and areas, a darker carpet for the jungle, a lighter area for the plain, a sun-capped, shadow-filled mass for the mountains.

He found himself flying toward those distant peaks that rimmed the northeastern horizon. In the midst of his breathless enjoyment and elation, he wondered why his course came so easily. Then he remembered a previous experience, and guessed that the nest of the eagle lay somewhere among those towering crags and gorges.

He was about to change his line of flight when his far-sighting gaze was drawn to the puzzling actions of three birds. The birds swooped to earth in single file, rose, looped over, and dipped again. It dawned on him that the birds were airplanes miles distant; and their maneuvers could best be explained if they were indulging in the luxury of ground-strafing.

Fifteen minutes later, drifting at an altitude of approximately a mile, he found his surmise correct. The airplanes, fast bombers equipped with machine guns, had evidently resorted to ground-strafing for lack of any considerable target worth bombing. He estimated the region to lie twenty miles north of where he had met the raiding column the day before. But it was only a guess, for small landmarks could not be distinguished at all from his height, and the large ones he viewed from a different perspective.

Gorges, basaltic extrusions, lava flows,

and jagged hills formed the terrain, as though a giant hand had built turrets and scattered massive blocks in random formation. Why any nation should want that lonely, unlovely land mystified him. Even from his height, however, he detected tiny ants here and there on the hilltops, or crawling from bush to bush in the valley bottoms. He heard the stutter of machine guns and saw answering wisps of smoke puff up from the ground. Now and then one of the ants stopped crawling.

He spiraled lower, the peril from stray shots forgotten in the anger that again welled inside of him. Leif Abbot had more than one contradiction in his make-up. As a footloose adventurer and trader, he had always been alert to strike a shrewd bargain when he could; but he was just as eager to leap into fray on the side of the underdog when someone else was taking an unfair advantage.

Still circling downward, he wondered if there was anything he could do about the one-sided battle. His intentness on getting a closer view and his preoccupation with means of counter-attack brought him to the danger zone before he realized it. The song of a sky-riding slug passed too close for comfort.

ONE of the bombers completed its power dive and its burst of firing. It zoomed upward for position. Its nose was tilted toward the eagle. Leif Abbot clearly saw the leather helmets of its crew, and a surprised expression behind the pilot's goggles as he noticed the eagle. Leif Abbot dropped the emerald figurine. It fell straight to its target.

There was a crash and a *zing*. Glittering green fragments and a flash of gold streaked the air. It was as though the propeller had rammed a stone wall.

The bomber leaped under its own momentum, lost speed, and went into a tailspin. It plunged toward the ground from its altitude of only a few hundred feet. The pilot frantically worked the controls and had just got the craft straightened out when it crashed.

All its bombs must have exploded at the instant of impact. A gigantic fountain of flame roared up. Grass and bushes flattened as a wall of wind rushed in. The concussion numbed Leif Abbot even before he felt the skyward surge. The air filled with blasted objects, débris, shards of metal, bits of flesh. The second bomber, diving to do its own ground-strafing in the wake of the first, was caught over that inferno, tossed as by invisible hands. Some hurtling missile must have struck the bomb rack, for the machine disintegrated in another great geyser of flame and smoke and erupting metal.

He never knew the fate of the third bomber. Tossed around in the violent currents from those blasts, he fought for control.

Then the world became quiet. It seemed to reel and grow fuzzy. His thoughts began to wander. How had he managed to hear at all? So far as he knew, birds were not equipped with auditory apparatus akin to man's, yet he had distinctly heard Burton speak.

His wings felt sticky. He wanted to fold them in and plummet to earth. It would be so easy. He could straighten out just before he crashed—but he wouldn't straighten out any more than the bomber. He didn't even know if he was flying in the camp's direction, but he kept to a straight line. The emerald was gone. Why should he go on, with the treasure for which he had endured so much shattered into a million irrecoverable bits? What insane impulse had made him throw it away? At least *they* wouldn't be able to take it away from him now.

LEIF ABBOT awakened from a dream that he had been flying through the air and sinking toward the green shadows of the jungle. He was not at all sure that he had wakened. Instead of flying, he found himself in suspension. He floated, not in air, but amid a denser medium. He saw the shadowy green twilight, but it was the obscurity of water, not of forests.

Beast, bird, fish—what did it matter?

One nightmare was no worse than another. He had survived the others, and he would live through this, until the delirium left him and he opened his eyes again upon the world as he knew it.

Try as he might, he could not close his eyes, now that a measure of awareness had returned. While he was brooding, he was consciousness of somber twilight. As his thoughts became coherent, he was forced to abandon evasions.

Travers and Burton had cheated and betrayed him. They had used their fiendish discovery to deprive him of his rightful body for the third time. They had locked him up in the guise of a fish.

He tried to turn his head to see what sort of finny creature he had become, but his head would not turn. A flip of the fins and he faced the opposite direction. He rose, dived, circled, wriggled, and spun around until he was dizzy with exasperation. His eyes could see only forward and upward. He could not turn his head.

Had they placed him in the headwaters, the ground springs, that formed the source of the river he had followed in his original flight? He became aware of a gentle lazy current, and allowed himself to drift along.

The water swarmed with life. He was appalled by what his human eyes had missed when he had drunk of necessity at tepid pools and streams during his years in the tropics.

A great horror of these strange depths overcame him. He could not follow the stream to the sea. He could never watch beneath or behind. He had no weapon to fight lurking monsters. He had no desire to find out what terrifying life-forms infested the deeper parts of the river, or what rotting hulks and bones littered the sea-bottoms. Once he left his present position, he would never be able to find his way back.

A flip of the tail brought him face about. A fiercer horror assailed him, but he had no voice to cry out, no time to flee. A sort of dumb and paralyzing madness quaked through him as he saw the jaws of the crocodile close—

Burton looked worried. He watched the body of Leif Abbot which was twitching grotesquely. The arms and legs made spasmodic movements. The mouth gaped like that of a fish out of water.

The body flopped weakly all at once, with a quiver and a horrible finality.

Burton sprang to his kit, seized drugs, and worked for an hour in sweating anxiety. His efforts produced no results.

"What happened?" asked Travers.

"I don't know. I'm afraid the vitality of the fish was of too low an order to direct a highly developed and complicated organism."

Travers filled his pipe irritably. "He was done for, no matter what. Why the devil couldn't he have left the emerald?"

# BLIND MAN'S BUFF

By

J. U. GIESY

**Now you see it—now you don't: Officer McGuiness was not a drinking man; but the vagaries of Professor Zapt were one too many for an honest Irish cop**

"SIGHT depends upon the etheric vibrations which we are wont to denominate light," said Professor Xenophon Xerxes Zapt, the eminent investigator of the unknown (sometimes called "Unknown Quantity Zapt" by his associates by reason of the double "X" in his name. He spoke from the reading chair wherein he had been browsing over the pages of a scientific journal, in the living-room of his home.

"Good thing it does, too," declared Bob Sargent, fiancé of the professor's daughter Nellie, surveying the young woman in appreciative fashion. "If it didn't, I suppose we couldn't see a thing."

"Exactly." The professor nodded. "There are times, Robert, when you have a gratifying manner of perceiving the main point of a deduction to be arrived at by the consideration of already established facts. Light being the main instrument of vision, its absence from the scheme of things would rob us of one of the five recognized senses beyond a doubt."

"And yet," said Bob, "they tell us that black is an absence of light, don't they, professor? So if they're right why is it we can see a negro—"

"Wait." The professor held up a slender hand. "We were speaking of light, not color, Robert."

Bob nodded. "Well, yes. But if black is an absence of color, why call the negro a colored man?"

Xenophon Xerxes Zapt indulged in a frown. Displeasure shone in his spectacled eyes. There were times when he disapproved strongly of Nellie's choice of a future husband—when he was more than a little annoyed by the particular sense of humor possessed by the young attorney. And now that annoyance flamed. "If it were not for the facetiousness you at times exhibit, Robert," he said with a sudden stiffness, "I would be far more satisfied as to the amount of light contained in what you are pleased to consider your mind. There are occasions, when in endeavoring to discuss some scientific problem in your presence, I am reminded of the saying in regard to casting pearls of price before—er —porcine appreciation. Levity is the last characteristic of personality with which we should approach the consideration of natural problems." He reached up and began pulling at the graying mutton-chop whiskers on either side of his cleanly shaven chin.

Nellie gave Bob a warning glance, though her blue eyes were dancing.

And Sargent heeded the sign. "Well, really, professor," he said, "I had no intention of acting like the proverbial swine. Just what's the notion, will you explain?"

"Invisibility!" Xerxes Zapt pronounced the word with a force hardly to be expected from a man of so slight a frame. He was a little fellow, was the professor, customarily clad as now in baggy trousers, a loose coat and roomy slippers, in which he went puttering about the experiments that had won him a certain sort of fame.

"Invisibility," he repeated, eying Sargent. "Have you any conception, Robert, of all that may be embraced in that term?"

"Why—er," said Bob; "if a thing's invisible you can't see it—like a gas, or—"

"Exactly," the professor helped him out; "or the workings of some people's brains. Invisibility is the state wherein a substance defies the operation of the visible sense. What, then, if instead of arriving at such a state through the vaporization process as in the instance of a gas, substances should be rendered invisible, and at the same time their solidity were to be maintained?"

"It would be rather awkward, wouldn't it," Sargent suggested. "People would always be bumping into things."

"Eh?" Once more Xerxes Zapt eyed him in an almost suspicious manner. "Well, perhaps—perhaps they would, Robert. And in that fact lies the advantage to be gained. Now this article on camouflage, I have been reading would make it appear that camouflage depends on the ability of man to present a baffling aspect of ordinary appearance to the perceptive centers of the brain, through the visual function of the optic nerve. Am I plain?"

"I believe that is the generally accepted explanation," Sargent assented weakly.

"Exactly. But what if, instead of changing the aspect of natural objects, they were rendered incapable of being seen?"

"Holy smoke!" said Bob and paused in sudden comprehension. "I guess I begin to get your notion."

Xenophon Xerxes Zapt leaned forward. "It would revolutionize the entire system of defense which might be employed by a nation. It would enable a fleet of an army to disguise its presence completely. I think it was known to the ancients. Merlin, whom Tennyson mentions, had a cloak of invisibility, you remember. Robert—my mind is made up. I am going to do it."

"Make things invisible?" Sargent questioned.

"Exactly." The professor rose and shook down his baggy trousers. "And when it is accomplished I am going to give it to this nation. The United States of America is going to be rendered—"

"Not invisible!" Robert interrupted.

"Certainly not." Zapt gave him a withering glance. "I was about to say that to Xenophon Xerxes Zapt it was reserved to render his nation impregnable from attack."

"By Jove, professor, that's a wonderful thing if you can do it," Robert exclaimed.

"If—if?" the professor bridled. "Just so. In all ages progressive minds have had to contend with the doubt of scoffers."

Having delivered that parting shot, he turned and stalked from the room.

"Well"—Sargent looked at Nellie—"as long as he doesn't render you invisible, sweetness."

Miss Zapt glanced down at Fluffy, the beautiful Angora cat she was holding in her lap, tweaked one pink-tipped ear with her fingers and—flushed.

"If you don't quit making him cross he's apt to squirt some of it on you when he gets it finished," she cautioned.

Bob laughed. "Small danger. He's too wise. If he did that he couldn't tell when I was hanging around the prettiest little brown-haired girl in town."

And after that—well, quite a while after that—he said: "Good night."

Yet late as he departed, a light still burned in the room Professor Xenophon Xerxes Zapt had converted into a laboratory of sorts, on the second floor of his home.

A month went by, however, before anything came of the professor's scheme, and Sargent had put the thing completely out of his mind. Then on a certain evening he mounted the steps of the Zapt residence, found the door open, and save for the unguarded condition of the house, no sign of anybody home.

With the freedom of long acquaintance, he stepped inside and glanced around.

The sound of a soft voice calling struck his ears. "Fluffy—Fluffy—kitty—kitty—come here—come on and get your supper, honey. Drat it—where has the creature gone?"

Sargent grinned in pleasurable anticipation, and followed the sound to the rear.

"Won't I do as well?" he questioned, entering the kitchen where Nellie was standing with a brimming bowl of milk in her hands.

"Oh, hello, Bob," she answered, turning toward him. "I can't imagine where she is. It's time she was fed, but she doesn't come when I call her."

"Oh, well, she'll come back. It's a way with cats," Bob told her. "Put the milk on the floor where she can get it when she does. I've got something for you."

"What?" Miss Zapt set down the bowl as he had suggested, and came to stand beside him, as he produced a box from his pocket, and from the box a ring.

"You said you admired it the other day when we saw it in a window."

"Bob!" Miss Zapt seized it and slipped it on a different finger from the one where her betrothal solitaire already blazed. And then she put her arm around Bob's neck and stood on tiptoe to kiss him.

Sargent met her halfway, lifted his head and stiffened a trifle, and stood holding her still in his arms, until at length he let out a slow ejaculation: "What th' deuce!"

"What's the matter?" Nellie raised her eyes, then turned them in the direction his were already staring, to find them resting on the bowl she had placed on the floor.

And that was all—except that for some unaccountable reason—the milk was disappearing! Even as she stood as rigid now as Sargent—it's blue-white level went down!

"Bob!" she whispered in a tensely sibilant fashion; "do—do you see it?"

"That's the trouble," he said rather thickly. "I don't see a thing, and yet—that bowl of milk is going to be empty pretty soon."

And then as they stood arrested, scarcely breathing, it must be confessed, in the face of the inexplicable thing occurring before them, if they were to accept the evidence of their senses, Nellie's ears caught a faintly rhythmic sound.

"Listen!" Her blue eyes widened. Her hand crept up and laid hold of Sargent's fingers.

"Lap, lap—lap, lap." The milk sank lower and lower.

"Fluffy!" sad Nellie all at once.

"Fluf-fy?" Bob repeated.

"Yes." Nellie set her soft pink lips together. "She's there—drinking that milk. I've got to catch her, but—don't you let go of my hand."

She began to tiptoe forward, and Sargent followed. "Fluffy," she wheedled softly. "Fluffy—honey." She bent her knees and reached out groping fingers. And suddenly she tore her hand from Sargent's grasp and made a swiftly clutching gesture. "I've got her," she announced and straightened.

"Where?" said Bob a trifle blankly.

"Right here. I'm holding her in my hands. Never mind, Fluffy—muddy's got you."

"Well—" Sargent accepted the information. "You sound like it, and you look as if you were holding something, but darned if I can see her."

"Of course not." Miss Zapt's tone was one of quickening exasperation. "Silly, don't you understand?"

"No, I don't," Bob said rather shortly, hesitated briefly and went on again in dawning comprehension. "Unless it's some more of your father's—"

"It is," Nellie declared with conviction. "That invisibility stuff he was talking about last month. And he's—he's tried it on Fluf-fy, and—" Her voice began to quiver.

"Good Lord!" Bob gasped. "Well, never mind, sweetheart. If he did it he can undo it. Where is he?"

"I don't kno-ow!" said Nellie in a fashion suddenly savage. "But—I'm going to find him and make him bring back my cat!" She turned and ran out of the kitchen, into the hall that led to the front of the house.

Sargent caught up with her in a stride. For a moment he had felt shaken, by the uncanny way in which the milk had vanished, but now that he knew the explanation, the whole aspect of things was altered. He grinned as Nellie raced ahead, apparently holding nothing to her bosom. And then he put out a hand and drew her to a stand.

"Listen!" he said.

"Swish! Swi-i-ish!" A fresh sound broke upon their ears.

"What is it?" Nellie questioned as the thing continued.

Bob shook his head. "If you ask me, somebody's washing the front of the house with a hose."

"Father!" Miss Zapt emitted the one brittle word, shook off Sargent's detaining hand and darted toward the swishing noise.

Bob followed—just as he had been following Nellie ever since he knew her first. Side by side they reached the front door.

Side by side they paused and gasped as a sweeping spray of fluid met them.

"Swish! Swi-i-i-ish!" Again the deluge.

"Get back!" Half-blinded, Bob reached for Nellie, caught her and dragged her to him. "Get back!"

As he turned to regain the protection of the hallway, he had a blurring vision of a slender figure with mutton-chop whiskers and spectacle-rimmed eyes, playing the drenching liquid toward them from a length of rubber tubing; then—

"Swish! Swi-i-ish!" The stream caught them again—this time in the back, and—he found himself apparently still holding Nellie's arm, but—Miss Zapt had disappeared.

"Nellie!" he faltered. It was unbelievable. He could touch her, but he couldn't see her!

"Bob—oh, Bob—where are you?" He heard her.

"Right here," he said as a horrible thought laid hold upon him. "Nellie—can't you see me—dear?"

"No-o-o. I can feel your—fingers," she whimpered. "But—I—oh, Bob—I'm so wet and—frightened. You—you just faded out—all at once, after—father—"

"Father? Yes, father," was the answer.

Sargent saw the whole thing all at once. Father had decided to make a practical demonstration of his new invention or discovery, or whatever one wanted to call it—and he had started spraying the infernal stuff on the house. Well—it was his house, and he could do what he pleased about it, but when it came to using the thing on human beings—

Father's voice cut into his swirling consideration: "Robert—am I right in thinking I saw you and Nellie on the porch just now?"

Bob turned. The little man had switched the direction of his hose and was staring toward the house with near-sighted eyes.

"You're dead right, you saw us," he flung back a none-too-gentle answer. "But you can't see us now. You turned that confounded stream into our faces, and—"

"Why bless my soul—I didn't see you,"

said Zenophon Xerxes Zapt; "not until it was too late—that is—then I thought I saw you—and then you disappeared."

"Exactly," Bob agreed, very much as Zapt himself might have done it. "That's exactly *what* we did."

"Turn around then, Robert," the professor advised. "The substance only blots out what it touches."

"We did that, too. We turned around and were blotted out about the time you gave the porch its third dose," Bob rejoined, and paused in consternation. All at once he became aware that he couldn't see the porch floor or the steps, or Nellie, or himself. About all he seemed able to see was the little man standing there on the lawn squirting some sort of diabolical fluid out of the hose he now perceived came down from the laboratory window. And without the least warning he found that the sight filled him with a sort of quickly upflaring rage.

In a rush he was off the porch, which seemed to be there, whether he could see it or not, and flinging himself toward the source of his and its disappearance.

"Put down that hose!"

"Robert, to whom are you speaking?" Professor Zapt peered toward the changing sound of Sargent's voice.

"I'm speaking to you," Bob told him almost roughly. "Put down that hose or turn it off, or—something."

"Remarkable—remarkable," said the professor, smiling. "Robert, I cannot see you, though I hear you plainly. You appear to be actually very near me. If anything had been needed to clearly demonstrate the unqualified success of my recent investigations, this—"

"Put down that hose!" Bob said it for the third time and seized the rubber tubing in his hands.

And for some reason best known to himself, Professor Xenophon Xerxes Zapt chose to resist. He struggled to retain possession of the hose, exerting his frailer strength against that of the unseen, yet stronger man who was dragging on it. He tugged and Bob tugged, and all at once the

professor lost his balance and sprawled upon the ground, while the nozzle released from his controlling guidance, whipped round like a serpent striking, and drenched him to the skin.

"Oh, I say, professor, I didn't mean to do that," began Bob, and broke off—because apparently he was speaking to nothing. Professor Xenophon Xerxes Zapt had vanished.

From the porch where she had been an unseen watcher Nellie screamed the one word "Father!"

Sargent put down the hose and groped toward where he had last seen "father" on the ground.

"Father!" Once more Miss Zapt was calling.

And Sargent's fingers made contact with something clammily wet and very active that bounced away from his touch and emitted a most irascible exclamation. "There, now, you impudent young whelp, see what you have done!"

"I—I can't—professor," Bob stammered, straightening and drawing a hand across his seemingly useless eyes. "I can hear you all right, but I can't see you."

"Father!"

"Yes, yes," Zapt answered his daughter's frantic query. "I'm—I'm all right, my dear."

"But—I can't see you—or Bob—or *myself*. Where are you?"

"Here. Sargent, where are you?"

"Here."

"Why bless my soul," said the professor. "We'd better get into the house and talk this over. Nellie where are *you?*"

"Right here where Bob left me," said Nellie in a tone of incipient hysterics.

"Well, stay there, and we'll come to you," Sargent advised her. "I can't see the porch or the steps, but I can make out the door. Are you there, professor?"

"Of course I'm here," Zapt assured him none too sweetly.

"Then come along." Bob began moving toward what was still visible of the house, feeling with shuffling feet for the vanished steps, in order to ascend them to the equally vanished porch, where Nellie waited, to all appearances no more than a disembodied voice.

"Bob!" that voice came to him.

"Here—coming," he answered, and found the steps, and went gropingly up, hands outstretched before him. "Nellie?"

"Here!"

Beside the door he found her. She gasped as he touched her.

"It's all right now," he said, "I've got you. Talk about blind-man's buff!"

Behind him came a sound of two objects colliding, and the professor cried: "Ouch!"

"Father!" Miss Zapt stiffened inside the arm Bob had slipped about her; "did you hurt yourself?"

"Not irreparably, my dear," said Zapt in somewhat sarcastic fashion. "And I trust I have not badly damaged the steps. Where in thunder are you?"

"Right here by the door."

"Huh!" The sound of tentative foot-steps came nearer. "All right—now I touch you."

"As a matter of fact," said Sargent, "that's my hand you're holding, but it's all the same. I'm holding Nellie. We'd better stick together."

The professor grunted and removed his clutching fingers. "We'd better get some place where we can locate ourselves by means of definitely known objects. Go into the living-room," he said.

They passed inside. At least they could now see where they were going. They gained the door of the living-room and passed through it. Bob led Nellie to the couch and seated himself beside her.

"Father, where are you?" she inquired.

"Here," came the voice of the professor. "In my usual chair, my dear. I presume you can see it, at least. Sargent, what are you doing?"

"I'm holding Nellie's hand." Bob told him the literal truth.

Xenophon Xerxes Zapt quite audibly sniffed. "At least," said he, "I can't see you."

"Well—you've nothing on me there, professor," Bob retorted. "Here's a pretty kettle of fish."

"Exactly," complained the professor. "If you young people hadn't interfered—"

"That's hardly the point now," Sargent interrupted. "The question now seems to be, how do we get rid of the stuff?"

For a time Xerxes Zapt made no answer, and then he sighed. "That is the point, Robert, of course," he assented. "But you see, I hadn't gone into it fully, and—"

"Father!" Nellie's voice cut into his confession.

"See here," Sargent half rose and sank back as her panic-tightened fingers held him. "Do you mean we've—got to stay—like this, till you think up an answer?"

"That's it, Robert," said Xenophon Xerxes Zapt in a tone he plainly strove to make soothing. "I think that I had—er —that I had better try to think."

Nellie began laughing. There was nothing of humor in the sound. It was just the cachinnation of jangled nerves and ended in a sob.

Bob put his arms about her and drew her head against his shoulder.

"Don't leave me, Bob," she murmured. "Promise me not to leave this house till I see you again."

"I won't," said Sargent. "I won't leave till your father has thought of something to get us all out of this fix." He drew his arms tightly about her shaking figure, and held her. The situation was rather eerie, to say the least. He could see everything in the room quite plainly—everything, but the professor, and Nellie, and himself.

And yet the sound of another sigh wafted to him from the reading chair beside the table, where presumably Zapt was thinking. It was followed by mumbled words: "Milk? —no—certainly not. Benzine?—scarcely. Ether?—"

"Ether ought to do it," Sargent caught up the suggestion. "You said it was etheric vibrations that were responsible for sight."

The professor grunted again, but made no further comment. Silence came down again. Dusk had fallen. The sound of shuffling footfalls struck on Sargent's ears —the snap of a switch. A sudden illumination filled the living-room and hallway. Plainly Zapt had turned on the lights. Bob listened while he padded back again to his chair and sank into it with a creaking of springs.

And then Zapt was speaking: "All things considered, Robert, I think we had best go upstairs and change our clothes."

"Simple? It was as simple as that. Bob saw it in a flash. "Of course," he exclaimed, as Nellie stirred in his embrace at her father's words, "that will be all right for you and Nellie, but I haven't any extra clothes here, myself.".

"I can lend you a bathrobe, Robert," Zapt replied. "Such a step will at least give us an opportunity to once more establish ourselves. The solution being mainly on our clothing, either their removal or their covering with an unsaturated texture, will render us visible in a major extent, even if it does not restore the visibility of our faces and hands. And, of course, I shall think of something in time. Alcohol might do it—"

"Exactly." Judging by sounds, the professor rose. "You will come with me, Robert. Nellie will go to her room."

"Come, dear," Robert prompted and helped Nellie to her feet. And then, as the fall of a heavy body, followed by inarticulate grunts and mouthings and mumbles came from the front porch, he paused.

The sounds went on. They might have been a scuffle to judge by their nature, or they might have been occasioned by some object trying to right itself. There was a clumping reminiscent of heavily shod feet —the rasp of stertorous breathing—then—

"Phwat th' divil?" a self-interrogation.

"Sssh!" One could fancy Xenophon Xerxes Zapt was the source of the sibilant warning. "Officer McGuiness. He's noticed the house, confound him. Quick now before he comes inside! Upstairs!"

In his last statement, Professor Xenophon Xerxes Zapt had been absolutely right. Danny McGuiness, large, florid, Irish, and a careful officer, *had* noticed the house, as a matter of course—as during his hours of duty patrolling the street on which it stood, he noticed it and half a hundred others every time he passed. And to-night as he approached it, just after dusk and

the assumption of his tour of duty, he had noticed something about it, such as he had never beheld in all of his life.

He came to a halt and stared. And then quite slowly he lifted a massive hand and passed it across his eyes. Seemingly, he was gazing upon the roof and the second story of a house, without visible means of support, as the judge of the city court was wont to say of certain individuals brought before him. The roof and the upper story were quite familiar. Danny had seen them every night for many months, since the night he saw them first, but—the rest of the picture had disappeared. Everything below that strangely buoyant part of the structure was seemingly wiped out, very much as a drawing might have been sponged from a slate.

Hence Danny's instinctive gesture to his eyes. He knew he couldn't be seeing what they said he was. He had heard of such catastrophes overtaking a man in the past. Hemi—or semi—or something like that, the doctors called it. Anyway, a man saw only half of what he looked at, and quite plainly he was seeing—or he wasn't seeing—something like half of Professor Zapt's house.

He put down his hand and laid hold of the fence that ran in front of Professor Zapt's yard. All at once, regardless of the roof and upper story of the mansion at which he was staring, Danny felt a need of support. For a moment he stood clinging to it, and then—he decided on a test. Slowly he turned his vision away from the floating superstructure of a modern residence, and directed it across the street.

Then he let go of the fence and drew a long breath. He could see the other side of the street all right—all of it. Under such conditions his eyes did nothing by halves. He could see the houses from top to bottom, the boles as well as the tops of the street-fringing trees. Then—what in the name of all sense was the answer? Perhaps a temporary seizure merely—something he had eaten, maybe, that had caused a passing semiblindness. He turned back and once more faced in the original direction, and stiffened before the original effect.

"Well, sa-a-y!" said Officer McGuiness, and decided that the trouble must be with the house and not himself. He decided, also, to investigate.

He knew Xenophon Xerxes Zapt. Several times before he had known the professor to produce some odd results by his experiments—had even profited by them to some extent, when Zapt had seen fit to hand him sundry bits of neatly engraved paper, as a mark of appreciation of the interest Danny had displayed. Having recovered from his first shock of surprise, McGuiness was half-minded that he was facing some such condition now.

"Funny little feller," he muttered to himself, as he went up the walk from the gate. "Always fussin' wid some sort of contraption. Lookit this now, wull ye—lookit—hull bottom of th' house gone—rest of it floatin'—"

Abruptly he collided with something and sprawled forward on what felt, even if it did not look like the steps of the missing porch.

For a moment he lay with the breath nearly shaken out of him, and then he began to feel tentatively about.

"They're here—even if I can't see 'em," he decided at last, the conviction driven into him by his fall and the verdict of his groping touch. "They're here, but—phwy is ut, I can't see 'em? Shure, now I'm here, I'll mention ut to th' perfissor. 'Tis a dangerous state of affairs indade, whin an honest man can't see where he's goin', an' moighty near breaks his neck."

Whereupon McGuiness got up and felt his way with searching feet to the top of the steps, and across the equally invisible porch, to the oblong of the door, beyond which glowed the lighted hallway. It was all most peculiar to be walking on something he couldn't see, and despite him, it affected Danny oddly.

"Phwat th' divil?" he voiced his bewilderment in a heavy rumble and stiffened in his tracks at a warning "Sssh!"

It was a sound of caution—a sibilant plea for quiet.

Danny considered quickly. His official instincts wakened. He strained his ears. The rasp of whispering came to him.

"Sssh! is ut—whisper—whisper? Be gob there's somethin' moighty funny goin' on about this house." Danny thought the words rather than spoke them, gave over his first intention of ringing the bell if he could find it, laid hold of the screen door and dragged it open and stepped inside.

The hall ran straight back before him. He saw the upward sweep of a flight of stairs. To the right lay an archway giving into a lighted apartment. McGuiness turned toward it, made his way into the living-room and gazed about him. So far as he could see he stood alone in a room otherwise deserted, and yet—dimly it seemed to him that he detected a sound of suppressed breathing.

He frowned. It was like being in a darkened room with some unknown person—only this room was brilliantly lighted and still he could perceive no one. A peculiar tingling, prickling sensation began to run up and down his spine. Somebody had whispered, and they must have been close indeed, for him to have heard it—somebody or something was breathing not ten feet from him. He was sure of it now.

The pad of a careful footfall! He whirled, tightening his grip on his club—to find nothing at all—or at least no one, before his starting eyes.

And yet that softly padding sound went on. It was as though unseen enemies were creeping upon him. Tiny drops of moisture started on his cleanly shaven upper lip. He spun about again at a rustle of movement from a new direction. His respiration quickened. A few moments ago his eyes had tricked him and now, seemingly, he couldn't believe his ears. Or could he? Those whispers—of breathing—of unseen footfalls were all about him. Surely someone or something was moving in the room. Something? McGuiness began to lose some of his ruddy color. He wasn't a coward, but this unseen, this unknown, this apparently unknowable thing was getting on his nerves.

"Father?"

He jerked himself up at the sound of the articulated word—no more than another sibilant sighing, but none the less something within his comprehension.

"Sssh!"

There it was again—that plea for silence —caution—from the hallway now, or else his ears had utterly failed him.

He twisted himself toward it. "Perfissor —are ye there, perfissor?" he questioned hoarsely and advanced on legs that shook the least bit for all his dogged effort to control them. At the worst, he told himself now, he was facing something human.

And yet, when he reached the hallway and groped along it, searching, searching heavily for what he couldn't see, there was no one, and—a stairboard creaked. He lifted his eyes quickly. He could see the stairs and—there was nothing on them!

All at once McGuiness found himself shaken by something like a chill, and clenched his teeth.

"Aw go to th' divil," he snarled a gritting surrender, "shure an' I wasn't hired to go chasin' after ghosts."

A giggle—an unmistakable giggle—was wafted to him from the second story. And yet to his baffled imagination it was the gibbering of a disembodied something. Kicking open the screen door he stepped outside, removed his helmet to draw a none too steady hand across a sweat-dampened forehead, and took a deep and somewhat uncertain breath. Then very slowly he found the steps and went down them, retraced his way along the walk to the street, and turned to look back at what he could see of the house.

It was just the same as it had been, only now McGuiness knew that no matter how it appeared, the bottom part was there, and —it wasn't the same after all—there was a light upstairs!

He regarded it for several minutes before he understood. When he had gone inside it had not been there—and there was that creak on the stairs! Somebody had whispered "father," and somebody had "sshed" the speaker into silence, and— somebody had giggled when he said he

wasn't chasing ghosts—and the recollection of that giggle wasn't at all the same now as it had seemed inside the house. It had been a sound of amusement with nothing of menace about it. The officer was greatly puzzled.

All at once Danny McGuiness set his Irish jaw in determination. "Begob," he declared to no one but himself, "I'm goin' to get to th' botthom of this now, do ye moind. I couldn't see anywan at all, at all, but—by th' same token I couldn't see th' steps. An' yit, I found thim."

Jerking open the gate, he found the steps again with groping feet, went up them and reached the door and let himself once more inside.

Upstairs, he told himself. Upstairs he would find them. He would go up, and this time he'd demand an explanation. Sshes would not deter him any longer. There was somebody up there. Ghosts didn't turn on lights. He'd go up and find the lighted room, and—

Something brushed against his leg!

He started, checked himself, and stooped swiftly with reaching fingers. They closed on something furry—something silken soft —something that drew back and emitted an unmistakable hiss.

"A cat!" said Danny. "A kitty, d'ye moind now—an' I can't see her—I can't see her any more than I could thim steps— but—I can feel her—or I could. Kitty— kitty—come here, kitty." Still bent he began feeling in all directions, turning on heavy feet as he sought to come once more in contact with her. "Come, kitty—come to Officer McGuiness. Where th' divil did you go to?"

"Why, officer, such language! I'm surprised."

McGuiness straightened slowly. He glanced upward, quite to the head of the stairs—and remained staring while his heavy jaw sagged.

Because something stood there—only it was hard to say what it was—except that it appeared like the dress of a woman— just that—just a dress leaning a little toward him across the railing. Or no. There seemed to be a pair of feet beneath it—a pair of feet, but neither hands nor head! There was nothing at all above the neck of the garment save a little triangular spot, as white as—as white as a virgin reputation. And that was all. There wasn't anything else. There was just that tiny white triangle, and a pair of feet, and the dress.

So much he saw and then the dress was joined by two other garments—a jerkily moving bathrobe and a suit of clothes. The three formed a group and began descending.

"Whuroo!" Danny let the sound out of his chest in a sighing exhalation and stood watching. But it wasn't a battle-cry of combat—it was just the last stand of conscious volition. And after that, as the three headless figures marched down the stairs toward him, Officer Danny McGuiness was volitionally paralyzed. He stared with a never-shifting vision, but he neither spoke nor moved. He was past all speech or movement, until, suddenly—the lady's garment laughed.

"Why, officer," it said, "you look as if you were seeing a ghost."

Hope waked anew in Danny McGuiness's breast. He stiffened his shaking knees. The voice had nothing of whispers, of "sshes" about it. It had a distinctly human note. It sounded suspiciously like that of Professor Zapt's daughter.

"Shure, I—I don't know what I'm seein'," he stammered. "Fer th' lasht fifteen minutes ut's been pretty much now you see it an' now you don't wid me, miss—but mostly don't."

"Of course." And surely that was Xenophon Xerxes Zapt's voice emerging from the suit of clothes. "That's the substance on our faces, McGuiness. Come into the living-room and I'll explain the matter to your better understanding."

"All roight, perfissor," Danny assented. "It is yersilf, isn't ut, perfissor?"

"Of course," said the suit of clothes.

"An—th'—th' bathrobe?" Danny questioned.

"Mr. Sargent," said the lady's garment.

"Av course," accepted Danny. "I moight

hov knowed it, if I hadn't been so—surprised."

"Come on in and sit down while father explains it," the bit of rayon crêpe said. And Danny followed while it led him in and gave him a chair, and seated itself on the couch at the bathrobe's side.

"You see, officer, I have discovered a substance which, applied to any object, nullifies sight," began the suit of clothes.

McGuiness nodded. "Shure, I don't know phwat nullyfies means, unless you put ut on th' steps, an' used phwat was left on yersilves an' th' cat."

"Exactly," the suit of clothes responded. "I suppose you noticed the house?"

"I did thot—phwat there was of ut, so far as I could see," said Danny. " 'Twas that made me come in to see was I goin' bloind or phwat. Was ut you sshed when I was standin' on th' porch?"

"Yes," the suit of clothes replied. "We were just going up-stairs to get some fresh garments so we could see ourselves, at least in a measure." They went on and explained fully what had occurred.

Danny grinned when the narrative was finished. "D'ye mean," said he, "thot you don't know yit phwat wull take ut off?"

"Exactly," the suit of clothes admitted in a somewhat apologetic manner.

"Nellie seems to be coming out of it better than the rest of us, anyway," the bathrobe suggested. "I can see her nose."

"I—I powdered it!" The lady's garment giggled.

"Powdered ut?" All at once Danny chuckled. That explained the white triangle above the garment's neck. Everything was coming clear at last.

"But see here, perfissor," he inquired, turning to where the suit of clothes was sitting rather limply in the chair beside the table. "Won't ut wash?"

"Wash?" the suit of clothes made irascible rejoinder. "Of course it will wash. It has to wash. I've been thinking about whether it will wash best in a solution of naphtha or gasoline. I—"

"But—I was speakin' of wather," Officer McGuiness interrupted.

"Water!" The suit of clothes literally bounded upright. "Why—why bless my soul! I dissolved the reagents in water. Water will take it off, of course! Here—" There was a brief pause and suddenly a neatly engraved bit of paper was seemingly floating just below the end of a sleeve extended in Danny's direction. "McGuiness, you're a wonder. Take this as a little mark of my appreciation of your assistance. I—er—frankly, McGuiness, I never before realized that you had a scientific mind."

Officer McGuiness took it. He rose. "I'll be gettin' back on my beat now," said he.

"But I'm shure glad to have been of assistance to ye, perfissor, an' I'm glad I understand th' sityation, or I reckon I'd be spendin' this here now to have a doctor examine my eyes."

"Well—all's well that ends well," remarked the bathrobe.

Danny, moving toward the hallway, paused.

"Thrue for ye, Mister Sargent, an' if you'll accept th' suggestion—maybe besides washin' yer hands an' faces, ut would be as well to use a little wather on th' front of th' house."

www.ingramcontent.com/pod-product-compliance
Lightning Source LLC
Chambersburg PA
CBHW080912020726
47502CB00008B/2433